THE JACKRABBIT BOOGIE

THE JACKRABBIT BOOGIE

A NOVEL BY

DOUGLAS BUCKLAND

CHAPTER 1

WE WERE SITTING IN A third floor conference room at the Byron Rogers Federal Building, which is located at 1961 Stout Street in Denver. The people attending the meeting were the United States Attorney for the District of Colorado, the Drug Enforcement Agency's Special Agent in Charge of the Denver Field Division plus myself and the four other guys on my DEA Special Operations Division (SOD) team. We were there to finalize the preparations required to serve a no-knock warrant at a location in the Capital Hill neighborhood located not far from where we were now sitting.

The person we were preparing to apprehend was not a violent criminal, in fact he and his crew seemed to go out of their way to avoid any violence whatsoever. The problem was appearances and the loss of face. The target, one Juan Cortez, a.k.a. the Jackrabbit, had been making fools out of the DEA in general and my team in specific, for several years now. Every time we got a lead on Jackrabbit we would hit the location, but Jackrabbit was never there. What was always there was a red envelope giving us a lead to a much more serious crime; sometimes this would be a sex trafficking operation concerning illegal alien women and girls, often it would be a large fentanyl load being brought into Colorado and occasionally Jackrabbit would give us the details about one of the 1% outlaw biker gangs putting together a load of guns to smuggle into Mexico.

Jackrabbit only sold dope, very high-quality dope; Kona Gold from Hawaii, Northern California Sinsemilla, Godfather OG, GG4, Bubba Kush, Bruce Banner #3, Strawberry Banana and so forth. He only supplied to order, and as such his clientele were the more upmarket white-collar stoners. As you can see, this was more of a face-saving bust than a serious criminal interdiction. Never discount the 'loss of face' penalty when you are considering taunting the law enforcement community, it can lead to more attention than you bargained for.

Jackrabbit had been seen going into the end unit of a fairly nice red brick rowhouse consisting of six connected townhouses at the corner of Sherman Street and East 11th Avenue, three blocks south of the Colorado State Capital Building, every Wednesday around 3:00 in the afternoon. He would have some visitors until roughly 6:00 in the evening, but then he'd stay at home until around 7:00 the next morning when he would walk over to a diner on North Broadway for breakfast. The plan was for my SOD team, the relevant personnel of the Denver Police Department and two ambulances to rendezvous at the parking lot at Grant Street and East 11th Avenue at 9:00pm to go over the plan one last time before breaching Jackrabbit's door at 9:30pm. It should have been a walk in the park, but never forget to take Murphy's Law into account as it'll bite you in the ass every time.

Everything went smoothly up to a point. Everyone met up in the parking lot on time to go over the plan. It was a dark night, well as dark as it gets in a city at night, and the weather was good. A watcher across the street radioed a sitrep and told us that the lights were on in the living room to the right of the door, but the drapes were closed and that the light was on in the foyer behind window in the front door as well. This was good information since we wouldn't be able to use our night vision goggles with the lights on as they would just 'wash out' in the light and blind us. A support vehicle took us to the target address and dropped us off before parking halfway up the block on our side of the street, under the large trees that grew curbside there. Another support vehicle parked just out of sight of the house on 11th Avenue ready to give additional support if required. We were good to go.

At 9:30pm we stacked up in front of the door and got ready to breach. We were positioned directly in front of the door because there was no room to stack properly on either side due to the ornamental railings bordering the doorstep. The breacher was positioned in front of the door with the Kodiak battering ram. I was at the front of the stack and the three remaining members of the team were behind me. Everyone except the breacher and myself was holding onto the guy in front of him with his left hand, weapons were ready in the right hand. I faced the breacher and held up my left hand with my fingers spread while holding my HK MP5 in my right hand. I 'counted down' by folding my fingers into my palm, our usual signal. When I folded my thumb into my palm, making a fist, the breacher slammed the battering ram directly above the doorknob. The door flew open, and we charged aggressively through the door to begin 'slicing the pie' or covering our assigned arcs of responsibility to neutralize any threats.

Normally this would have worked beautifully just as it did in practice, except for Jackrabbit. How he knew we were coming is something that would need to be addressed later, the fact was that he did and that he had prepared for our visit like a pro. The first thing that happened after the breacher had rammed the door open is that the lights in the entire townhouse went out. Remember we had raised our night vision goggles to the standby position on top of our helmets since the lights in the foyer and the living room would have made them useless. Now, just as we breached, we were essentially blind until our night vision recovered, which would have been fine if we had the time for it to do so. In a breach like this, once the door has been rammed open you rush through the opening as quicky as possible to get out of the 'fatal funnel' where you are silhouetted in the doorway, and take up your assigned positions. Which is what we were attempting to do.

The problem was that Jackrabbit, at some point, had cut out the entire foyer floor and the underlying crossbeams. As we were momentarily blind due to the lights going out and in the middle of a breach, we didn't immediately notice this. The entire team, including the breacher who had dropped the ram and became the last man through the door, took an immediate 10-foot vertical trip into the basement due to the effects of gravity and no means of support underfoot. Thankfully Jackrabbit had the kindness to pile a bunch of mattresses on the basement floor directly underneath the hole which he had created. The landing in full battle rattle was softened but still painful, especially to me the team leader, who was the first one to hit the mattresses with the remaining members of the team dropping on top of me adding injury to insult. The breacher was the last to drop and as his finger was on the trigger of his HK MP5, he suffered an accidental discharge of his weapon and shot the number four guy right in the butt. It was a through-and-through so although bloody, was not life threatening and the support guys got him into an ambulance within minutes.

After the casualty was in professional hands, we turned on the Surefire lights mounted under the muzzles of our MP5's and took a look around. Sure enough, in the middle of the room was a wooden kitchen chair with a red envelope on it. Jackrabbit was just letting us know that he was getting out of the dope business as the profit margin was getting too low since Colorado had legalized pot. He suggested that we had better things to do than chase him in the future. By the way, there was a big fentanyl shipment coming in two days from today at Union Station in LoDo, hidden in the bottles of several oxy-acetylene welding sets. He gave details and locations for when and where the welding sets would be delivered.

We found out later that Jackrabbit and his crew had knocked holes in the five walls in the attic spaces separating each of the individual units. Jackrabbit had simply prepared his tiger trap then climbed up in the attic, crawled through the holes to the unit at the far end of the building then climbed down and walked out the front door to a waiting vehicle. The guy was a legend as well as a pain in my ass.

CHAPTER 2

MY NAME IS JOHN FISHER, which naturally led to the nickname 'King'. The original John 'King' Fisher was a gunman, outlaw and lawman in Texas back in the Old West who was shot and killed in San Antonio on March 11, 1884. My parents had a strange sense of humor. I'm roughly 5'11 tall, tipping the scales at about 175 pounds with an athletic but not beefy build. I've still got a full head of brown hair that I keep in a flattop simply because I like the look and its low maintenance. People tell me I sort of look like a younger, smoother and more intelligent version of Jason Statham, with much more hair.

I grew up in the little town of Bern, Idaho doing all the things that young guys do growing up in a rural environment; hunting, fishing and rodeoing, which I was never any good at. My father was the ranch foreman for a big cattle ranch to the northwest of Bern while my mother taught English at Bear Lake High School in Montpelier, the high school I eventually graduated from.

Like many young people who grow up in a rural setting, I wanted to go see what the world was like outside of our little corner of Idaho. Since my family could not afford to send me to college, I did what many young guys in my circumstances do, I enlisted in the Army. After basic training and all that nonsense, I was assigned to the infantry with a Military Occupational

Specialty (MOS) of 11B, infantryman. I eventually became airborne qualified and before my enlistment was over, I had progressed to an MOS of 11B2P or Light Infantry Paratrooper Team Leader assigned to the 101st Airborne Division, 2nd Brigade Combat Team out of Fort Campbell, Kentucky. As an E5 sergeant I was responsible for the physical and mental readiness, weapons proficiency, medical skills proficiency and the leadership development of the members of my team. This was very good training not only in weapons and tactics, but in leadership as well. The problem was that this is not a very marketable skill set in the civilian world.

Once my enlistment was over, I shopped around and decided that I'd try to hire on with the DEA and then get into their Special Operations Division (SOD), which I did. This is what led to me to being face down in a pile of old mattresses with the other humiliated members of my SOD team piling down on top of me.

After surviving Jackrabbit's tiger trap and being totally fed up with the current 'catch and release' mentality where criminals were apprehended and then released with little or no bail, to simply go out and repeat whatever had led to them being apprehended in the first place, I finally decided that since I was now 33 years old that I needed to do something else with my life.

Due to my upbringing in rural Idaho and my chosen career path, I was something of a 'gun enthusiast' and decided to try owning and operating a gun shop, with the idea that at some point I would get into gunsmithing and eventually manufacturing my own brand of custom firearms. With this in mind, I got my FFL, my federal firearms license, and bought a small shop in Loveland, Colorado on the corner of 14th Street SW and Highway 287, a good high traffic area. I also rented a small farmhouse about a mile from the shop as the crow flies. The farmhouse was set off by itself in the northwest corner of a large field, about 50 acres, that was planted in wheat during the season. The nearest neighbor was another farmhouse about half a mile to the south, which gave me a lot of privacy. The rented farmhouse also had several outbuildings which allowed me buy, refurbish and then sell old cars and trucks which I found on the farms in the area. It was something which I always enjoyed doing and gave me another source of income while the gun shop got going.

About a year and a half after the tiger trap incident, I came home to the farmhouse around 9:00pm, after locking up the gun shop and making sure that all my stock was secured in the basement. I parked my old '65 Dodge D100 stepside pickup, possibly the ugliest American pickup truck every built, in front of the farmhouse. The truck was so ugly it actually grew on you after a while so I'd been slowly but surely bringing it up to speed mechanically. I hadn't gotten around to trying to make it cosmetically appealing yet, assuming that this was even possible.

Anyhow, as soon as I walked in the front door, I could tell that something wasn't quite right. The lights were out so I couldn't see anything amiss, but there was something wrong with the smell, it had a coppery taint to it. Walking to the kitchen in the back I turned on the light and all was revealed. There were two older Hispanic guys, both about 60 years old I would say, sitting at my kitchen table. Sitting may not be accurate, they were actually slouching back in the chairs with their legs splayed out in front of them, one on each end of the table facing me and they were both looking the worse for the wear. The smaller guy on the righthand side of the table was actually bleeding all over the old linoleum floor, while the guy on the right was trying to hold an old, single action Colt revolver on me but he could barely hold it up and the muzzle was making figure eights in the air while he tried to hold it steady.

"Looks like Pancho and Lefty may have bitten off more than they could chew somewhere," I observed. They obviously didn't get the connection to the old Willie Nelson tune so I continued. "Boss, why don't you put that hog leg down before you drop it and shoot one of us in the foot. Can I get you guys a beer or something?"

Laying the gun on the table, the big guy said, "I probably don't have the strength left to pull the trigger in any case. A beer would go down well, what do you say, Miguel?" He asked the other guy. Miguel said that a beer would be most welcome, so I grabbed three beers out of the refrigerator and passed them out. After everyone had taken a few swigs I asked, "You guys want to tell me what this is all about?"

"Well, what you are witnessing here is the result of a business meeting with some old colleagues from back in the day which did not go the way that we thought it would. The other party was not receptive to our suggestions and took it personally. We managed to disengage from the negotiations after a violent confrontation and here we are," said the larger, un-perforated guy.

"Okay, I can see that your meeting went a bit sideways, but how did you decide on my humble abode as your sanctuary and how did you get here?"

"To answer your second question first, you will find an old Ford F-150 backed into the shed on the south side of your house. It is not stolen, but our disgruntled ex-business partners may be looking for it. Perhaps you should leave it in the shed for a little while. The answer to the first question may be a bit confusing. The fact is that you came highly recommended. To answer your unvocalized third question, I picked the lock on your front door. I thought that you would appreciate the finesse as opposed to just kicking it in."

I had to think about this for a second as I was sure that I had never had any dealings with these guys, or anyone associated with these guys. "Thank you for your consideration concerning my front door, it is appreciated. I think mystifying is more appropriate than confusing regarding my first question, but let's leave it at that for now and let me go get my trauma kit before your buddy bleeds to death on my kitchen floor."

The big guy just waved me on, so I went into the living room and got my trauma kit out of the cabinet in the corner. Since my old Army days, I had always kept a trauma kit handy and made sure that it was comprehensive and nothing was past its use-by date. Going back into the kitchen I knelt in front of the smaller guy and used my shears to cut his jeans from the hem to the knee exposing his entire shin. Getting out the hydrogen peroxide and some gauze I cleaned up his lower leg and it was obvious that he had a through-and-through gunshot wound through his calf muscle. There was no pulsing blood flow so the guy hadn't been hit in an artery, which made things a bit easier.

After cleaning both wounds thoroughly with hydrogen peroxide, I then asked the big guy to come over behind his partner and to hold him down by the shoulders as the next step was going to hurt. I explained that I needed to apply a clotting agent and for the clotting agent to work I needed to secure it in place. Clotting agents work by creating heat which cauterizes the wound, this means that it is very painful. I applied the clotting agent, Miguel whimpered while the big guy held him down and eventually the pain died down to a dull roar. At this point I pulled the edges of the wounds together and secured them in place with SteriStrips and applied antibiotic cream to both of the holes. I then covered the wounds with an Israeli bandage, one hole covered by the gauze built into the dressing and the other covered with added gauze. The Israeli bandage itself provided the required pressure. This was the best that I could do for Miguel, and he'd be fine until he could get to a proper doctor.

"Remind me never to go to a business meeting with you guys, that is a gunshot wound. Miguel is going to be okay for a day or so, but he needs to get some professional medical attention as soon as possible. Right now, I'd say that if you don't want to go to the emergency room and explain this GSW to the staff there, the best thing you two can do is try to get some sleep. There is a bed made up in the guest room and the couch is available. If you do not feel that you can trust me, then one of you will need to stay awake and make sure that I don't do anything foolish. I'll let you guys' figure that one out."

Coming downstairs in the morning I saw the big fella was asleep in the recliner with the footstool attachment kicked out while Miguel was snoring on the couch. Good for them, they were both at the end of their tethers last night. I went into the kitchen and made coffee and a huge plate of scrambled eggs and half a loaf of toast. Going into the living room I shook the big guy awake and told him breakfast was ready if he'd help Miguel into the kitchen.

We managed to polish off all the eggs and toast with Miguel eating more than his share, which was good. While sitting around afterwards drinking coffee I asked them what their plan was.

"We need to get to Trinidad by tonight. If you can drop us by the bus depot, we'll get headed that way.", said the big guy.

"There is no way that you will be able to keep Miguel comfortable on a bus for that length of time and there is no guarantee that you'd be able to get to Trinidad by tonight once you purchase tickets and with the stops in Denver, Colorado Springs and Pueblo."

"Then what do you suggest?" asked Miguel. "Our options are somewhat limited at the moment."

"Why don't you guys take my truck. Once you get to Trinidad call me and tell me where you left it. I'll report it stolen and you can call in an anonymous tip to the sheriff in Trinidad and tell him where he can find it. I'll drive your truck around if I need to."

"That is very thoughtful of you. Why are you doing this for complete strangers?" asked the larger of the two who still had not given his name.

"Well, to be honest, I am intrigued by your comment last night that I came highly recommended. Secondly, you guys were in a bind and were no threat to me so I did what I could for you."

"What do you mean that we were no threat to you? I had the revolver sort of pointed at you occasionally when you first walked into the kitchen."

Reaching behind my back I took out my old re-worked Colt Gold Cup. "You never even thought to pat me down, but in any case, it was not necessary."

Shaking his head, the big guy said, "Sometimes it baffles me as to how I have managed to live this long."

Walking them out to the old Dodge I gave them the keys then shook hands with both men and wished them well. I also reiterated that they needed to let me know when they were finished with the truck so that I could report it stolen. The big guy told me not to worry about it, he'd have it delivered back to me with a full tank of gas within a week.

As they drove off, I wondered who my house guests were and what they'd been up to. I'd probably never know, but it had made for an interesting evening.

CHAPTER 3

FIVE DAYS LATER I DROVE their old Ford F-150 home from the shop at the end of a fairly profitable day, to find my ugly old '65 Dodge pickup parked in front of the farmhouse. It had been detailed inside and out, although detailing the outside was a waste of time at this point since I had only rebuilt it mechanically and hadn't gotten around to the body yet. The gas tank was full as promised and there was an envelope taped to the dashboard. Parking the F-150 back in the shed, I walked back out front and grabbed the keys and the envelope from the Dodge, went into the house and got a beer out of the refrigerator before sitting on the couch to see what was in the envelope. I was surprised and intrigued, the note in the envelope read as follows:

'Mr. Fisher,

Thank you for your kindness and assistance last week, it was much appreciated. Miguel is healing nicely and would like me to convey his thanks to you for the expert medical care you provided during his time of need.

I would like to offer you employment that I think you would find both financially rewarding as well as professionally satisfying. If you think that this would be of interest to you, could you meet me at the Mission Deli Mesa

Steak House in La Veta this Saturday for lunch, say around 12:00pm? Lunch is on me.

If you do not show up, I will take that to mean that you are not interested in my offer although I think you should hear me out first and give it some thought.

Again, thank you for the kindness which you showed to Miguel and I.

Sincerely,
The big one with the pistol'

For a variety of reasons, I would have to go to this appointment. I was curious as to what role he had in mind concerning the employment and you should never dismiss an opportunity, but I was also curious as to who this guy was and how I had been recommended to him.

Since it was roughly 225 miles from Loveland to La Veta, I hit the road around 6:00 the following Saturday morning. It is basically a solid metroplex driving south on I-25 along the Front Range from Fort Collins in the north until you break out of it just north of Castle Rock in the south. Since I had left early and it was a Saturday, I made good time all the way to Walsenburg. Taking the Walsenburg exit off I-25, I looped around and got on State Road 160 heading west-southwest. After a scenic 15 miles or so on 160, I cut left onto State Road 12 and had gone about a mile when I saw a candy apple red '66 Mustang pulled off the side of the road with the hood up and a rather shapely blue jean clad female rear end poking out over the front bumper while the owner of said rear end was looking at something in the engine compartment. Pulling off the road a few yards in front of the Mustang I got out to see if I could offer assistance. By this time the owner of the rear end, and apparently the Mustang as well, was leaning back against the front of the car with her arms across her chest waiting to see what I was going to do.

At this point it is only fair that I describe the woman leaning against the front of the Mustang. She was dressed in snug, well-worn Wrangler jeans over brown laced up roper boots with an Aztec patterned V-necked Boho blouse tucked into the jeans. I'd say she was about 5'9" tall, slender yet shapely with long black hair down past her shoulders that was riotously curly. This was to be expected as although she looked Hispanic at first glance, there was some other blood in there as well, either Caribbean or Brazilian I would guess. Her skin was slightly darker than that of a pure Hispanic, her lips slightly fuller, but her hips and backside were not as pronounced as they are on many Caribbean or African girls. Her backside looked about the size and shape of a properly inflated 12" Pilates ball, which is the definition of a perfect female derrière. I'd guess her bust size as a 32B, but at this point that was only an educated guess on my part. Think of a darker, sexier version of Jessica Alba in 'Into the Blue' mixed with a less voluptuous version of Halle Berry in 'Die Another Day' and you wouldn't be far off.

"What seems to be the problem?" I asked.

"I really don't know. It was running just fine, then it just quit."

"Do you mind if I take a look, I know a little bit about these things?"

She hesitated for a second, which is understandable when you consider that she was an attractive woman alone on a deserted road with a strange man offering to help. The world has gotten very distrustful these days. I guess that since I had not approached too close and was being polite, she said she'd be grateful if I could help her out.

As she moved out of the way to let me lean into the engine compartment, I could smell some sort of sandalwood and jasmine perfume. Not only was she incredibly easy on the eyes, she smelled good too. Anyhow, after a cursory inspection of the engine I noticed that the lead to the center of the distributor from the coil had pulled loose from its socket on the distributor cap. Plugging it back in I asked her to see if it would fire up. It did and was running fine. I told her to just hold on a second and I'd get some duct tape out of my truck and tape it in place although she should probably replace that lead once she got to where she was going.

I shut the hood as she got out of the car to thank me. "Thank you very much, that was very nice of you. By the way, my name is Kassandra. I'd offer to buy you lunch, but I am in a big hurry and I have to run." I told her that the pleasure was all mine and that I hoped we'd run into each other again some time. She said that would be nice and drove off. If girls like Kassandra grew wild in Huerfano County, I'd take whatever job was on offer just for the scenery.

Anyhow, after sitting in my truck on the side of the road while I drank a bottle of water, I finally got back on the road and pulled into the parking lot of the Mission Deli Mesa Steak House. Lo and behold, that same red Mustang was parked out front. Life was getting interesting. I parked beside the Mustang and walked in to find Kassandra sitting at a table with her back to the front door talking to the man I had come to see.

Kassandra turned around in her chair when she heard the door chime ring as I walked in. "That is the man who helped me out with the car, Papa." She said to the older Hispanic man at the table. Looking at me she asked, "Are you following me?"

"Kassandra, as enjoyable as it would be to follow you and the view it would provide while doing so, the fact is that I have a business meeting with the gentleman sitting across from you at that table."

She turned back to her Papa, "Do you know this man? What business are you going to discuss?"

"Kassy, I know of this man but do not really know him personally at this point. He is here at my invitation to discuss employment with our trucking firm. Now be a good daughter and go help Maria in the kitchen as she prepares lunch for Mr. Fisher and I."

Kassandra got up and walked back to the kitchen. I was mesmerized by the wiggle in her walk. "Mr. Fisher, although I can fully appreciate your interest in my daughter's backside, I must warn you that this sort of attention is fraught with danger. Not so much from me, although she is my only daughter, but I warn you that her bark and her bite are both formidable.

"Now that we have that out of the way, perhaps we can get down to business. My name is Hector Archuleta and you've met my daughter Kassandra. I own a very successful trucking company based in Walsenburg.

During the past year I have incurred significant losses due to some of my loads getting hijacked. I would like to hire you as a security consultant to help me remedy this situation."

Hector was probably in his early 60's, about 6' tall with broad shoulders and a beefy build that looked to be mostly muscle. He still had a full head of salt and pepper hair. His hands were large and the forearms below the rolled-up sleeves of his Levi work shirt were corded with muscle. Even at his age I'd bet he'd be a handful if he got annoyed.

I thought about this for a second before replying, "Mr. Archuleta, although I appreciate the offer of employment, the position which you describe would seem to require someone with a much different set of skills than a yet to be successful gun shop owner."

"That is true, Mr. Fisher, but let's not play games here. You were an Army E5, a sergeant, with an MOS of 11B2P or Light Infantry Paratrooper Team Leader. After leaving the military you joined the DEA's Special Operations Division and spent six years with them as a Special Agent/Team Leader. I believe that you have the skill sets that I require."

I just sat there and looked at Hector for a minute before asking how he could possibly know all of that?

Hector smiled at me then simply said, "I'm Jackrabbit."

You could have knocked me over with a feather, but everything was starting to fall into place; the comment at my place in Loveland that I had come 'highly recommended' and the comment earlier to Kassandra that Hector knew 'of this man'. It also went a long way toward explaining the condition that he and Miguel were in after their "business meeting with an old colleague from back in the day which had not gone the way that they thought it would."

"May I call you King? The reason that I was so successful in my past enterprise, which intersected with your previous line of work, was that I made sure that I knew who was targeting me, what assets they had available and their logistical concerns and constraints. I actually knew where you were going to be before you did. Yes, I had informants within the DEA and the

SOD, it was money well spent. Granted, I dealt in dope and was therefore a person of interest to the DEA, but I got out of that business shortly after you and your friends fell into that basement in the Capital Hills neighborhood. Seriously though, now that marijuana has been legalized in Colorado and considering that was all that I dealt in, my past should be forgiven. Furthermore, no one in law enforcement or any of my crew was ever injured by my actions except for the unfortunate man that was accidentally shot in the butt when he fell into that hole in Capital Hills."

"Feel free to call me King if I may call you Hector. I really don't know what to say."

At this point Kassandra hip checked the door to the kitchen open and came into the room carrying a big plate on each forearm. On each plate was a large green chili pork burrito with a side of refried beans, it smelled terrific. Placing them on the table she turned to go to get the drinks.

"Thanks, Kassy," I said, it seemed like the proper thing to say at the moment. She jerked to a stop, turned around and sauntered back over to the Hector's side of the table before leaning down with both hands flat on the table looking me right in the eye.

"You do not know me well enough to address me as Kassy, and maybe you never will. In the future, please refer to me as Kassandra. I do not know why my father feels we need to bring a stranger into this situation. Please keep in mind that I am part owner of the trucking company and as such if you work for Papa, you also work for me."

Kassy turned around and walked back into the kitchen. When the door closed behind her, I looked at Hector and asked, "Is she always like that?"

"Actually, no. This is the first time I have seen her fired up in a long time. I am thinking that perhaps she finds you interesting, even though you are a gringo," Hector said with a chuckle.

"If that is what she is like when she interested in someone, I'd hate to see her if she is disinterested in them."

At this point Kassy butted the door open again and came to the table with a tray that held two glasses with ice and a pitcher of iced tea. Setting this on the table she started back to the kitchen while saying over her shoulder, "You really do not want to see me when I am disinterested in someone. Keep that in mind always, Mr. Fisher." She had obviously been eavesdropping on our conversation.

"Hector, I'm not sure I need the headache of working with Kassandra, but let's hear what you have to say and take it from there."

"I heard that!" Obviously, Kassandra was still eavesdropping from the kitchen.

Hector laid out his proposal. I would move down to La Veta and re-open my gun shop here. Hector would provide the location for the shop as well as suitable accommodation rent free for a year. While in La Veta I would be expected to come up with a strategy and the tactics to combat the recent hijacking problem. Financially Hector would remunerate me on the basis of a consultancy paid for each day, or part thereof, spent in the service of Hector's trucking company working on the security problem.

"What rate would you be paying for the consultancy service?" I asked.

"I'm thinking $1,000 per day. Keep in mind that your shop and accommodation are rent free for the first year. We would need to re-evaluate the rate once we get a better idea as to what your job will require and the time you would need to spend at your consultancy duties."

I thought about this, then said, "La Veta is out of the way and not on any travel corridor, I can't see where a gun shop here would ever be profitable."

"I am a very well-respected resident of Huerfano County with both the residents and the elected officials. I believe that I can guarantee you a reasonable amount of business although it would be handy if you were a gunsmith as well. We do not have a good one in the region at the moment and this would definitely increase your business."

We went to work on our burritos while I considered the offer. Eventually I asked Hector when he needed an answer. Hector said that the hijacking was getting out of control and was costing him big money, so the sooner the better. I replied that I'd go back to Loveland tonight to run some numbers and do some research on how much paperwork was required to get my present stock from Loveland to La Veta, but that I would let Hector know by the following Wednesday.

Hector and I stood up and shook hands. I said that I would need Hector's number to stay in touch, so Hector sent me a WhatsApp message with his contact details. Checking my phone to ensure it had arrived I asked, "How's Miguel getting along these days?" Hector said he was recovering just fine and that there didn't appear to be any lasting damage thanks to my timely ministrations.

"That's good, tell him I said hello, would you?"

"Consider it done," said Hector.

"One last question, is there an auto parts store in town?"

"Sadly, no. We need to go to the NAPA in Walsenburg to get parts. Why do you ask?"

"Kassy needs a new lead from the coil to the distributor. Maybe one of the guys at your shop in Walsenburg can bring one down. She runs the risk of it conking out every time she drives at the moment."

"Good idea, I'll call the shop this afternoon."

Kassy stuck her head out of the kitchen door where she had been eavesdropping and informed me that I seemed to have forgotten our earlier discussion where she had made it clear that as far as I was concerned, that I should address her as Kassandra. When she had gone back into the kitchen Hector looked at me and said, "I think you may have a problem there amigo. Be brave. I will pray for you."

From the kitchen someone said, "I heard that, Papa!"

CHAPTER 4

AS I DROVE BACK TO Loveland, I thought over the proposition that Hector had made. At first blush it didn't make any sense to pack up and relocate my gun shop, which had only been established in Loveland for just over a year and a half, simply on a verbal promise of a reasonable amount of business in La Veta. That said, Hector seemed like a stand-up guy and the idea of earning a grand a day for doing what I had been trained to do seemed too good to be true. I'd have to run the numbers, but a year's rent free for both the shop and accommodation would allow me to bank some money in any case. I'd just have to see how much of a hassle it would be to move my business and stock from Loveland to La Veta.

On the personal side of things, I was intrigued by Kassandra. Not that I thought we'd ever be an item or form of a relationship of any kind, but just being around her would be interesting and likely entertaining. First things first, I'd have to run the numbers like a rational adult to see if the move made financial sense. If it did, the taming of the shrew, or the attempt thereof, would simply be icing on the cake.

Sunday rolled around. Sitting at the kitchen table I got out my laptop and began running the numbers. If I could sell the present gun shop and break even on the shop and pay off the present loan, then that would be a wash. If I happened to make a little on the sale, that would be a bonus. I'd also end up saving the rent on the farmhouse which was running about a grand a month. From that point on, everything I made on the security gig or from the new gun shop would be profit, at least for a year. Last but not least, the scenery around the Spanish Peaks was absolutely beautiful and there was plenty of hunting to be had in the fall and good fishing to be had all over the Sangro De Cristo range year-round. The more I thought about it, the better it looked and then there was still the Kassandra component to consider. As politically incorrect as it may be, there is nothing wrong with 'eye candy' in the workplace.

After building a spreadsheet to weigh the financial pros and cons, I started researching just what paperwork and hassle would be involved in moving my present business and the stock of guns and ammunition from Loveland to La Veta. The movement of a large number of firearms and ammunition within Colorado was not sufficiently addressed on the internet, so I called a buddy of mine in the ATF (Alcohol, Tobacco and Firearms) to see if he could help me out. I was told that moving weapons and ammo between states was not an issue, but the rules did not directly apply to moving these items from one FFL shop to another new FFL shop within a state. He suggested that I contact the local sheriff and see what he said.

That seemed like a good idea, so I called up the sheriff's office in Larimer County and had a chat with Sheriff Justin Smith. He suggested that I get a shipping container and set a date for the trip down to La Veta. On the day that the shipping container was to be loaded up, the sheriff would provide a deputy to be on hand to witness the loading of the container. The deputy would then place a metal strip seal through each of the two lock rod handles once the container was loaded. An off-duty deputy would then accompany the container to the final destination and cut the seals off once there. He would remain on location until the shipping container was empty and all the weapons and ammo were again in another secure FFL location. I'd need to feed, water and pay the deputies for their time, but Hector could organize the shipping container, truck and trailer, and hopefully some help. So far, so good.

On Wednesday morning I called Hector on the number that he'd given me on WhatsApp and told him that I'd like to take him up on his offer, but if he wanted me down there as soon as possible I'd need some help. I explained the deal with the shipping container and truck as well as the fact that I could use some manpower. I'd also need to put the old gun shop on the market and stop the lease on the house. As I'd be moving around $300,000 dollars' worth of guns and ammo to an undisclosed location in La Veta, that location would need to be secured with things like burglar bars on the windows, steel doors and doorframes and if it had a basement that would be great, but it would have to be burglar proofed as well.

Hector was quiet for a moment as he pondered my requests. Finally, he said, "First, don't put the old shop on the market, I have somebody in mind that would like to buy it. Second, you pick the day that you want to move the guns and such and I'll have a shipping container on a truck parked in front of your house the night before with a crew to help you out. I'll send Miguel up to ramrod the crew and he can also bring back my old F-150 that we left up there earlier. I have already purchased your new gun shop here in town and will have it brought up to secure FFL gun shop specs by the time you get here. Let's plan to get this all done and dusted by the end of next week." I like a guy who will take charge, this was almost too easy, then I heard someone talking in the background.

"Hold on, King, somebody wants to talk to you." I could hear the phone changing hands then Kassandra was on the line.

"Hello, Mr. Fisher. How are you today?"

"Ah, it is the delightful Kassandra. What can your newest indentured servant do for you this fine day?"

"First off, you can quit being a smartass. I believe that we may have gotten off on the wrong foot. That said, you still technically work for me, and I need a favor." Interesting.

"Well, Ms. Kassandra, I technically only work for you when I am on the Azteca Trucking Lines clock. Other than that, I work for myself. Now how may I be of assistance?"

"You are an impossible man; do you know that? I bet you spend much time alone."

"I do. Now how can I assist the person who seems to be determined to make my new circumstances as irksome as possible?"

"Keep it up, Mr. Fisher and I'll show you what irksome really looks like. Now back to business. I have placed an order for some clothing at Cloz to Home in Loveland since I knew that you would take the job here, it was simply women's intuition. The shop is at 129 East 4th Street next to the Chophouse. Would you mind picking the order up and bringing it down with you when you come?"

"Well, that depends. What do I get out of the deal?"

"My undying gratitude for starters and I'd owe you one."

"Do I get to pick the form of payback, or is that too risky for you?"

"I think that you are pushing your luck, Mr. Fisher."

I heard the phone being passed back to Hector who was chuckling. "I don't know what you said to her, but she is pulling her hair out in frustration. I haven't seen her this animated since she beat the crap out of the guy at the rodeo who grabbed her butt. I can't wait until you get down here, this is promising to be a very interesting summer!"

"Please inform Kassandra that I must be getting soft in my old age, but that I'll pick up her stuff for her and bring it down with me. Tell her that I was just winding her up and that she had better get used to it. Can you send the truck, container and crew up to my place next Tuesday? I'll put every one up at my place and we can then drive over to the shop and get an early start on Wednesday."

Hector was still chuckling when he told me that sounded like a good plan and that he'd talk to me over the weekend.

I'd finalized things with Hector over the weekend, and had settled the plans with the sheriff's department to get my guns and ammo down to La Veta on Wednesday. Miguel would be at my place Tuesday evening with the truck, container and crew, so Tuesday afternoon I got the grill ready to fire up and put a case of beer in the refrigerator after making sure that the spare bedroom and couch were ready for guests. I'd also had to get four surplus Army cots earlier in the week from the Army-Navy Surplus store in town to give the boys somewhere to sleep.

Around 6:00 Tuesday evening a fairly new Freightliner truck with a shipping container on a flatbed trailer pulled up in front of the house followed by a F-250 crew cab with four Hispanic guys in it. Both trucks had the Azteca Trucking Line logo on their sides, a stylized thunderbird. Miguel was driving the semi with a guy riding shotgun and he hopped out as soon as the truck stopped and hobbled over to shake my hand. As the other guys came over, he introduced them. I am terrible with names, especially when they are all Hispanic. I decided to rename them Bashful, Doc, Dopey, Grumpy and Happy

I showed them the sleeping arrangements and gave them a tour of the house so that they would know where everything was at before I headed out beside the house to get the grill fired up. After the cheeseburgers were devoured, apparently they didn't get enough burgers down in La Veta as they were all gone in a flash, we sat on the front porch and had a few beers while we went over the plan for tomorrow. Around 10:30 everyone decided to call it a day and we all went in to get some shut-eye and prepare for a long day tomorrow.

Miguel had gotten up at the crack of dawn and had coffee, eggs and bacon ready by the time the rest of us showed up in the kitchen. After breakfast, Dopey drove the semi over to the gun shop while Bashful, Doc, Grumpy and Happy drove over in the F-250. Miguel and I cleaned up the house before locking it up for the last time then Miguel jumped in the old F-150 that he and Hector had left here on their original visit and drove over to the shop. I took a last look at the farmhouse and followed everyone in my old Dodge pickup.

Dopey expertly positioned the trailer so that the end of the trailer carrying the shipping container was up against the loading dock at the back of the shop and we could simply carry everything from the shop directly to the open shipping container without having to go to down to ground level and hand everything back up. I'd packed everything as securely as possible over the past week, so it was simply a matter of carrying each box or crate from the shop to the shipping container and placing them carefully on the shipping mats which Hector had provided. I'd boxed up all the ammo by caliber, so it was easier to move than the guns themselves. It took us about three hours of constant work to get everything loaded up and secured, so we were ready to head south at around 11:00 in the morning.

The sheriff's deputy, Deputy Bridgeman, sealed the container and noted both seal ID numbers before declaring that we were good to go. Miguel and I drove over to MacDonald's in his F-150 to get enough burgers, fries and Cokes to provide lunch for everyone while we were on the road. We would eat en route to La Veta. Dopey got back behind the wheel of the semi with Bashful riding shotgun, the other dwarves piled into the F-250 and they all pulled out of the loading area onto 402 heading about 5 miles east to catch I-25 south and begin the long run to La Veta. Since he was off duty, Deputy Bridgeman got into his personal vehicle and tucked in behind the F-250 for the 5 hour trip.

Miguel rode with me into Loveland to pick up Kassandra's order at Cloz to Home before I took him back by the old shop to pick up the F-150. We got back on 14th Street SW, which became 402 east of the old gun shop, and made our way to I-25 south as well.

The convoy pulled over at the Air Force Academy Airfield Overlook just north of Colorado Springs and we all got out to stretch our legs and eat our cold McDonald's burgers and fries. Miguel and I had caught up with our shipping container and the boys just outside of Del Camino and we had been running south in a convoy at a constant 60 miles an hour ever since. We had about another 2 hours to go until we arrived in La Veta.

Miguel and I were sitting on the tailgate of my ugly old Dodge pickup sharing a bottle of water, which I took as the perfect opportunity to try and pick his brain regarding Kassandra, the La Veta shrew.

"Miguel, I'm flying a little blind at the moment and could use some information and advice." I thought this was an acceptable lead-in to an interrogation, but Miguel was way ahead of me.

"You are going to quiz me about Kassy, aren't you?"

"Well, technically I am not allowed to call her Kassy, so to be accurate I was about to interrogate you concerning Kassandra."

This got a smile from Miguel. "Listen closely, gringo, I only want to go through this once. Kassy, Kassandra to you, is an angel. I realize that this may come as a surprise to you, but it is so.

"As you may have noticed, Kassy is not pure Hispanic. Her mother was from the Dominican Republic, Hector met her mother in Santo Domingo 30 years ago when he was smuggling all matter of things around the Caribbean. Kassy, Kassandra to you, is mixed race Caribbean and Mexican and this is where she gets her unique features. I find her to be a very captivating young lady.

"Her mother Yolanda passed away from breast cancer 10 years ago when Kassy was 19 and attending the University of Colorado at Boulder, because of this Kassy is very protective of Hector. You should be writing this down.

"Kassy has earned a Bachelor of Science in Business Administration with a Master's degree in Accounting; she is a very clever girl. She does all the accounting and bookkeeping for Hector's trucking firm.

"Kassy was engaged to be married to some hijo de puta frat boy her senior year at college, but the useless pendejo managed to do us all a favor when he got drunk at a frat party before getting into the Porsche that his father had bought for him and running off the road on the way to Denver doing about 120. There was not much left of either him or the Porsche.

"Eventually Kassy got over this and came home to help out Hector with his businesses. To my knowledge she has never shown any interest in another man although every male between the ages of 14 and 64 in Huerfano County has shown an interest in her at one time or the other. You really can't blame them.

"That's all you are getting out of me now. Do with it what you will. For some unknown reason you seem to have lit a fire under our Kassy. Whether you get burned or not remains to be seen. I will light a light a candle for you."

We pulled into La Veta about 4:00 in the afternoon, but I didn't know where the new shop was located. Not to worry, Miguel did. We convoyed through town on South Main Street then hung a left on High Street then hung another left into the driveway of what appeared to be a very large single story old brick house that, according to the sign above the front door, was the old VFW meeting hall. This house was set in a huge yard exactly in the middle of the block on the northern side of High Street. The only other houses on that side of the street were at either end of the street. The driveway ran up the right, or eastern side of the house, so that is where we parked the semi. Kassandra's little red Mustang was unoccupied and parked in front of the house on High Street, which meant that she was probably inside waiting for us. Sure enough, as the tractor trailer came to a halt beside the house, Kassandra opened the front door and yelled, "Welcome home, boys! You too, Mr. Fisher."

Now I should have been annoyed at being an afterthought to her salutation, but the fact was that Kassandra was dressed in what appeared to be her professional office attire; a black pinstripe pencil skirt that came down to a few inches above her knees, no hose to detract from the natural wonder of her legs, wedge pumps that tightened an already shapely calf and a tailored white blouse that showed off her figure while highlighting her caramel skin. The result was so stunning that I think that I may have gone into mild hypovolemic shock for a second.

Once I had recovered, I followed everyone into the house and took a look around. The place was open planned and at one time had been equipped with a bar along the wall to the right as you walked in the front door. Hector had been busy and there was a counter built about 5 feet out from the wall to the left running almost the whole length of the room from front to back, with a small office at the front of the building in the southwest corner. The top of the counter was made from shatterproof glass and would be ideal for showing off handguns and smaller items and a hinged gate had been installed in the middle to allow access behind the showcase counter. Behind this freestanding case they had built a set of lockable cabinets about waist high, also with shatterproof glass fronts, which would be perfect for displaying ammunition. This also provided a narrow waist high counter against the left hand, or western wall. Above this, the builders had installed industrial pegboard where I could present my rifles and shotguns horizontally simply by adjusting the provided pegs to fit any specific firearm. This was a very good start.

In the back was a kitchen that was much too big for a family residence, so I guessed that when the place had a bar, the bar had also served food. There were bar-type bathrooms on either side as you walked through the little passageway to get to the kitchen. Just before the kitchen, on the left hand side of the passage just past the restrooms was another door that opened to a set of wooden stairs leading down to a full basement. This was an incredibly good start to my business.

That said, running down the middle of the main room, from front to back was a little wooden wall about waist high with a swinging door in the middle of it. It reminded me of what you would find in a courtroom separating the lawyers' tables and judges' bench from the spectators, court reporters and riff raff. I was looking at this when Kassandra came walking out of the kitchen and over to where I was standing.

"Well, Mr. Fisher, what do you think about your new shop?"

"First, would you please just call me King like everybody else does? I'm really not into the formal address thing like some others here who will remain nameless. Secondly, the work done on the western half of the building is outstanding. I may have to install some freestanding shelves and so forth running out perpendicular from in front of the showcase counter, but that can be sorted out later. Finally, I'm trying to figure out why they built this courtroom divider and gate running down the middle of the room," I answered.

"Well, if you prefer to be casually addressed by your adolescent nickname, then I will accommodate you. The courtroom divider and gate as you call it is very easy to explain. We will be in business together. I will open a Caribbean themed taqueria on the eastern or right-hand side of the room while you run your gun shop from the other side. I think it has promise, you can shop for guns with your family and have a convenient breakfast or lunch either before or after you shop." She was not only serious when she said all this, she was positively beaming.

I just turned around and walked out the front door to begin unloading my guns and ammo. I think I was going into shock again and it had nothing to do with the Caribbean-Hispanic stunner standing in the middle of what I thought was going to be a gun store. I'd need to speak to Hector quickly before this idea actually took hold.

"I've already got a name for it, 'Kassy's and the Caribbean King's Taqueria and Gun Shop'," she proudly announced as I left the building.

CHAPTER 5

WE HAD ALL THE GUNS and ammo securely locked up in the basement of the new shop by 8:00 that evening. I'd paid off Deputy Bridgeman and he took off back to Larimer County and home while I walked with Miguel and the dwarves to the Mission Deli Mesa Steak House where I had been interviewed by Hector and harassed by Kassandra a couple of weeks earlier. It was only one block over, at the corner of Oak Street and Cucharas Street, from the new gun shop cum taco stand. I bought the guys dinner and beers, and thanked them for all their help. After dinner we returned to the shop to get the truck and trailer back to wherever it needed to go, which just left Miguel and I standing in front of the new shop in the dark.

"Miguel, is there a motel in town? I just realized that unless I sleep in the shop that I do not have a place to lay my head this evening."

"I forgot to tell you, Hector booked you in this evening at the bed and breakfast over by the library on South Main Street. I've got the key in the truck. We'll all meet up at the gun shop and taco emporium tomorrow morning," Miguel said with a laugh as he climbed into his pickup, handed me the motel key and drove away.

The 1899 bed and breakfast was a lot more than you would have normally expected in a town the size of La Veta. Honestly it would have been a pretty upmarket bed and breakfast in Denver. I got a good night's sleep then got up around 8:00 for a shower and a shave before dressing in jeans and a black t-shirt. Tugging on my Timberland boots, which were obviously going to be a rarity in this cowboy town, I strolled to the dining room for a breakfast of scrambled eggs, bacon and coffee. After finishing my meal and relaxing with a second cup of hot, black coffee I went back to my room and loaded up my duffle bag and rucksack before checking out and driving the 5 blocks back to the new gun and grub store in town.

Arriving at the shop around 9:30, I saw Hector's F-150 parked beside the shop with a late model Toyota Tundra pulled up behind him. I also noticed that the door to the shop was open. It seems that I was not the only one with a set of keys to my new shop. Going inside I found Hector and Miguel sitting in the little office in the corner, Hector behind the desk and Miguel on the little sofa across from it, eating sopapillas from a paper bag on the desk and drinking coffee which they were pouring into Styrofoam cups from a huge thermos which was also on the desk.

"Good morning, gentlemen! May I join you?"

They kept munching but pointed at the paper bag and thermos, so I helped myself before sitting down on the sofa beside Miguel. While we enjoyed the sopapillas and coffee I politely asked if perhaps I could have all the keys for my shop.

"You already have all the keys to your shop, the ones we used were for Kassy's side," smirked Hector.

"And that brings up another issue. At which point did you fail to mention the fact that I was having a business partner? This was not mentioned when we discussed the job earlier." Miguel was trying not to laugh.

"May I point out that technically you do not have a business partner as Kassy will be responsible for the taqueria while you have sole ownership of the gun store," replied Hector.

"Hector, you are avoiding the issue and splitting hairs. What is going on here? As of now I am seriously thinking about heading back to Loveland since you have, in my mind at least, breached the contract and are not being transparent as far as I am concerned."

"Don't get your panties in a wad, King, this caught me by surprise as well. I had originally purchased this property with the idea that it would only be a gun shop. When Miguel and the boys ran up to Loveland to sort out moving your stuff from Loveland to here, Kassy sat me down at the kitchen table in our house and she showed me her well thought out business plan including the required capital outlay and the earning potential. She is good at this sort of thing. Anyhow, it looked good on paper, you were out of town, she is my daughter and technically you do not own this building until you have first right of refusal in a year," explained Hector.

"Have you ever heard of a phone, Hector? You could have called me at any time to discuss this issue."

"That is true, but the main reason I did not want to discuss this with you is that Kassy is hard-headed and impossible to deal with once she gets an idea in her head and the bit in her mouth. I would much prefer for you to deal with her than me. She is wearing me down in my advanced age."

"So essentially you are playing the senior citizen card while growing a set of slopping shoulders and sliding this whole gun shop and burrito boutique thing onto my plate. Is that correct?" I asked.

"Good, you see the whole picture clearly now so I can leave it to you," Hector replied with a smile. Miguel was grinning from ear to ear.

Hector continued to ruin my previously pleasant morning. "Kassy will be here sometime this afternoon to discuss this issue with you in detail. Try to keep an open mind, who knows it may even work."

"Fine as long as you two peons, I believe that is the correct terminology in this part of the country, are here to back me up if I conclude that this taqueria idea is not going to fly."

"We'd love to, King, but sadly our presence is required in Walsenburg today on business. I'll stop by later to see how it went," said Hector as he motioned for Miguel to make a move.

As they walked out the front door Miguel turned back to me and said, "I tried to tell you amigo, but don't worry I did light a candle for you." He was laughing his butt off as he headed out toward Hector's truck.

I spent the next few hours setting up my long gun displays on the pegboard above the waist high counter along the left-hand wall. I also brought up all the ammo, segregated it by caliber and stored it in the cabinets below the long guns. After a quick lunch at Corners Diner, I was back at the shop putting my handguns in the free standing display counter where the actual business would be transacted.

Around 3:00 Kassandra walked into the shop. Not seeing me in the main room she sauntered over to the office where I was making notes of what I still needed to do. She leaned against the door jamb while I studiously ignored her although I was kind of curious as to how she was attired today. That pencil skirt ensemble the other day was sensational, so I wondered what was on display today.

"What are you doing there, Mr. Fisher, I mean, King?" she asked.

"I am writing a book," I replied.

"What is the nature of this book you are writing, may I ask?"

"It's a short story concerning how to survive in either a personal or business relationship with Caribbean-Hispanic people. It is entitled, 'Run!'." At this point I put down my pen and looked up. Big mistake.

Kassandra was dressed in one of those Puebla Mexican peasant dresses, this one was bright yellow with embroidery across the breasts and up along the shoulders as well a bit in the middle below the breasts and another bit in the area that would politely be termed the lap. She paired this up with some flats that I really didn't pay much attention to. On any other women this attire would likely be less than remarkable, on this one it was rather awe inspiring.

Okay, at this point she already had an advantage over me as my heart was beginning to palpitate. She had stopped leaning against the door jamb and was now standing in the door with her arms straight down beside her with her hands made into fists. Her face was not pleasant and I thought that she was either going to throw a tantrum or go grab a gun out of my display case and shoot me.

"What is wrong with you! I try to be nice, and you just throw it back in my face. I came here in good faith to discuss our business arrangement and you sit there and heckle me. Can't you ever be serious?"

Sitting back in my chair, I decided to nip this in the bud before it went any further.

"Sit down on that sofa and don't say a word. I'm going to tell you how the cow ate the cabbage and then you are going home to contemplate what I have told you."

I was guessing that nobody had spoken to her that way in a quite a while. She moved over to the couch without another word and sat down with her back straight and her hands folded in her lap.

"I came down here at the request of your father. We were acquainted a few weeks ago when I helped your father and Miguel out of a bind up in Loveland. I never asked for any praise or reward for doing what I did as it was simply the right thing to do. I also helped you out on the road the other day because again, it was the right thing to do. Since that time, you have been acting like an entitled little shrew. You can do what you want to do simply because you are somewhat attractive and happen to be Hector's daughter. You agree to call me by my nickname, yet I cannot call you by yours for some reason. I'm guessing that it allows you feel superior.

"I made a business deal with your father not you, yet for some reason you feel that it is fine to change the terms of the contract by browbeating your father and without even considering asking me if I was interested in your proposal.

"Regardless of how attractive you may be, in my mind you are nothing more than damaged goods. Your character is flawed from what I have seen so far. At this point I am not interested in being your business partner and if you think that you can intimidate me into doing so all I can say is that you don't really know me. I'll be back in Loveland so fast it will make your head spin.

"That is all that I have to say to you. I suggest that you go home and give what I've said some thought. Don't let the door hit you in the butt on the way out."

I went back to making notes on what I still needed to do while she quietly stood up and walked out of the office without a word, then out of the shop. Maybe I had been a bit harsh on her without knowing her full story, but I was not going to put up with that nonsense for a year.

At 6:00 I was still at the shop getting things sorted out when I heard a vehicle drive up. Shortly thereafter Hector walked into the shop, and he was obviously troubled. We went into the office and I sat down behind the desk while he took a seat on the couch.

"I just came from the house and apparently your business meeting with Kassy did not go so well. She is up there sitting on the porch with tears streaming out of her eyes and will not talk to anyone. That is my only daughter, King, she is all that I have left. What did you say to her?" he asked.

"Hector, I told her what you and the others around here should have told her a long time ago. That life is a struggle and nothing that comes easy is really worth it. She is a very educated woman and also a very attractive woman, she could have made it on the 'outside' but apparently did not have the faith in herself to become successful in the world outside of Huerfano County. Perhaps she got caught up in this liberal crap while she was at CU, it is an intellectual cesspool and maybe they made her think that her bloodlines made her second rate, who knows? I think that she used the passing away of her mother as an excuse to come back here and take care of you, knowing that you would take care of her and she wouldn't need to expose herself to the possibility of failure outside of Huerfano County. She needs to develop some faith in herself that is not tied to the great Jackrabbit.

"I told her that I do not appreciate someone arrogantly telling me how to address them, nor do I appreciate them changing the terms of a contract that they were not party to. There is absolutely no way that I was going to last a year here under those conditions. I simply told her the truth. If you want me to leave, just let me know and I'll be gone."

Hector sat there with his head down for a few minutes before looking up at me and responding.

"King, you are right, and I hate to admit it. Since Kassy's mother passed, I may have not done the right thing and shielded her from the world as it is. I blame myself.

"Would you agree to stay and abide by our contract while I try to sort out this mess that I have made with Kassy? I'll likely need your help in this matter as you seem to be the only one who has the cojones to confront Kassy and try to get her to see herself for who she really is, and for me to see her as well."

I could tell Hector was hurting now. It wouldn't cost me a thing to ride this out for a few weeks and see where it went.

"I'll stick around for a few weeks in any case to get this shop up and running and to see where this situation with Kassy goes. Like I said, I don't actually think that Kassy is a bad person, and I really don't think that she realizes just how attractive she would be if she simply let herself be herself, developed some faith in herself and just pulled the whole package together. She just seems to have lost track of who she really is. Anyhow, when she's ready, tell her that we'll get together and go over her proposal, I am not averse to it although it is a bit different."

Hector stood up and we shook hands. "Thank you, gringo, this is something that I have no experience with and can use all the help I can get. It looks like I may be owing you again."

"Well seeing as how your bill is still pending for the first time, I guess we'll just put this one on your tab as well," I said with a grin.

As Hector headed out the door, he told me that my house would be ready to move into tomorrow afternoon, so I should book into the B&B for this evening again.

CHAPTER 6

AFTER ANOTHER NIGHT IN THE B&B I was back at the shop around 9:00 and trying to get a carpenter in the area to build me some stand-alone shelving and racks to go in front of the display counter to hold cleaning kits, gun oil, tactical gear and so forth. I'd set up the register and everything was coming together except I still had that court divider and gate running right down the middle of the shop, which was a problem. I also had to figure out an alarm system and how to secure the basement which is where I'd be storing the guns each evening.

Hector came in about 11:00 with coffee and donuts, so we retired to the office to take a break and enjoy them. Just to get the 800-pound gorilla out of the room I asked him how Kassy was getting along today?

"Well, she sat out on the porch by herself until very late last night and did not want company. This morning she seemed to be very bright eyed and bushy tailed and it appears that she has recovered from your tongue lashing and has made some sort of commitment to herself. This could go one of two ways; either she decides to take what you said to heart or she beats you like a piñata the next time she sees you."

"I can think of worse ways to go than being beaten like a piñata by Kassy."

"True. Kassy is not much of a procrastinator so I think you should be prepared to meet your Maker from this point going forward."

With that said, Hector got on the phone with a local carpenter and organized my shelving units as well as called the security company that he uses in Walsenburg to come down and build us an alarm system that would send an alarm not only to my new house, but to Hector's as well. We were thinking ahead to if Kassy's taqueria became a going concern.

Once that was in hand, Hector took off back to his and Kassy's house off County Road 431 to the west of town while I decided to install some serious burglar bars on the four basement windows, one on each side of the house.

When that was done to my satisfaction, I drove over to Charlie's Market on South Main Street to get some provisions for my new house which was supposedly somewhere off Cherry Street. Loading the grocery bags in the back of my old Dodge pickup, I drove back down South Main then took a left on East Garland Avenue and followed it to the end where it swung left and became Cherry Street. There was a turnoff to the right, so I took it and saw an Azteca Trucking Line company Toyota Tundra pickup in front of the only house on the righthand side of the little cul-de-sac I found myself in. Pulling into the driveway I hopped out, took two bags of groceries out of the bed of my truck and took them into the house. There was a little foyer just inside the front door with a small table and a coat rack to the right. Continuing on, there was a formal dining room to the left and a cozy living room with a fireplace on the right. As you walked back toward the kitchen through a short passageway, the stairs leading upstairs were to the left with a half bath to the right before you got into the kitchen proper. Dumping the groceries on the old fashioned Formica kitchen table, I continued surveying my new abode. Upstairs was a master bedroom and ensuite bathroom taking up the entire back of the house, which would be to the left as you came up the stairs and took a right onto the small landing at the top. Across from the landing was a full bathroom and at the end of the wide hallway going toward the front of the house was the door to the guest room.

The house was furnished in a rustic western sort of fashion, not fancy but comfortable and meant to be lived in. It was fully furnished, and had obviously not been lived in for a while but someone had been in and cleaned it up, aired it out and put towels and toilet paper where towels and toilet paper were supposed to go. Going back down to the kitchen I found an unopened bottle of water in the refrigerator and drank half before going back out to my truck to get the rest of the groceries. After putting these down on the table as well I went looking for my house guest.

I found Kassy up on a step ladder in the guestroom with a broom sweeping the cobwebs out of the corners of the ceiling.

"What are you doing up there, Kassy?" I asked while perusing her phenomenal cut-off blue jean clad backside while she was trapped on the ladder.

"I am sweeping for cobwebs dough head, somebody needs to do it," she replied without looking down at me while she kept sweeping the corners.

"What are you doing?" she asked.

"Just bringing in some groceries so that I don't have to keep going out to eat." While keeping a close watch on her rear end I suggested that she had missed a cobweb further to her left. The ulterior motive here was to get her to stretch as far as possible over the top of the ladder while I kept a close watch as her shorts stretched higher and tighter over that outstanding posterior.

"There, I think you got it." I only said this as she was at full extension by this time and the view was as good as it was going to get.

Once she was down off the ladder, we went down to the kitchen where I poured her and myself a Coke over ice, in actual glasses which I found in a well-stocked cabinet beside the stove. After we put the groceries away, we sat at the kitchen table and I asked her if she had been the one to clean the place, air it out and make it livable. She had, so I thanked her.

"What are you doing for dinner tonight?" she asked.

"No plans. I was thinking about staying in and just taking it easy," I replied while desperately trying not to stare at her sweaty, clinging t-shirt.

"If I go out and pick up some dinner, would you consider going over my business proposal for the taqueria while we ate here?"

I reminded myself that there are such things as stupid questions.

"That sounds like a fine idea, and it will give me a chance to clean up a bit while you're gone."

She looked down at her sweaty t-shirt and made a face. "I need to clean up as well, but I'll be back in about 30 minutes," she said as she grabbed her purse off of the little table by the front door and ran out to her truck.

I went outside to my truck again and got my duffle bag and rucksack out of the cab and threw them on the bed in the master bedroom. Jumping in the shower I washed off the day's grit and grime before putting on a fresh pair of jeans and t-shirt out of my duffle bag. I figured shaving would be too forward so I just ran a comb through my flattop and went back into the living room and sat on the couch while I waited patiently for Ms. Archuleta to return.

45 minutes later she came strolling back through the front door with a big bag of something that smelled like real Mexican food, not that TexMex variety. I noticed that she had also cleaned up and was now wearing a different peasant dress than the one she had on yesterday. A nice one in blue with the requisite embroidery with flip-flops on her feet. I followed her into the kitchen watching the wiggle in her walk. While she got the enchiladas and tacos out of the bag and onto proper plates, I grabbed us each a beer from the refrigerator.

She must have phoned in the order then rushed back to Hector's to shower and change before hurrying back to collect the food and getting back here in 45 minutes. I definitely appreciated the effort.

We had a nice dinner with no antagonism whatsoever, it was as if our discussion in my office yesterday had never occurred. After dinner, while I cleaned up the kitchen, she went back out to her truck and got her messenger bag. I grabbed us another beer then met her on the couch where she laid her proposal out on the coffee table and gave me her spiel. It was exceedingly difficult to concentrate with her sitting there rubbing shoulders, hips and thighs with me as she leaned over the coffee table to point out some salient points in her proposal. This creature had absolutely no idea of the effect she had on the male of the species, well me anyhow. Furthermore, she now smelled like Chanel No. 5, which is nothing more than distilled pheromones to discerning gentlemen like myself.

I forced myself to act my age and started paying attention to what she was saying. She was a risk taker; I'll give her that. There were many Mexican food places in Huerfano County, but no really good ones in La Veta. There were no taquerias anywhere that she knew of that served Mexican food with a Caribbean twist. The gun shop would be the lure that drew them in and got the word-of-mouth advertising going. Kassy was supposedly a remarkable cook, according to Miguel, and she had already earmarked and spoken to some other ladies to help her out, I was starting to see that she was good at this business stuff and that this was now a crusade for her. Perhaps my little talk yesterday gave her the little kick in the tush she needed to give it a go herself without Hector backing her up all the time.

I thought that the whole idea was just unique enough that it might actually work. Having Hector in the background couldn't hurt either. I would really feel like an ass if I shot her dream down at this point.

"Okay, Kassandra, let's give it a go. I'm going to be busy getting my side of the shop ready to open up soon, so I'm afraid that you'll need to get your side sorted out yourself," I told her. She just beamed at me like a kid with a new bike. I never really paid attention before, probably because my attention had been directed elsewhere, but her teeth were perfect and unbelievably white.

Getting back on track, "Kassandra, you realize that it is against the law to serve alcohol anywhere that firearms are sold, don't you? You can't even offer beer with the meals. This may be a bone of contention with the menfolk."

"You can feel free to call me Kassy now," she said with a smile. "You don't know the power that Hispanic women have over their menfolk. I guarantee you that the men on my side of the divider will be behaving themselves as if they were at Mass."

Kassy got busy putting everything back in her messenger bag as she prepared to go. As she got up to go to the door, I followed her acting as a proper host. Once she got outside on the porch she turned around and with a serious demeanor said, "Look, King, I apologize for acting like a jerk since you've been around. I really needed to hear what you had to say yesterday although it was painful. Would it be possible for us to start over? It would be nice if we could be friends as well as business partners."

I cocked my head to the side and thought about that for a moment with a pensive look on my face. "Is this 'friends with benefits' or just friends?" I asked jokingly, sort of.

Smiling as she put her hand out for me to shake, she asked, "You really are an impossible gabacho, aren't you?" I wasn't sure what a gabacho was, but she was grinning when she said it, so it couldn't have been too bad, whatever it was.

As I shut the door, I wondered why she just couldn't be your typical arrogant, egotistical, spoiled little brat? Those you could deal with or just simply ignore. When a woman is outrageously attractive and doesn't seem to realize it, it simply negates all the usual strategies. Not that I thought that I had much of a chance to start with, but now I had to play out this hand just to see how it ended up. You never know, I may get lucky and draw to an inside straight.

CHAPTER 7

AFTER 10 DAYS OF WORKING together, Kassy and I finally got both the gun shop and the taqueria ready for business and we were planning on having a grand opening on the following Saturday. Kassy was set on the name 'Kassy's and the Caribbean King's Taqueria and Gun Shop'. No amount of arguing with her, or browbeating her, would get her to change her mind. I figured that this was not a hill I wanted to die on, so I caved in. Anyhow, everybody was just referring to the shop as 'Kassy's and King's' so whatever was on the sign out front in the yard was simply the formal designation.

Friday was spent cleaning the shop up after the various construction issues required to get all of the taqueria equipment up and running; stoves, ovens, deep fryers, ventilation and so forth had been resolved. Kassy also had her crew arranging tables, putting on tablecloths and hanging decorations. My side was an easy matter of making sure that everything was presented correctly and was clean and tidy. I also drew the short straw to clean the restrooms and make sure that there was toilet paper, soap, hand sanitizer and paper towels as required. I had hired Miguel to help me out and to run the shop when I needed to be away to sort out the hijacking issue, which was something else that I'd need to address shortly.

Kassy had hired her friend Maria away from the Mission Deli Mesa Steak House, which didn't appear to have caused any hard feelings and had hired three younger girls to act as the waitress, cashier and hostess. I did notice that one of the young girls seemed strangely attached to Kassy.

Around 2:00 in the afternoon, everyone took a break and Maria fixed us all tacos and iced tea. Kassy came into the gun shop office where I was going over some invoices with a plate of tacos and iced teas for the both of us. She pulled up the old cross backed chair that had somehow made it into the office and sat across the desk from me as we discussed the grand opening tomorrow. What those jeans and t-shirt were attempting to conceal was much more interesting than invoices.

During the conversation I asked her about the young girl who seemed to be somehow attached to her and asked if she was family? Kassy looked at me for a moment before getting up and closing the office door. Sitting back down she told me the story.

"Her name is Xocoyotl, pronounced 'coco-yo-til', but we just call her Coco. She's 15 now, but I brought her here when she was 13. I'd been down in Raton to see some friends and was coming home north on I-25. I had just passed the exit for the Trinidad Golf Course when a little girl ran across the highway in front of me, and I almost hit her. I slammed on the brakes and pulled off on the right side just before the overpass and jumped out of the car to make sure that she was okay. Coco was squatting in the middle of the median between the north and the southbound traffic. She was almost catatonic when I got to her, but I managed to carry her back to my car and we drove to the next exit and circled back to the McDonald's on West Cedar Street. We went through the drive-through and I got us some breakfast then I drove over to Cumino Park to figure out what to do.

"Coco was famished, so I gave her my McMuffin and orange juice as well. After she had calmed down, I asked her what had happened. Apparently, Coco and her mother had made it all the way from Colombia to Trinidad and were supposed to meet their connection for the last leg of the journey into Denver at the Days Inn near the golf course exit. Once Coco and her mother were in the room, there were two traffickers who explained that Coco and her mother needed to pay the remainder of the 'coyote fee' that had gotten them to Trinidad. The mother told them that she had paid the full amount of $3,000 before she had left Colombia and had a receipt. The two men just laughed and told her that the money she had paid was only good for as far as Trinidad. To get to Denver, and then to find work in Denver, would be another $1,000. Coco's mother told them that she did not have the money.

"At this point the traffickers informed Coco's mother that the only other alternative was for her and her daughter to be sold into the sex trade in Denver and that they could earn the money by working on their backs. As they said this, they started unbuckling their belts and told them that they would need to be 'broken in' before being delivered to Denver.

"Coco's mother threw herself at the men, going for their eyes with her fingers while she yelled for her daughter to run. Which is when I almost ran over her.

"While we were at the park, I called Hector and told him what had happened. He told me to get back on the road and head toward the trucking office in Walsenburg. He would have some of his guy's head south immediately and they would track my phone coming north and tuck in behind me once they found me. I was to go directly home, and he would meet me there in the afternoon.

"Later that day Hector arrived home to find us in the living room, me in one of his reclining chairs with Coco asleep on the couch. The little girl jumped up in fright when Hector came into the room, so Hector just stood still while I explained that Hector was my father and that he owned the house that they were in.

"Coco eventually relaxed enough so we could all take a seat; Hector across the coffee table from me and Coco on the couch. Coco looked at Hector and asked where her mother was. Hector told her that he had spoken to the police in Trinidad and that her mother had been brave. She had gotten a knife into one of the traffickers and killed him, but the other one had shot her, and she had died at the hotel.

"Coco has nowhere to go and no identification to use even if she did. Coco has been living with us ever since and everyone thinks that she is somehow related to Hector and I and we continue to let them think that."

I just sat back in my chair and let that story sink in. I think it was the saddest story I'd ever heard.

"So, you're saying that she is essentially a ghost with no identification at all and nowhere to go? She's almost an adult, this will get very problematic in the near future," I said.

"That's true, King, but what can we do? We can't send her back to Colombia and we don't have the paperwork required to get her a green card."

"Can you bring her in here? I'd like to meet her."

Kassy got up and opened the door and called for Coco, who walked through the gate in the courtroom divider and came over to the office. As she walked over Kassy put her arm around her shoulders and walked her over in front of the desk and introduced us.

"I am pleased to meet you, Mr. King and I am looking forward to working with you in the shop."

Coco was a cute little thing, only about five and a half feet tall, with curly black hair to rival Kassy's. Since she was Colombian by birth, Coco had Indian features, but she was well on her way to being a little heartbreaker.

"Coco, how much would it cost me to just have you call me King?"

"Do you prefer King, or would you prefer to be addressed as 'el gringo', 'el bobo' or 'that impossible gabacho'? Kassy has used all of these to refer to you at one time or another recently." Coco was trying hard not to laugh, and Kassy was looking at Coco in shock.

"I can't believe you just said that?" said Kassy looking sternly at Coco. "She really didn't mean to say that."

I just winked at Coco and told her that I thought that we'd get along just fine. Kassy was frustrated and told Coco to get back to work, which she did while laughing all the way across the shop. After Coco had gone, I asked Kassy if she could write down everything that she knew concerning Coco; her actual legal name, her actual birthday, her address in Colombia when she left, just anything that she could think of. "Oh yeah, I'll need about a dozen good quality passport photos as well," Creed added.

"Why? What are you going to do with all this?" Kassy asked.

"Don't you worry about it, but I may have a plan to retire our resident ghost. I call it the 'Bobo Plan'. Doesn't 'bobo' translate to 'fool' or 'foolish' in English?"

She turned bright red, well as red as someone with her coloring allowed.

"When is Coco's next birthday?" asked King.

"She'll be 16 in a month, again why?" she queried.

"Because it will take a few weeks for this gabacho to execute the Bobo Plan."

As she headed out the door and back to her side of the shop, she was mumbling something about 'imbécil gringos'.

Saturday morning bright and early, Kassy, Coco and the rest of her crew plus Miguel and I, were at the shop ensuring that everything was in order for the grand opening of 'Kassy's and the Caribbean King's Taqueria and Gun Shop'. A notification had been put in the 'World Journal', the local county newspaper servicing Huerfano County as well as on the local radio station KSPK 102.3 FM in Walsenburg. Other than that, our advertising campaign relied on Hector and word-of-mouth advertising.

People started to trickle in around 10:00 with curious guys and their families coming in to take advantage of the free sopapillas and coffee. They'd park their wives and kids over on the taqueria side of the divider then come over and take a look at what I had on display. Around noon the taqueria was doing a booming business, but the gun shop had only sold some ammo. I was perplexed as I thought that I had a good, high quality selection of rifles, shotguns and pistols. I noticed that there were a couple of tables where the local guys were huddled up drinking coffee after having had their lunch, so I asked Miguel to go over there and find out what they were discussing. About half an hour later Miguel and the entire group of guys who had been sitting at the tables came over to the gun shop side and cornered me behind the display counter. Miguel nodded to an old bow-legged, weather-beaten Hispanic guy in old jeans and a snap button western shirt with an enormous rodeo belt buckle. I supposed that he was the spokesman.

"King, we appreciate what you have done and the fact that we now have a decent gun shop in town, but you've missed the mark concerning your clientele. You have a very nice selection of fancy weapons, but most of us cannot afford these guns and would hesitate to use them on a regular basis even if we could."

"Now I do not mean to offend you but let me give you some examples. You have a very nice LaRue AR-15 rifle on the wall behind you chambered in 5.56mm NATO. A good rifle to keep in your truck while mending fences or clearing irrigation ditches. It is good for coyotes, skunks, prairie dogs and any of the other varmints we have around here. The problem is that it costs over $2,000 and you just wouldn't feel right throwing it around the truck or strapping it to a tractor or four-wheeler.

"The same goes for shotguns. We all love to go duck, dove, turkey or pheasant hunting, but we simply can't afford to shell out $2,500 for a Browning Cynergy over and under.

"You've got some fine handguns in your case as well, but that Model 27 Smith & Wesson wheel gun runs about $1,100.

"I guess what I am trying to say is that the guys in this county are more your 'Ruger and Remington crowd'. A Ruger Mini-14 will do just about anything a fancy AR rifle will do, yet only runs about $1,300. Your standard Remington 870 pump gun will run you around $500 and a good, dependable Ruger GP100 will only set you back about $950.

"What we would like to suggest to you is that you get the latest catalogues from your mainstream manufacturers, let us come is and discuss things with you, then you go out and get what we want. You'd become more of a 'supply on demand' type of shop, which would also keep your overhead low. I'd keep what you have on hand now for the odd graduation, birthday, Christmas sort of purchase.

"You are stocking way too much ammunition of calibers that just aren't too common around here. I can't think of any guy around here who shoots a

.338 Lapua or a 6.5 Creedmore. Why don't you let us make you up a list of the ammo we shoot down here and you can make sure that you have it on hand. If someone does buy a rifle chambered in an uncommon round, he can make arrangements with you to get some in.

"Last, but not least, we really need a gunsmith in town to keep what we've already got up and running. You should think about that as well."

Well, they all just stood there looking at me for a while waiting for me to say something. I knew that this would either make or break not only my shop, but Kassy's side as well.

Leaning against the back counter I contemplated what the old guy had said, and I knew that he was right. I had misread my potential clientele and had arrogantly figured that they would be in the market for what the folks in Loveland were. It was my mistake and it was a serious one.

"Guys, you are absolutely correct. I read my potential customers wrong and worse than that I didn't make the effort to go out and find out what you guys actually wanted or needed. I'll download the latest catalogues from every mainstream manufacturer that I can think of, and when you guys think that you need something, we'll just sit down in my office and figure out what you actually want or need and then I'll order it and have it delivered.

"Concerning ammunition, I'd really appreciate it if you guys could let me know what you actually shoot and I'll make sure that I keep enough on hand to keep you happy. As far as the gunsmithing idea, I'd already planned to start taking courses online and becoming an NRA approved gunsmith, but you'll need to give me a little time on that as I need to sort out something for Hector first. You guys willing to give me a second chance?"

The old guy looked around at his buddies before he turned back to me and said, "You've got it, young man, but don't take too long as some of us are getting a little long in the tooth and won't be able to wait on you forever. That said, you're probably safe as long as Kassy's side of the shop stays open. It's nice to have a local place to sit and drink coffee, talk guns and watch Kassy and Maria scoot around, if you know what I mean," he said with a twinkle in his eye.

I told him that I knew exactly what he meant and thanked him and the guys for setting me straight and I'd look forward to seeing them all again in the future. They then went back over to Kassy's side. It was now lunchtime and I suppose they wanted to try out the new menu and watch Kassy and Maria scoot around. Heck, it sounded like a pretty good idea to me as well, so Miguel and I joined them.

About 3:00 in the afternoon business tailed off in the taqueria. It had been pretty dead on my side all day although I did sell some more ammunition. While her crew was cleaning up on her side, Kassy came over to my side and asked me how it went. I told her that it could have been better and what the old cowboy had to say.

"So old Joaquin took you to school, did he? He's a smart old guy and has been around for 60 years or so, you'd better listen to him. By the way, did I mention that I have a degree in business administration? Feel free to consult with me at any time," she smirked.

I told her that I'd lock up after she and her crew were finished and shortly thereafter, I was on my own putting guns down in the basement to secure them. It has been an educational day. Tomorrow was Sunday and I was looking forward to finally getting back to my morning workout routine and maybe even getting a run in. Locking the shop up I drove home, had dinner and then an early night.

CHAPTER 8

I WOKE UP AROUND 6:00 without the benefit of an alarm clock. I then climbed into my old DEA running shorts and an old Army t-shirt before I sat down and laced up my Asics Kayano running shoes. Since this was the first run in a while, I did some stretching in the front yard before taking off at a reasonable pace.

I'd earlier mapped out a route from my house south on Cherry Street to West Grand Avenue. After a block on Grand I turned south on Oak Street and took it just past the Mission Deli Mesa Steak House where it swung west going out of town and reverted back to State Road 12. I stayed on 12 as it swung south again after about half a mile, then ran along it for another half mile or so before I hung a right onto County Road 420 headed west. This was a straight stretch of roughly one and a half miles of dirt road before I hit the cut-off for 421 to the right and headed north-northeast for just over a mile until I came to 430 heading east and back toward town. When 430 dead ended at South Aspen Street I ran about a half block north to West San Francisco Street, a quarter of a mile east on San Francisco until I hit Oak Street before hanging a right on Oak and following it for 3 blocks then another block west on East Garland Street until it turned into Cherry Street and I was home. About 6 miles exactly.

I barely made it home that first day. My breath was coming in gasps, my thighs were on fire and I was fairly certain that my heart was about to give out. As I struggled up the steps to my front porch, I found Kassy sitting on the porch swing, swinging back and forth dressed, and I use that term loosely, in what I discovered later were little tight black yoga shorts and a black sports bra modestly covered by a loose grey muscle shirt. This did not do my pounding heart any favors. Things would be so much easier around this town if Hector's daughter would have been as ugly as a mud fence.

"This is what happens when you get old and out of shape. Perhaps you should do this more often and give yourself a reasonable chance of seeing the big four-oh."

Stumbling over to the swing I told her to scoot her butt over and let the walking wounded sit down and recover. She reached into her backpack and handed me a bottle of water and I downed half of it in a single gulp.

"How old are you anyhow? Hector wouldn't tell me. ", she asked.

"At the moment I am 35 going on a hundred."

"How far did you run this morning?"

"About 6 miles."

"Oh, I didn't realize you'd run so far, I was thinking maybe a block or two. My apologies. That said, living in a small town is not conducive to staying in shape, you'll need to keep working at it."

Okay, now it was my turn. "Noted. Now how old are you? Hector wouldn't tell me either, and how do you keep in such fine shape?"

"You should never ask a woman her age, but as you are simply a rude gringo and cannot be expected to know this, I will answer you. I am 29 years old. Now as to how do I stay in shape? Do you call this 'in shape'?" Grabbing my hand and pulling it down toward her navel with one hand while pulling up the bottom of her muscle shirt with the other, she continued to lecture me.

"Here, pinch this piece just below my belly button. See, you've got almost a quarter of an inch of unsightly fat between your fingers! Disgusting. I try to maintain some sort of fitness by doing Bikram yoga three times a week at the yoga studio at the corner of East Ryus Avenue and Main Street. You should stop by some time." Looking down at my hand she told me that I could let go of her now.

I didn't want to, but I did. This miniscule roll of belly fat was well camouflaged by an incredibly attractive and well defined abdomen. But giving my head a shake, I came back to Earth and let go of that little piece of paradise.

"Chica, we'll be lucky to have any time to work out in the next few weeks. I've got Miguel to watch my side of the shop, but you'll need to be there most of the time on your side. If I'm not mistaken, both of us will be required in Walsenburg on Monday, you to do your day job and me to get working on the hijacking issue."

"I can actually do most of the bookkeeping and accounting online from home, although I'll need to get up to the office in Walsenburg at least once a week," she informed me. "So, sticking with my workout routine isn't an issue."

"Lucky you. I'll need to get up early every morning to do my calisthenics, then fit in a run whenever I can."

"Determination, I like that in a business partner." Getting up off the swing she grabbed her backpack and swung it onto her shoulder. "I need to get to the studio now and work on my asanas. I'll see you around."

I'm not so sure that was a good idea. As much as I enjoyed her company, I wasn't sure my heart was up to it yet. I'd better keep up with the running. Life would be so much less stressful if all the women were unattractive and resembled Jabba the Hut. Women like Kassy are the principal cause of heart attacks in men under forty.

Afterwards I'd showered up and was sitting in the kitchen with a cup of coffee when Hector called and asked if I could come over to his house for lunch so that we could discuss the hijacking issue. I told him that I'd be there around noon.

Hector lived with Kassy and Coco about 4 miles west of town in the foothills. His home was a 3000+ square foot log home with 3 large bedrooms and 3-1/2 baths. Hector and Kassy each had a master bedroom with an ensuite bath upstairs while Coco had the large bedroom downstairs just off the living room, which also had an ensuite bath. The half bath was beside the kitchen. It was a unique house plan as the only rooms on the second floor were Kassy's and Hectors bedrooms, one on each side of the house connected by a walkway. The rest of the upstairs area was open from the rafters to the ground floor. The foyer, kitchen and living room were all open plan with the stairs to the upper level just to the right of the front door. There were two steps up to a landing, after making a 90 degree turn to the left the stairs brought you up to the righthand side of the walkway, closest to Hector's room. The front of the house had a generous porch that faced back across the valley toward La Veta. It was an odd yet beautiful house.

I got to Hector's place just at noon and parked my ugly old pickup on the driveway in front of the porch. Climbing the steps up to the porch I knocked on the door and Coco came to fetch me.

"Hector is in the living room, King. I heard you and Kassy had a date this morning?" she informed me before quickly turning around and going back into the house before I could quiz her on how she knew about Kassy's unscheduled visit.

Going back through the kitchen to the living room at the back of the house, I found Hector sitting on one end of the couch, so I sat down on the other and we got down to business. Hector explained that he was averaging about a truck a month being hijacked. Each load was a high dollar load usually containing electronics, pharmaceuticals, liquor, high-end sports apparel, or specialized auto parts. In every case the truck was forced off the road early in the morning and in each case the driver was forced out of the truck at gunpoint. The hijacking crews usually consisted of two vehicles with one either pulling in front of the truck to force it to stop or pulled across the road to accomplish the same thing. There was always a vehicle at the back of the truck with two guys in it. These guys performed the actual jacking at gunpoint with one of them being the new driver who drove the hijacked tractor and trailer away.

Hector had just finished his dissertation when Kassy came out of her room and crossed the walkway before coming down to the kitchen and going to the refrigerator to get something to drink. Now keep in mind that the foyer, kitchen and living room were open plan so I could clearly see into the kitchen. Kassy apparently had just gotten out of the shower and had on a short dressing gown, fuzzy rabbit motif slippers, no makeup on whatsoever and damp shower hair. She didn't see us sitting in the living room until she closed the refrigerator door which opened her line of sight to the couch. Once she saw me sitting there staring at her in her less than flattering attire, she gave an ear-piercing squeal, dropped her glass of juice and flew back up the stairs. We watched her as she hit the walkway upstairs and flew across it and into her room. My angle was good, but she was moving too fast to see what she had on under the dressing gown.

Coco came out of her room to clean up the mess caused by the plastic glass of juice that Kassy had just dropped and said that she guessed that she had forgotten to tell Kassy that I was there. Judging by the mischievous look on her face, this was intentional. Hector just suggested that we get back to business now that the entertainment was over.

I questioned Hector as to how he contracted loads and how he assigned them. It seemed rather straight forward as he had contracts with many well-known companies which supplied the items getting hijacked. They would call the office and speak to one of three schedulers who would use an operations research based algorithm to put the nearest or most economical truck at the client's warehouse or place of business as soon as possible. I asked if there was a difference between the nearest truck and the most economical truck. Apparently, there was and it all had to do with full loads versus partial loads, the final destinations of the full or partial loads, and the possibility of another client having another load which needed delivered in the same area.

"Have any of your drivers even been hurt during these jackings?" I asked. Hector told me that a few drivers had been roughed up or pistol whipped when they hesitated to get out of their cabs, but so far nobody had been shot or seriously injured, although that possibility was always present.

At this point we heard Kassy's bedroom door open and we looked up to see her dressed in jeans, t-shirt, no bunny shoes and minimal make-up. Her hair was back in riot mode. She came down the stairs, through the kitchen and over to the couch and told me in no uncertain terms that I had not seen her earlier and did I understand what she was saying?

"But I did see you earlier in your little dressing gown, rabbit slippers and shower hair. Do you want me to lie?"

"I think that in this instance that lying may be your healthiest option. Are you hearing me now?"

"What happens if I choose to stay on the straight and narrow and decide to tell the truth and remain an honest man?" I needed to know my other options.

"I would have no other recourse other than to beat you senseless."

"Would you be wearing the dressing gown and bunny slippers as you beat me? That might make it worthwhile."

She'd had enough of my childish bantering, threw up her hands in defeat and stormed back into the kitchen where she ran into Coco who simply looked at her and said, "King one, Kassy zero."

Getting back to the hijacking thing after the interlude with Kassy, I told Hector that I'd give it some thought and meet him at his office at the depot in Walsenburg on Tuesday morning. Kassy should be there as well, but she should leave the rabbit slippers at home.

"I heard that!" Kassy informed us from the kitchen.

After the four of us had a nice lunch of grilled cheese sandwiches prepared by Kassy and Coco, I headed toward the front door. Bidding everyone goodbye, I walked out to my truck with Coco following close behind me. Getting into the driver's seat I shut the door and Coco leaned into the truck with her forearms on the window frame.

"What are you going to do about Kassy?" she asked.

"And what do you mean by that, my troublemaking little friend?"

"You really are muy stupido, aren't you? She wants you to ask her out on a real date, are you blind as well as stupid?"

"You should never call your elders stupid; it's rude. Kassy would not pick me up if I was hitchhiking in the middle of the Sahara Desert. Furthermore niña, I'm too old for her and she is definitely out of my league," I informed the child.

"We all know she is out of your league; the problem is that she doesn't. If you play your cards right you could still have a chance," the child informed me.

"Do you always play matchmaker or are you just trying to cause trouble again?" I asked Coco with a smile.

"A little of both I guess, but this would be good trouble if you'd just listen to me."

I told her that there was no such thing as good trouble. She told me to give it some thought as she stepped away from the truck and I drove away.

CHAPTER 9

I ARRIVED BACK AT MY house on Cherry Street and backed the truck up to the porch. The old girl hadn't had a thorough cleaning since I left Loveland so I thought I'd give her a wash. As I mentioned before, I hadn't had time to do any real body work to her so giving her a wash was really just maintenance. Once she was cleaned up, I popped the hood to check fluid levels and filters. The outside didn't look so great, she hadn't been very attractive when she was new, but underneath the hood she was a beauty. Under the hood she was sporting a 5.7 liter Eagle Hemi engine putting out 372 horsepower and 400 foot-pounds of torque. This was routed through a A-855 Passon Performance manual 5-speed transmission turning a custom Strange driveshaft. The power got to the rear wheels through a Chrysler 8-3/4" 3.73 rear end. Suspension was a 4 link set-up with coil over kits at each corner. A transmission crossmember had been added to help hold everything together.

That chore finished; I called an old buddy of mine from my DEA days. Dennis was working for ICE, the US Immigration and Customs Enforcement outfit, when I was with the DEA Special Operations Division. We'd worked together on a few jobs. His girlfriend, now wife, had been illegal when they met, and he would have been bounced out of ICE if his bosses knew about her back then. I knew, but never said a thing. Dennis called in some favors and got Felicia a green card under the table so that they could get hitched. Now I needed a similar favor. I called him at home as it was a Sunday and it was probably still illegal to tap a guy's phone for no apparent reason. After the usual salutations and catching up, I got down to business.

"Dennis, I need a favor. Something like what you did for Felicia. Can you help me out?"

"You do realize that you are asking a federal agent to engage in illegal criminal activity, don't you?" he retorted.

"To be more accurate, I am asking the federal agent to break the law again. I'm guessing he needs the practice." He was laughing now.

"Okay, buddy, give it to me, lock, stock and barrel."

I gave him the whole story from when Kassy almost ran Coco over, the traffickers going to break them in before selling them into the sex trade in Denver and the fact that Coco was now living high on the hog in Huerfano County and would not be a burden on the American taxpayer.

"That story just sucks. We should be allowed to shoot these assholes on sight. Okay, you've plucked my heartstrings, what do you need?"

"Can you get me a valid Colombian birth certificate, a US social security card, a valid green card and a valid US driver's license?"

"No problem, when do you need it?"

"Is within a month possible? Her birthday is coming up."

"Not a problem. Fedex me all the details and photos tomorrow and I'll have everything ready for you in two weeks."

"What do I owe you for coercing you to once again participate in an illegal enterprise?"

"To be honest, I've been wanting one of those Charles Daly Honcho triple barreled shotguns for a while now. They're as rare as hen's teeth up here. Get me one of those and we're square."

"I'm sure that you realize that those things run about $1,500. But I've been looking at those Honchos as well so maybe I'll just order two and get the pump gun for me. Anyhow, when it gets to my shop, I'll run it up to you and I can collect that paperwork at the same time."

"Sounds like a plan, see you in a couple of weeks."

Okay, that was me done until I had to get up and start my calisthenics routine tomorrow morning. Time to sit out on the porch swing with a beer.

I got up at 5:00 the next morning to get back into my fitness routine. I had done some research into training regimes which would allow me to work out at home, that fit my schedule, did not require any equipment and would keep me in shape and flexible if I watched my alcohol intake and diet. What I settled on was a Marine Corps daily workout routine developed by a Sergeant Collins. This consisted of side straddle hops, regular push-ups, mountain climbers, weight count body builders, flutter kicks, dive bombers, leg lifts, squat thrusts, bicycles, regular grip pull ups and dips followed by a 30-minute run. I had rigged up both a set of dip bars and a pull up bar near the garage behind the house under the trees, so I was set to get into my routine today.

I managed to complete the workout and the run by 7:00, but I think I damn near killed myself. I'd need to keep it up since I really hadn't done any serious exercise, except my 6 mile run a few days ago, since I had left Loveland.

After a shower and a shave, I drove over to the gun shop and taco stand to meet with Miguel and Kassy to discuss shop business before getting to work on the hijacking issue. Kassy, Coco, Maria and the other girls were already at work and had the coffee, sopapillas and other snacks prepared. There were already a few old guys sitting at a table just shooting the breeze, drinking coffee and reading the newspaper. This was a good sign. I ordered a coffee and sat down at another table to wait for Miguel to show up.

A few minutes later Miguel showed up with another guy, who he introduced as Antonio. Shaking hands with Antonio I sat back down and waited for an explanation. Miguel ordered coffees for Antonio and himself before getting around to business.

"King, you'll be tied up with the hijacking business with Hector for at least a month or so if all goes well. I'll need a helping hand around here while you are away and I thought of Antonio. He is recently back in town and could use a job. I have known him and his family from since he was knee high to a small duck. I thought that I would bring him around today and let you meet him and interview him if you thought that a second hand would be useful around the shop."

Miguel was absolutely correct that for the next month or so I'd be stretched a bit thin, but we still had a cash flow issue as we had just opened and apparently, I had read the local market entirely wrong according to old Joaquin. I explained this to Miguel in front of Antonio as I wanted to be as transparent as possible. Miguel told me that Antonio had agreed to work for the new minimum wage of $15 per hour until the shop got up and running if Kassy would provide breakfast and lunch for free. Once the shop was in the black, we'd renegotiate his wages. Since he was presently living with his parents in town, he did not need to worry about rent or dinner.

I told Antonio that this was very considerate of him, but he'd need to know something about guns of all types as well as ammunition, did he have a background that supported this?

"Mr. King, I enlisted in the Air Force just out of high school. I did my basic training at Lackland in San Antonio before being selected to attend the Special Warfare Preparatory Course, also at Lackland. I then passed the Special Warfare Assessment and Selection course. During my enlistment I completed the Combat Dive Course, Airborne School, the Free-Fall Course, SERE training, both Pararescue EMT courses as well as the Pararescue Apprentice course. I am a fully qualified PJ."

"Impressive, Antonio. I don't think familiarity with guns and ammo would be an issue for you. Now don't take this the wrong way, but you seem to have had a great career ahead of you as a pararescueman and you are too young to be retired, so why did you leave the military?"

"You're right, Mr. King. I'm 27 now and I had no intention of leaving the military." As he was speaking, he reached down and pulled up his pants leg on his left leg. "And then I jumped into Syria in 2018 and this happened."

I felt like a fool. Antonio's left leg from the knee down was a prosthetic. "I took a few PKM rounds in the leg, and it had to be taken off below the knee. I was allowed to stay in for a while, but they finally gave me a medical discharge a few months ago. I'm fine with that and loved being a PJ, but sitting around doing admin work was making me nuts."

"Antonio, I apologize but I had to ask. You're hired as of right now. You'll be working directly for Miguel until we get a few things sorted out here. You know that we are just getting up and running at the moment, so you'll just have to bear with us. Let's go over to the office and let's see where we stand at the moment."

As they strolled over to the office in the corner, I went over to the taqueria counter to order some sopapillas, three more coffees and to pay the bill. Coco rang me up and took my money before looking at me with a smirk before informing me that I may now have competition for Kassy with Antonio being around. I suggested to her that I was not involved in any competition. Kassy was a grown woman and had free will, if she chose to associate with Antonio, I'd wish them luck. It would save me the mental anguish of trying to figure Kassy out.

As I walked away Coco hit me on the back of the head with a dishrag. The child had no respect for her elders.

Once Miguel, Antonio and I were in the office I went through the lecture that old Joaquin had given me the other day. We would now need to transition to a 'supply on demand' type shop as opposed to a typical retail shop. We'd still display and market a selection of fine firearms of all types, but we would definitely let our present level of stock reduce through sales until it was at a more reasonable level for the situation we now found ourselves in. Our 'bread and butter' would be filling specific orders for our customers while assuring that we always had a supply of the ammo which they actually used or wanted.

I also reiterated Joaquin's request for gunsmithing services. I'd planned to take the required courses online to become an accredited gunsmith, but I just didn't have the time. I asked Antonio if he'd be interested in becoming an accredited gunsmith by taking the courses online? Once he was accredited, he could then teach Miguel and me. The shop would cover the cost of the course. Antonio just grinned; he was all for it.

"Okay, guys, get to work. I need to figure out what to do about Hector's hijacking problem. I'll be in the office all day unless I need to run over to Hector's."

A few hours later I was slowly but surely coming to grips with the hijacking issue when Kassy knocked on the door and came in.

"What are you doing there, Mr. King?" she asked.

"It's just King, and I'm trying to figure out a way to fix Hector's hijacking problem. Do you have a few minutes to spare?"

She did, so I asked her to pull the old X-backed chair over beside me so that we could go over some things. This may have been counter-productive as she was looking as delectable as ever in her old jeans and t-shirt today. She was also smelling like coconut and vanilla. This had my mind wandering toward beaches and bikinis as opposed to truck hijackings. Anyhow, I managed to get back on track and started asking her questions.

It appeared that Azteca Trucking Lines employed 3 dispatchers, each covering different geographical regions. Dispatchers have a variety of responsibilities, but the two that I was interested in were listed on their job description as:

'Coordinating and managing the most efficient loads to remain cost effective as a company, combining shipments based on their routes and timeline to minimize how many trucks or drivers are out.' and 'Determining the best delivery methods and negotiating rates directly with the vendors and customers.'

I asked Kassy if these people would know what was being picked up or dropped off, the value of each load and the route which would be used? She said that they would need this information to do their job. I then asked her how long the 3 dispatchers had been employed by Azteca Trucking Lines? She must have started thinking along the same lines as I was.

"Bob Sanders has been with us forever, since I was a child. Richard Sax came onboard about a year and a half ago and John Greene hired on a year ago," she told me.

"And when did the hijacking begin?"

She looked at me as it dawned on her what I was getting at and said, "About a year ago."

"I think I'd better go have a word with Hector. Is he home today?" I asked.

"Yes, he has a meeting with someone this afternoon, but I am sure that he will see you."

As she stood up to put the X-back chair in its place and went to leave, she stopped at the door and leaned against it with a mischievous look on her face.

"Who's the cute new guy in the shop this morning?"

With a straight face I replied, "That's Antonio, he'll be working with Miguel from here on. Would you like his phone number?"

She looked exasperated as she stormed out and slammed the door. A few minutes later Coco opened the door and informed me that I was still an idiot before she closed the door again. I guess that I must have done or said something that I shouldn't have. Oh well, I had things to do so I called Hector to let him know that I was coming over before going out to my truck.

CHAPTER 10

I ARRIVED AT HECTOR'S PLACE and once he invited me in, we went back toward the living room to discuss the hijacking issue. I noticed that there was another gentleman sitting on the couch by the coffee table positioned ninety degrees to what I called the main couch, which was positioned with its backrest toward the floor to ceiling windows at the back of the room. As Hector and I moved around the coffee table to sit on the main couch, Hector introduced me to Hernández, who happened to be the office manager for Azteca Trucking Lines in Walsenburg.

I laid out my plans for educating the drivers on how to react and respond when they got hijacked. I suggested that we do this in Walsenburg at the depot when the drivers could fit it into their schedule, with the caveat that they must attend the lecture within a month of it being offered. At the moment I did not want the driver's to be armed. To date nobody had been seriously injured during a hijacking and the last thing we needed was for the jackers to start shooting first and then hijacking the load. Finally, I wanted to ensure that each driver had a cell phone hidden on him and not for his normal day-to-day personal use. The reason for this was that many of the jackings were taking place on remote stretches of road early in the morning. I wanted the drivers to simply give up their loads without resisting, but they needed a way to contact help afterwards and to let us know where they were so that we could get someone to them quickly.

Hector said that this was all well and good, but this would not stop the hijackings. I agreed. Which is when I got into the 'meat and potatoes' of my little presentation.

"Somehow, someone seems to know which of your loads are high value. They also know exactly what is in the load, the worth and the exact route it will be taking. After speaking to Kassy this morning, it seems to me that the only people with this information readily available to them are the dispatchers. Kassy said that you employ three; one has been with you for a very long time, one came on about a year and a half ago and the other has been with you for about a year. By your own admission, this hijacking issue began about a year ago. Do you see where I'm headed with this?"

Hector said that he did, but to continue. "Okay, I assume that your trucks are LoJacked or something similar, is that correct?"

LoJack is a stolen vehicle recovery and IoT connected system that utilizes GPS and cellular technology to locate users' vehicles.

Hector said that both the tractors and the trailers were LoJacked.

"Would the dispatchers know where the LoJack recovery systems are located on the trucks?" I asked.

"There is really no need for them to know where the LoJack device is located, but I guess they could easily find out simply by talking to the Spireon reps or to go out to the shop while the system is being installed."

"So, when you have a truck jacked, does the LoJack system keep on transmitting or does it stop functioning at the point of the hijacking?"

"They have all stopped transmitting shortly after the hijack. When the tractor and trailer are eventually found, the systems have been disabled."

Sitting back on the couch, I looked at Hector and Hernández and told them that I thought the hijackings were an inside job. It seemed to me that the only position in the company that had access to all the information required to successfully target the loads were the dispatchers.

Hector wanted to know what we were going to do about it. I told him that we needed to identify which dispatcher was actually assisting the hijackers before we did anything. My plan was for Hector to somehow pull one of the dispatchers at a time off duty for a week. During this week the other two dispatchers would be given a high value shipment to organize. If the load was jacked while a specific dispatcher was not on duty, then we could safely assume that he was not the culprit. We'd then rotate through the dispatcher roster until another hijacking occurred, this would give us probable cause to suspect a certain dispatcher and investigate him further.

"But this still means that I am losing loads while your investigation is in progress," Hector rightly mentioned.

"This is where I earn my money. I will be riding along with the high value shipments, and I'll be armed. Hopefully I can convince the hijackers that these particular loads are not worth the effort."

At this point Hernández interrupted. "King, regardless of your skill set, one armed man alone will not stand a chance against these hijackers. In every case there were two vehicles involved with two men in each vehicle. Your plan is not tactically sound."

"What do you propose then?" I countered.

"I'll ride along with you; this will give us a much better chance. Furthermore, I doubt that you can drive a rig and we need two guns. I'd better tag along as I've had a commercial driver's license for 10 years now and can handle these rigs pretty well."

"That's all well and good Hernández, but can you also handle yourself when the shooting starts? I don't mean to be rude, but it has to be asked."

"I was a designated marksman for the Houston Police Department SWAT teams for 10 years before I joined Hector's company. Good enough?"

Hector was laughing at us by this time. "Okay, enough of this pissing contest. Let's go outside and see if either one of you two studs can actually hit anything that you are shooting at. I assume that you both have your preferred pistols in your trucks. Get them and come with me."

After going to our respective trucks and getting our handguns, we followed

Hector around to the back of his house. Hector had picked up a stack of paper plates and a stop watch on the way out, and now stopped by a tool shed in the backyard to get a staple gun. Going over to the split rail fence at the end of his backyard, Hector stapled 7 plates to the top rail. There was about a three foot gap between each plate.

"Here's the deal. Each of you will put two rounds into each of the first three plates going left to right, skip the middle plate, then put two rounds into last three plates going left to right before coming back to your left and putting two rounds into the center plate. This is a timed event, the one with the best time, assuming he successfully completes the challenge as described, will get the bragging rights. Who will start?"

Hernández and I flipped a quarter. I won so I let Hernández go first. Getting his Sig Sauer P226 MK25 from his case, Hernández shoved in a 15-round magazine and racked the slide. Doing a press check to ensure that a round was chambered he walked up to a spot about 7 yards in front of the center plate with the weapon in his right hand down at his side and waited for Hector to say 'go' and start the stopwatch.

When Hector gave the word, Hernández flew into action, quickly bringing his weapon up and into a 'thumbs forward' grip while getting into an isosceles shooting stance and began firing. He was poetry in motion while he double tapped the first three plates, skipped the middle one, double tapped the last three before coming back and double tapping the middle plate.

"Very well done, amigo! Five and a half seconds. It is now your turn, King."

When I took my pistol out of the soft case, Hector immediately called a halt to the proceedings.

"King, you cannot possibly hope to beat him with that."

'That' was my old, reworked Colt 1911 Gold Cup National Match. I'd put in a stronger recoil spring and changed out the original Elliason target sights for a set of high visibility Trijicon Bright & Tough night sights in green tritium. What Hector was referring to was that instead of a 15-round magazine like that in Hernández's Sig Sauer, my Colt only had a 7-round magazine since it was chambered in .45 ACP, not 9mm like the Sig. I'd have to do a quick magazine change halfway through the shooting to be able to complete the challenge.

"It's all I've got, Hector, so let's just give it a go and see what happens."

Making sure that I had a second full magazine in a Blackhawk Single Mag Pouch looped onto my belt on my left hip and a full 7 round magazine in the pistol with one in the pipe, I re-checked the position of my magazine holder on my left hip before I took up the position in front of the middle plate. Signaling that I was ready, I waited for Hector to yell go.

When he did, I brought the old Colt up in the 'thumbs forward' grip, but unlike Hernández I transitioned into the Weaver stance, which I preferred. I double tapped the first four plates going from left to right, skipping the middle plate before performing a quick tactical reload and racking the slide before double tapping the remaining two plates on the right and transitioning back to the center plate and giving it a double tap as well.

Looking back at Hector and Hernández, they seemed a bit awed. "What's my time?" I asked.

"Five and a half seconds! It's a tie," exclaimed Hector.

"Not really, my friend," Hernández said. "He did a mag change in the middle plus he was shooting a more powerful weapon with significantly more recoil. I've been fairly beaten."

"Where in the heck did you ever learn to shoot like that?" Hector asked.

"Well, I grew up shooting in Idaho as a kid and just got better in the Army. Then the DEA sent me to all those shooting schools like the Gunsite Academy in Arizona and Rogers Shooting School in Georgia. I think I just have a natural aptitude for shooting, and I enjoy it.

"Regardless as to how impressive that was, you'll still need Hernández to drive the truck," Hector informed me.

"Hernández, you'll need to organize the schedules so that we can target the two newer dispatchers. You'll also need to get King set up with a conference room to go over his suggestions with the drivers concerning how to act when and if they get hijacked. Call King when you've got things set up in Walsenburg and we'll take it from there."

Driving back into town I stopped by the shop to touch base with Miguel and Antonio. It seemed that old Joaquin had stopped by and dropped off a comprehensive list of what type of ammo we needed to order and how much. I asked Miguel to place the order with the various vendors and to also order me two of those Charles Daly Honcho shotguns; one Tactical Triple, the scary three barreled break open 12 gauge and one Honcho Tactical pump-action. The pump action was for me while the other triple barreled version was for Dennis, the ICE guy sorting out Coco's paperwork. I was playing the Coco thing very close to my chest, so I didn't explain the order to Miguel.

While Miguel and I were talking, Kassy walked through the gate in the courtroom divider thing and sashayed over to where Miguel and I were having our discussion at the display counter. I was on the outside leaning against the counter while Miguel was behind the counter. Kassy leaned back against the counter beside me and crossed her arms across her chest.

"I just got a call from Papa. Should I still address you as King or do I now call you Señor Wyatt Earp?"

I was ignoring her by acting like I was reviewing Joaquin's order, difficult as that was, but Miguel was curious. "Why would you call King after a famous Wild West lawman?"

"Well, it appears that Mr. Fisher here just outshot Hernández out at Papa's place during a little impromptu shooting competition that Papa had organized in the back yard."

Miguel perked right up at this tidbit of information. "King, you must tell us the story now. Nobody has ever outshot Hernández before." Kassy wasn't going to let me off the hook either. "Yes, Señor Earp, enquiring minds want to know!"

"Look you two, I did not outshoot Hernández. The fact is that we tied on time shooting a bunch of paper plates, it was not a big deal."

By this time, Antonio decided to stick his nose where it didn't belong. "What were you shooting, King?" I reached under my t-shirt at the small of my back and pulled out the old Gold Cup. "I was shooting this."

"And what was Hernández shooting?" This guy was like a dog with a bone.

"A Sig P226 MK25."

"And how many paper plates were there?" Would Antonio ever shut up?

"Seven plates."

"And how many shots did you have to put into each plate?" continued Antonio.

"Two rounds into each plate. Are you finished with the interrogation yet?"

"No, not yet. So let me get this straight, you tied on time but to shoot twice into each plate you would need to do a magazine change in the middle while he did not."

Turning to Kassy, who was still leaning against the counter with her arms crossed, Antonio asked her if she knew the time.

"Papa said they both timed out at five and a half seconds."

Miguel and Antonio whistled. "Not bad for a white boy!" said Antonio.

"Well, if you guys are finished with the interrogation, I'd suggest that you get back to work before the white boy exercises his white privilege and fires you all."

"You can't fire me, I'm your business partner," informed Kassy.

"Then I might have to bend you over my knee and paddle your behind for being such an annoying co-owner."

This was a huge mistake on my part as she just got a big grin on her face and said, "That sounds fun, would you be gentle?"

I'd had enough, threw my hands up in defeat and told them I was going home and to call me if they needed me.

On the way out the door I heard Coco shout, "King one, Kassy one!"

CHAPTER 11

AFTER MY CALISTHENICS THE NEXT morning, I drove over to the shop to check in with Miguel and Antonio and get some scrambled eggs with chorizo from the taqueria. The tables were full this morning, so I guessed the word was getting out that Kassy and company served a pretty good breakfast.

I was planning to head to the Azteca offices shortly so I just checked to ensure that Miguel had made the ammo order as per Joaquin's suggestion and to see if we'd had any orders placed for firearms. Miguel said that he had an order for two Ruger Mini-14's, one in 5.56 NATO and the other in 7.62 x 39, which actually made it a Mini-30 to be absolutely correct. There was another order for two of the little Ruger SR22, .22 semi-automatic pistols. Ruger seemed to be the manufacturer of choice so far, but I'd need to get some weapons from some of the other manufacturers out there just to drive competition.

Going over to the taqueria side to get a coffee to go, I had the misfortune to run into the resident matchmaker Coco, who politely asked me if I was actually going to be gentle on Kassy as I paddled her behind or would I get rough with her?

"I don't know, Coco. How do you think I should play it?" I answered.

"Want me to ask?" she replied with a leer.

I just shook my head and walked out to my truck, got in and fired it up before getting on the road to Walsenburg.

The Azteca yard was a 6-acre lot with roughly a 500' x 500' open yard in the middle. The north side bordered on West 2nd Street, with a two story brick office building in the northwest corner facing east and a huge garage cum workshop in the southwest corner with the bay doors facing north, toward the office. Essentially the whole 3 acres on the western side was paved with asphalt to provide a big parking lot for the rigs as well as access to the workshop. The rest of the lot was left to nature, room to expand I suppose. The entire perimeter was fenced by an 8' tall chain-link fence with triple strands of barbed wire angled out at the top. Pulling through the front gates of the Azteca Trucking Lines depot, roughly in the middle of the northern side, I pulled into a parking spot in front of the office building and walked through the front door on the east side of the building.

I told the pretty young receptionist that I was there to see Hernández. She made a call then asked me to take a seat in the reception area until Hernández could come and get me. While I waited, I looked around. The building was very upmarket with polished wood floors covered with Mexican motif rugs. The interior walls had been left as rough brick and had been hung with good Old West genre art. Everything was clean and professional.

While I was waiting, the young receptionist girl came over and shyly asked me if I was the 'King' that Ms. Archuleta kept mentioning? I told her that I went by the nickname King, but that I doubted that my name had ever crossed Ms. Archuleta's lips.

She gave me a wink and said, "You'd be surprised," as she went back to her desk. Between this young thing and Coco my life, as well as any relationship with Kassy, was destined to become complicated.

Hernández came down the stairs on the south side of the room and came over to shake my hand before we headed upstairs to a conference room. There was a coffee maker in the room so we both grabbed a coffee before we sat down to strategize. He'd already informed all the dozen or so direct hire drivers that they would need to sit down with me soon to go over what would become the company policy when a load was hijacked. They would start scheduling themselves for the available slots beginning next week. It had not been necessary to try and isolate the two most recently hired dispatchers as one, Richard Sax, would be going away on his two-week annual vacation in a few weeks leaving John Greene and Bob Sanders to handle the dispatching responsibilities.

Next week I would begin the Driver's Response to a Hijacking seminar for the drivers, but the week after, Hernández and I would be picking up a load of liquor from the James B. Beam distillery in Clermont, Kentucky and bringing it to wholesale liquor warehouses like LDF in Wichita and Tulsa, and the various Costco Wholesale outlets located around the Denver area.

Whiskey comes in cases of 12 bottles each, and each bottle has an average minimum retail value of between $15 to $20. Assuming 750ml bottles, you can get between 98 to 117 cases on a pallet. Using 112 cases per pallet as an average and 24 pallets per 53 foot trailer to avoid overloading your trailer, you do the math and end up with 2688 cases or 32,256 bottles of whisky per truckload. At $15 dollars a bottle that is a value of $483,840 for the load. This should definitely be tempting for any self-respecting truck hijacker.

We would let John Greene handle this particular load from the cradle to the grave. If we got hit, it would be a sure indication that he was involved with the hijackings. We would fly into Louisville, Kentucky and then drive down to the James B. Beam distillery to relieve the regular driver, give him an airline ticket back home and the keys to our rental car so that he could turn it back in at the airport and we'd take over the load.

Since the load would become less valuable once we started hitting the warehouses and unloading product, we'd probably be hit somewhere early in the journey. We would be taking I-65 north through Louisville before getting off on 160 going northwest to Salem then getting on 135 heading north again. We would stay on 135 through Gnaw Bone and Nashville as we worked our way north and west to avoid the road works that were never-ending in the Indianapolis area until we hit I-70 and could take it west into Kansas.

Taking state roads north, as opposed to staying on the interstates, could send up a red flag as they would no doubt be tracking us, but avoiding Indianapolis was just common sense. The area between Salem and Morgantown is some of the most remote country in Kentucky. This would give the bad guys about 60 miles of lonely road to make their move. Now we just had to ensure we were on that particular stretch of road in the wee hours of the morning.

If we picked up the load at the distillery at close of business, say 6:00 in the evening. Faked a flat tire and then had a long dinner in Salem, this should put us on the road from Salem to Gnaw bone at about 10:00 in the evening. Not optimal, but acceptable. For a load this valuable they would be willing to take some risks.

With the plan in hand, I left Hernández in the conference room to make some notes on our discussion and walked back downstairs to leave. As I passed the pretty young receptionist, I asked her if she knew Coco the Clown that lived with Ms. Archuleta. She said that she knew her well and that they occasionally got together when her and Ms. Archuleta were in town. I told her that I thought that may be the case.

"Are you kids tag teaming me in regards to Ms. Archuleta?" I asked.

"That would be inappropriate, Mr. King," she replied.

"I notice that you did not answer my question, Candy." I had finally read her name off the receptionist sign on her desk.

"Very astute of you, Mr. King. Ms. Archuleta is my boss and I simply follow orders."

"That's what they said at Nuremberg. You see what that got them."

"I have absolutely no idea what you are you talking about." Obviously, history was not Candy's strong suit.

"Never mind. You can report to both Ms. Archuleta and Coco that all of you confuse me to no end. Have a good afternoon."

I got back to the shop just at closing time and went over to my side of the premises to check in with Miguel and Antonio. The ammo order had gone in, and a customer had placed an order for a Winchester Model 101 Field Grade over and under. It was good to see that we were selling something other than Rugers and ammo now.

I was leaning with my back to the display counter and was admiring the view of Kassy cleaning the tables. She was now wearing a pair of those black Nike running shorts with the built-in underwear and a pale blue Polo shirt. Anyhow, as Kassy would reach over to wipe down the tables, the shorts would ride up the back of her thighs. It was truly a sight to behold and it was without a doubt the most spectacular female backside that I had ever had the opportunity to ogle.

Women's posteriors need to fall within certain parameters to qualify as 'spectacular', I had given this subject a lot of thought during my formative years. Needless to say, they can't be too big or too small. Generally speaking, slightly larger than the size of a basketball is considered perfect, depending on their height. They must also be the just the right shape to fill out whatever type of covering they are hiding behind and to stretch that material in an alluring manner when required, such as when they are reaching over to wipe down a coffee table in a taqueria. This triggers the occipital lobe in the back of your head which is responsible for imagination. A proper female backside must also be firm and tight in all respects. Furthermore, and this is important, where the bottom of the backside in question meets the top of the thigh, it must, I repeat, must have that perfect 'curve and tuck'. A butt that is too skinny will not have any tuck and the butt just becomes an extension of the upper thigh. The perfect female behind will execute a perfectly shaped elliptical profile just before it tucks into the back of the upper thigh, at the vertex of the curve. A feminine backside that exceeds the absolute maximum of 90 degrees just as it tucks into the upper thigh will result in a slight but noticeable sag or overhang.

I was deliberating on this when Antonio came up behind me and said, "Take a picture, amigo, it will last longer."

Jumping up while giving my head a shake I said, "Okay, time to go home." So, I did.

CHAPTER 12

I GOT A GOOD NIGHT'S sleep and was up again at 5:00 to do my workout routine before showering up, shaving and getting down to the shop. I'd spend a few hours working up a PowerPoint presentation to give to the drivers the following week and then I had to run over to Fort Garland to check something out.

I'd been at it for a while when I walked over to Kassy's side to get a cup of coffee and a donut. Both Kassy and Coco were behind the counter, this could be dangerous.

"What's the chances of getting a coffee and a donut to go?"

"Pretty good," said Kassy.

While they were heating up my donut and pouring my coffee, I informed them that I had met yet another one of their co-conspirators during my trip yesterday.

"Oh, you mean Candy? What did you guys talk about?" queried Coco with an innocent look on her face.

"I'm sure that you knew the answer to that question before I even got out the front gate." Kassy had her back to me but was trying not to snicker, so I knew that I'd hit the nail on the head.

As Kassy handed me my coffee and my donut in a paper sack, she asked me what I was doing. I told her about the PowerPoint presentation I was composing. She asked if I'd mind if she took a look. Walking across to the office behind her I noticed a slightly suggestive swing of her hips, but that could have simply been a product of my overactive imagination.

"You do realize that I can see you eyeing my backside in the reflection from the display cases, don't you."

"Sorry," I said as I flushed up a bit.

"Don't be, I put a lot of time and effort into that part of my anatomy, and it is nice that someone appreciates the results." I just shook my head. You'd have to be a blind octogenarian not to appreciate it.

Getting into the office she took a seat behind the desk and brought up the presentation on my laptop while I sat on the couch and ate my donut and drank my coffee.

"This is pretty good, but I can clean it up some and make it a little more appealing to your audience. Do you mind?"

"Knock yourself out, I can use as much help as I can get."

About that time, I saw the Fedex guy come in with a package, so I left Kassy to it and walked over to where the guy was talking to Miguel at the counter. I showed him the proper documentation and paperwork before taking possession of the package. While I took out my Swiss Army knife and started to open the box, both Antonio and Miguel came over to see what was in it. Pulling out the first carton I opened it up and pulled out the triple barreled Charles Daly Honcho shotgun. I handed it to Miguel and asked what he thought of it?

Being a practical sort of guy, he said that although it had a certain 'shock & awe' quality to it, it was about as impractical a weapon as he had ever seen.

"You've only got three shots and you'd have to be a brave man to fire it one handed. That dueling pistol sort of grip might break your wrist. I'm assuming that they had the sense to equip this thing with a selective trigger and that you can't fire multiple barrels at one time," he said as he handed it to Antonio.

"All true," I agreed. "But you can get off those three shots much quicker than you can with a pump gun. The trigger is a mechanical reset and goes right, left then top. The whole thing is only 27" long which means you can conceal it pretty easily. As you say, the 'shock & awe' factor is phenomenal, but anyone getting hit by three loads of buckshot out of 3" magnum cartridges is not going to be getting back up any time soon and will be in no position to stop you from going for your pistol."

"Fair enough," said Miguel, "but why two?"

Pulling out the second carton I opened it up and took out the Honcho Tactical pump action shotgun. I was also only 27" long as well, with even a more laid back pistol grip similar to what you'd find on an old Moorish pistol, but whereas the triple barreled weapon had 18" barrels, due to the differences in the length of the actions, break-open as opposed to a pump, the pump gun only had 14" barrels. This made it a very nasty close-in weapon, plus it held five 3" magnum rounds in the tube magazine plus one in the pipe, twice the capacity of the triple barrel.

"Well, the triple barrel is for a friend of mine as payment for something that you'll find out about later, and the pump is for me."

About this time Kassy asked me to come into the office and see what she'd done with my presentation. One look at what she'd done told you that she'd gone to college and taken it seriously while I was simply digitally challenged. The presentation was only 9 slides now, but they had an eye catching background and the Azteca logo on the upper right of each slide. She'd boiled it down to 4 topics; what to look out for before you hit the road, what to look out for when you were on the road, what to do after the hijacking occurred and lastly, what you never do.

The first slide was just an introduction to the topic, each of the 4 topics were addressed by bullet points on each slide followed by visuals on the next. It was very professional and would take no longer than 30 minutes to run through with each driver. I'd give them a hardcopy to take with them.

"That is very well done. It would have taken me forever to get my version into this shape. Thanks a lot for this. What do I owe you."

"How about one day when we are both in Walsenburg, you take me to lunch at the New Century Chinese place and we'll call it even."

"You're on," I told her.

I started putting my laptop into my rucksack and getting ready to leave when Kassy asked where I was going. I told her it was a surprise. She got a big happy smile on her face, obviously she thought the surprise was for her. It couldn't hurt to let her keep thinking that, but all would be revealed in the not-so-distant future.

I got in my unsightly hotrod truck and took off out of town and headed north on 12 until it hit 160 then took it through and over the mountains to the west until I got to Fort Garland. After following the directions given to me, I found the little ranch south of town and pulled into the driveway. Getting out of my truck, I knocked on the door and when the old guy opened it up, I explained who I was. He said to hold on a minute while he got his old straw cowboy hat and we walked out to his barn. Walking inside he headed to a back corner and took the tarp off of an old vehicle which had been stored there. It was an old 1967 Volkswagen Beetle, also known as the Bug. Although the body was in excellent shape, the motor definitely needed work. It was one of the ones that came with an original sun roof and the pop out rear windows. It had belonged to his daughter, but once she married and moved to Denver, she had no place to store it and really didn't want it anymore. He said he'd almost pay somebody to tow it away as he needed the space in his barn.

"How about this, I'll pay you $500 dollars as it sits if you can get it towed or trailered over to my place in La Veta?" I offered.

"Cash money now?"

"In crisp one-hundred-dollar bills," I told him.

"Done and dusted. I'll let you know when I'm ready to deliver it to you. Is the weekend good for you?"

"That'd be fine and much appreciated."

Driving back to La Veta I could now check that off my list. My nefarious plan was to present Coco with her legal documents on her birthday, including her driver's license and give her the old VW Bug as a bonus. The problem is that I was running out of time for me to sort it out along with running the shop and sorting out the truck hijackings. I needed some help.

Getting back to the shop around 3:00 in the afternoon, I called Antonio into the office. When he came in, I asked him to close the door. From the look on his face, he had come to the conclusion that he had done something wrong.

"No, I'm not going to fire you. I actually need your help," I told him.

I explained my plan with the VW Bug, without mentioning the legal documents for Coco, and told him that I needed someone to restore the car back to mint condition by Coco's birthday in 3 weeks. The icing on the cake would be if they could put in a new interior and paint it in a flowing American flag motif.

"That's a pretty ambitious timeframe, King," he replied, but then he laughed. "My cousins own a restoration shop in Trinidad. If you can get the car here in a week, I'll tow it down to them and tell them that it is an important rush job. It'll cost you, but I guarantee it will come out looking and running as if it just rolled off the showroom floor. Do you have any photos of how you want it painted?

I reached into my desk and pulled out some photos that I'd printed off from some sites online and gave them to him.

"Thanks for that, Antonio, you just got me out of a bind. Not a word to Coco or Kassy, understood?"

"Understood, this will be kind of fun."

I was slowly but surely ticking items off my 'to do' list. I still had to get the documentation for Coco from Dennis, deliver Dennis' triple barrel shotgun to him in Denver as payment for the documentation, Hernández and I still needed to go get hijacked somewhere in Kentucky, and we still needed to resolve the issue with the dispatchers. All before Coco's birthday in about three and a half weeks.

Grabbing my new shorty pump gun and a box of 3" magnum 12-gauge shells in double ought buckshot, I left the shop in the capable hands of Kassy and Miguel and went home to do another 6-mile run while I contemplated life in general.

CHAPTER 13

THE FOLLOWING DAY I HAD to force myself to do my calisthenics routine as I was still recovering from the previous afternoon's 6 mile run. After performing the morning's ablutions after my run, I drove over to the shop to get a coffee and just check on things. As usual, I walked in the door and straight over to Kassy's counter to get a coffee and a couple of sopapillas.

As Kassy went to the machine to get my coffee, I saw that she was wearing what I thought was a very nice navy blue, knee-length blouson dress with the typical loose bodice and the cinched waist. On many women this dress would not have been remarkable, on Kassy it looked great.

While she still had her back to me, I asked, "Kassy, is that a new dress? I don't think I've seen it before. It looks very nice on you!"

The response I got was not at all what I had expected.

"Damn," said Kassy as she went to the register and got out a $5 dollar bill and gave it to a grinning Coco.

As she handed me my coffee and sopapillas I asked her what that was all about. Before she could answer, Coco piped up, "She bet me $5 that you wouldn't even notice the new dress. I told her that even you couldn't be that blind and took the bet. Thanks, King!"

They were both smirking openly now. "You two are going to drive me to drinking. I can never figure out what is going on with the two of you."

As I started to walk over to my office, Coco informed me, "Earth to King, that's the whole problem."

With that out of the way, I could try to get something done. Miguel and Antonio came into the office to discuss the shop economics. I thought that we may need to put some money into advertising, but Miguel said that word was slowly getting around the county concerning the unique taqueria and gun shop in La Veta and that Hector was still spreading the word. He suggested, and I concurred, that we give it a month or so to see how things progressed.

Later that afternoon my cell phone rang, it was Hernández. It seemed that we'd need to be in Kentucky on Monday and to plan accordingly. We had the early Delta flight out of DIA in Denver at 7:55am and would be in Louisville by 5:23pm after a stop in Minneapolis. This meant that we'd have to be on the road by 2:00 in the morning. We'd need to put whatever firearms and ammo that we wanted to take with us in a hard-sided, lockable case that we would declare at the airline check-in and ship as checked baggage. I told him that we wouldn't be getting much sleep that day if we planned to do all that traveling, pick up the load in Clermont then ensure that we were in deepest, darkest Kentucky at the optimum hijacking hours.

"It is what it is. Do you have a suitable case for the guns and ammo?" he asked.

I did. We'd meet up at my house on Sunday evening to get all of our kit together and he could rack out in the guest room until we hit the road early in the morning.

I remembered that I was supposed to start the hijacking seminars for the truck drivers next week, but I couldn't be at two places at one time. I called Hector and explained the situation to him. I suggested that since Kassy had actually re-written my presentation, that perhaps between both of them they could cover for me while I was out on the road with Hernández. He said he'd sort it out, but to be careful since it was almost guaranteed that the jackers would hit a load worth almost half a million dollars.

"Hector, one last thing. Hernández and I will be armed next week and may actually have to shoot some of these pendejos. How are we fixed legally concerning the carrying of the weapons and if we actually do shoot a few people?"

"Years ago, I made a decision that my drivers would not be armed. I would rather they just give up the load as opposed to try and protect it. But with the recent hijackings and the fact that some of the drivers have been beaten or pistol whipped I have had our legal department inform all of our clients and the authorities in each of the states that we operate in that the drivers could now chose to be armed. Nobody has complained about this new policy. If you do happen to shoot some pendejos during your journey, simply stay where you are at, call 911 and tell them the truth. If you get in a bind, I'll have you lawyered up quickly.

"Now let me ask you a question. If you do stop a hijacking, won't this be a problem with our ongoing investigations of the dispatchers? Won't this tip them off that we are looking at them?"

"I don't think so, Hector, in fact not taking any action would seem odd to them. They've been hitting you hard for about a year now and you have not taken any overt action, I think something like we are planning would be expected."

"Fair enough. Try not to shoot each other next week and I'll talk to you when you get back. By the way, how are you and my daughter getting along in the new shop?"

"To be fair, her side is making more money than my side at the moment. Their food is great, and people seem to enjoy going to the taqueria and just hanging out. Your daughter and her sidekick Coco seem to think I'm stupid, blind or both and I am not entirely sure why that is."

"Gringo, if you haven't figured that out by now then you are both stupid and blind. I suggest you take a closer look at what is going on around you when you get back," at which time Hector hung up. These Hispanics were very complex people.

Saturday, I chose to forego the morning calisthenics and decided to get the

6-mile run out of the way instead, which meant that I got to sleep in until 7:00. Getting on my running togs, I did a little stretching in the front yard before heading out into the countryside to abuse myself. I really didn't enjoy running, but I enjoyed being out of shape even less so I forced myself to do it.

I started my run around 8:30, so if I could maintain a 9 minute per mile pace, I should be back at home around 9:10, a perfect time for breakfast. I had just about finished the run and had turned off Cherry Street onto the cul-de-sac when I once again saw the little red Mustang pulled up behind my pickup and Kassy sitting on the porch swing going back and forth in her snug little yoga outfit. I stopped at the bottom of the porch stairs and leaned over with both hands on my knees to recover some sort of composure before climbing the stairs. I finally managed to do this and sat down on the swing beside Kassy.

"What brings you to my humble abode so early on a Saturday?" I wheezed.

"Well, I went to the early Bikram session, and I thought I'd stop by and see if you wanted to go to breakfast with me?"

"Where did you have in mind?"

"How about Corners Diner? We could walk there."

I told her that that sounded like a good plan as I started to push myself up off the porch swing. "I'll need to shower up before we hit the road," I informed her.

She shoved me back down on the swing and said, "Ladies first. I didn't get a chance to shower at the studio." Picking up her backpack, she walked into the house.

I was shocked, Kassy was going up to my bathroom to take a shower like she owned the joint. All I could think of to say was, "The towels are in the cabinet by the..." but before I could finish my sentence, she told me over her shoulder as she went up the stairs that she knew where everything was as she is the one that originally put them there.

I was sitting in the living room when Kassy came down the stairs still toweling off her mane and told me it was my turn, but this time Kassy had on a nice knee length filmy summer dress in a flowery design and was barefoot, not at all like the Kassy that had gone up the stairs in her yoga outfit. As I walked by her, I started to lift the hem of the dress up, but she smacked my hand away and asked what I thought I was doing?

"Well, I just wanted to see if you still had those little yoga shorts on under your dress or did you carry a complete wardrobe with you in that backpack?"

She was smiling now, "Some things are better left to the imagination, Mr. Fisher, don't you agree?"

"Not really. I just wanted clarification as to your mobile wardrobe and the contents thereof, but as I am a proper gentleman, I will not pursue this line of questioning further."

"Proper gentlemen finish last. Go take your shower."

I showered up, shaved, put on a clean pair of 505 Levis, my Timberland boots and a CZ USA t-shirt before going downstairs. Kassy was once again on the porch swing so after I locked up the house while she put on some flip-flops, we started walking to the diner. The diner was only about two and a half blocks away, but we had to go about a half block south on Cherry Street to where it became West Grand Street. Cherry and West Grand were dirt until you crossed Oak Street, so we just walked along the right-hand side of the road.

As we were walking, Kassy said that it would be proper if we held hands while we strolled along. I told her that due to my concern for her wellbeing I couldn't possibly do that.

"And why would that be, Mr. Fisher?"

"I've been told that for any young, nubile Caribbean-Hispanic girl to be seen holding hands with an older 'pote 'e leche' will, like the breaking of a mirror, bring seven years bad luck to the previously mentioned nubile young thing," I explained.

Kassy jumped in front of me and began walking backwards while she educated me on the proper 'walking to breakfast' etiquette. "Here's the deal, Mr. Fisher, either you hold my hand while we walk to breakfast, or I will beat you to a pulp here and now! You can be a frustrating man sometimes."

"As I don't want to get beat up by a girl in public, I will concede to your wishes."

As she resumed walking forward beside me as opposed to backwards in front of me, I held out my left hand, she put her right hand in mine and we continued walking to Corners Diner. Kassy actually began swinging our hands like we were a couple in high school. Before we even got to Oak Street she started laughing, "How do you even know what a 'pote 'e leche' is? That's Puerto Rican slang for 'can of milk'. You definitely didn't pick that up around here."

"I may have been studying some of that Caribbean slang, you never know when it might come in handy."

"Yeah? Like with a local girl?" There was hope in her eyes.

"More like if I ever go to the Caribbean for a vacation I was thinking."

The hope in her eyes transformed into the evil eye as she informed me that, "You are skating on very thin ice, Mr. Fisher. You had better hope that you have the nine lives of a cat."

We were on the paved section of Grand Street now, walking hand in hand along the sidewalk on the south side of the street, with Kassy closest to the street, when an older Kia Rio turned right off of Main Street onto Grand and stopped as it came abreast of us. The driver, a young Hispanic girl powered down the window and waved at Kassy.

"Is that him?" she asked.

Kassy was blushing big time as she made a shooing motion down by her hip with her left hand trying to get the girl to go away. She finally took the hint and drove off laughing.

"That is Angelina, don't pay any attention to her. She tends to gossip a lot."

"Really? She seemed pretty level headed to me. Who was the 'him' she was referring to?" I wasn't going to let her off the hook on this one.

"Who knows? It could have been anybody."

"I suppose so, but I couldn't help but notice that you seemed to have been blushing a little and I would have sworn that your hand began to perspire."

"I'm simply hungry, that is all."

We'd arrive at Corners Diner, oddly enough at the corner of Main and

Grand, so I held the door open for her and we walked in, took a seat and both ordered huevos rancheros and coffees.

It was a nice, relaxing breakfast but the local guys at the counter kept giving me the stink eye. I think that they were a little jealous that I was sitting with probably the prettiest, sexiest woman in at least a three-state region having breakfast and they were not. Not my problem, but it did make me feel a little smug.

We walked home after breakfast, hand in hand again so that I wouldn't get beaten to a pulp. When we turned into the cul-de-sac, we both noticed the old '67 Beetle sitting in front of my house. It must have been delivered while we were at breakfast.

"Why would someone drop off an old Bug in front of your house?" Kassy asked as I reached in and grabbed an envelope off the driver's seat. Opening it up I found a note from the previous owner letting me know that the title and a Bill of Sale were in the glove box.

"It's a project of mine. I'll restore it when I get around to it."

"An old Bug doesn't seem to be your style, but to each his own I guess," she said as we walked into the house. She walked over and picked up her backpack and we walked back out onto the porch.

"That was fun, King, we should do it again sometime." I agreed wholeheartedly.

Giving me an innocent kiss on the cheek, since we were officially out in public I assumed, she strolled over and opened the door to her Mustang, but before she got in, she leaned on the roof and turned toward me.

"By the way, I do keep a complete wardrobe in the backpack. The yoga shorts are now in the pack. I will leave it to your imagination as to what is, or is not, under this little summer dress. See you later!"

Okay, time for another shower, cold this time.

CHAPTER 14

AFTER MY COLD SHOWER I put on a pair of old cargo shorts, a t-shirt and some flip-flops before going back downstairs to fire up the coffee machine and get busy sorting things out so that I had everything covered while Hernández and I were away trolling for bad guys.

First, I called Antonio and told him that the VW Beetle had arrived, and we needed to get it out of here before Coco saw it. He said he'd be over in an hour with his truck and trailer. I then called Miguel and let him know the plan in regards to Hernández and I heading off to Kentucky. He said that he and Antonio could handle the shop while we were away, no problem. The old guy was worth his weight in gold. That done, I decided to call Kassy to let her know that I would not be in the shop for about a week as I'd be out on the road with Hernández. At least I told myself that this is why I called, I may have had an ulterior motive, but I was sticking to the 'responsible business partner' story.

When she picked up the phone, she opened with, "Are you missing me already?"

Two could play this game. "That goes without saying, but the real reason I called is that I found a pair of Calvin Klein bikini panties, the red with grey motif, in my bathroom. Since I am fairly certain that they are not mine I thought that perhaps they were yours and that they had fallen out of your backpack while you were showering this morning."

After a moment of silence, she icily replied, "I do not wear Calvin Klein, they must belong to another woman."

"Could be I suppose, I'll have to call around."

As I expected, she went ballistic and was saying some very colorful things while not actually using foul language once. That's either a talent or very good self-control. I let her go on until she ran out of steam and then simply said, "Gotcha!"

There was another moment of silence before I was told in no uncertain terms that I was the north end of a southbound mule. While trying to keep from laughing, she asked if there was a serious reason I had called. I told her about Hernández and I going to Kentucky and what we were going to be up to. Her, Coco, Antonio and Miguel would need to watch both the shops while we were away. She told me to be careful and to call her as soon as I got back.

About this time, I heard a vehicle pull up out front. Going out on the porch I discovered that it was Antonio with his truck and trailer. He'd backed his trailer up directly in front of the VW. I went back inside and got two mugs of coffee, one for me and one for Antonio before heading back outside to hand him his mug.

As we started to get rigged up to winch the Bug onto the trailer I said, "Thanks for this, Antonio, I'll owe you. I needed to get it out of here before that pesky Coco saw it and started asking questions."

Once the VW was in place and tied down securely, we sat on the back end of the trailer to finish our by now cold coffee.

"I heard that you and Kassy were walking hand in hand over to the diner this morning. You need to be careful amigo; Hispanic girls can be a handful. I can only assume that Caribbean-Hispanic girls would be downright dangerous."

"Damn man, that was only a few hours ago! How did you find out about that?" I asked.

"Angelina is my cousin. Once she saw you two walking down the street holding hands you can rest assured that the rest of the town knew about it before you got home from the diner. There are no secrets here amigo, you'll need to be very discreet." He was laughing as he said this.

"What have I gotten myself into, Antonio?" I asked while jokingly shaking my head.

"I think it is what our young Coco calls 'good trouble'."

Antonio took off with the old VW and I went back into the house to eat some lunch and then pack up my kit for the excursion to Kentucky. I had to remember where I had left my old hard sided rifle case suitable for flying weapons on commercial airlines. I finally found the Pelican V700 case under the bed in the guest room. Taking it to my bedroom I threw it on the bed and popped it open. This particular case was perfect for that little Honcho pump gun I was planning to take as well as my old Colt Gold Cup and whatever Hernández planned to take as well as the ammo for each. I laid the Honcho up toward the hinges and the Colt in the lower right corner. This left a spot in the lower left corner for what I assumed would be Hernández' Sig. Between the two pistols we'd store unloaded spare magazines, a box of 9mm for the Sig, a box of .45 ACP hollow points for the Colt and a box of 12 gauge 3" magnum double ought buckshot loads for the Honcho.

Leaving the Pelican case open on the bed, I loaded up my small wheeled Samsonite soft sided case and my rucksack with a couple pair of old jeans, spare underwear and socks, a couple t-shirts a couple old Levi denim work shirts and my shaving kit. I should be good to go.

Hernández showed up around 6:00 in the evening in his new black F-150 Ford Raptor. I'd cleaned out an old grill that I had found in the garage and had it ready to fire up when he arrived. We'd grill some steaks and bake some potatoes for dinner while having a few beers. But first things first.

Dragging his kit up to the guest room, I showed him where he would be racking that evening, then told him to get whatever guns and ammo he wanted to take, and we'd lock them in the Pelican case now. As I thought, he was only taking his trusty Sig Sauer P226 MK25 and a box of Federal hollow points, so they fit easily into the case. Hernández raised an eyebrow at the little pump gun, but I told him better safe than sorry. Locking the case, I put it on the floor at the foot of my bed alongside my Samsonite bag and we were ready to take off early the next morning.

We baked the potatoes and grilled the steaks before sitting down at the little Formica table in the kitchen to have our dinner and just shoot the breeze. After washing and drying the plates and silverware, we cleaned up the kitchen before grabbing another beer and going into the living room to rehash the plan for the next few days. Around 9:00 we called it a day and tried to get some sleep before the 1:00am get up and go.

We'd gotten some sleep by the time 1:00 the next morning rolled around, but not really enough for what we had ahead of us. None the less, we got up, showered and shaved before putting our shaving kits back in our bags and taking them downstairs and dumping them by the front door. While Hernández got the coffee going, I fried some eggs and bacon for a light breakfast. After cleaning up the kitchen we grabbed our kits, locked up the house and got in his Raptor for the long drive to Denver.

We rolled into the long term parking lot at the Denver International Airport around 6:00 and took the shuttle to the main terminal, known as the Jeppesen Terminal. Going to the Delta counter in Terminal East, we checked the guns in and collected our boarding passes prior to doing the TSA song and dance before being allowed to go downstairs to the train servicing the concourses. Getting off at Concourse C we proceeded to Gate 47 to await our flight.

Eventually we got onboard, airborne and on our way to Minneapolis where we would connect with the flight to Louisville. We landed in Louisville around 5:30 in the afternoon, picked up our checked baggage then rented a late model Impala and drove down to Clermont, arriving at the distillery at around 7:30 in the evening. When we arrived at the James B. Beam distillery office in Clermont, we were told that our load and driver were actually waiting for us at the Jim Beam Booker Noe Plant a few miles south outside of Boston, Kentucky. Getting back into the Impala, we drove south toward

Boston and ran into the Booker Noe facility about 2 miles north of Boston proper. We turned off Lebanon Junction Road into the entrance to the plant. Before we even entered the plant, we saw the Azteca Freightliner tractor and its trailer pulled off into a parking lot to the right.

Pulling up beside the rig, we got out and Hernández beat on the driver's door. The driver had obviously been taking a nap, but woke himself up and climbed down from the cab and shook hands with Hernández. They obviously knew each other.

"Jimmy, this is King, he's doing some consultant work for us regarding the recent hijackings."

Jimmy was in his early 30's, a slim and trim guy from Colorado Springs. Slim and trim over the road truckers were rare, the lifestyle does not lend itself to proper exercise or diet. Jimmy obviously worked to stay fit on his off time.

"Nice to meet you, King. The rig is fueled up and ready to go and the manifest is in the document compartment between the seats. Hope you have a good trip."

While Hernández was handing Jimmy his ticket back to Denver from Louisville and some travel money, I got our bags out of the Impala and threw them into the sleeper compartment in the cab.

Jimmy drove off a happy man and Hernández and I climbed into the rig. I had no idea how to drive a big rig and left that to Hernández while I climbed into the sleeper compartment and unlocked the Pelican case and laid out the weapons. Since Hernández was busy doing the driving, I loaded up two mags for his Sig, slotted one in the grip, racked the slide and did a press check before handing him the weapon and the spare mag. I did the same for my old Colt. We both put our pistols in the map pouches built into the doors for easy access. I then got the Honcho pump gun off the mattress in the sleeping compartment and loaded five 3" magnum double ought buckshot rounds into the tube magazine, jacked a round into the chamber and replaced that round in the magazine. Ensuring it was on safe I laid it back on the mattress. Now we only needed to see if we'd actually need all the firepower that we'd brought with us.

Since we had not anticipated the side trip to Boston to get the rig, we actually didn't get on the road until about 9:00 that evening. There was now no need to fake a flat tire or to have dinner in Salem. We were through Louisville and then Salem by around 10:30 and heading north on 135 toward Plattsburg and then Brownstown. This is what I referred to as Stage 1 of the potential hijack zone. It was a run of about 25 miles through lightly populated farmland and wooded hills. We kept alert and aware while we were on this stage.

We arrived in Brownstown at 11:00 at night and stopped at the Country Mark station, where 135 teed off at 50, for a pit stop, a coffee and some snacks. From there we took 50 west about 3 miles until we caught 135 north again for a run of roughly 25 or 30 miles through a lot of hill country perfect for a late-night truck jacking, this was Stage 2. We had just taken the sharp left hand turn at the Stone Head Nature Preserve when I noticed two sets of lights behind us. This stretch of road was very isolated, hilly and wooded for the next 3 miles, if the guys behind us were going to make a move it would be in the next few minutes.

I got my Colt Gold Cup out of the map pouch on my door, did a press check again to ensure that there was a round in the pipe then leaned forward and shoved it in my waistband at the small of my back. Hernández went through the same routine, but laid his pistol on the console between the seats. I reached back for the Honcho pump gun, pulled back the slide until I could see a cartridge inside the ejection port, then jacked the slide forward again and let the little shotgun ride muzzle down beside my right leg.

Sure enough, less than a minute had elapsed since we had tooled up when the lead SUV, a black late model Chevy Suburban passed us and disappeared up the road. The tail vehicle just hung back about 50 yards or so.

I happened to notice that we had just passed a sign for the Trinity Hill Vacation Cabin, when Hernández said, "Heads up."

Looking through the windshield I could see the stationary Suburban blocking the road about a quarter of a mile ahead of us.

While Hernández was downshifting to bring the rig to a stop on the side of the road, I told him that I'd bail out just as he stopped and head back along the trailer to deal with the guys in the vehicle behind us and for him to get out and sort out the guys in front. I'd join him when I was finished or vice versa. By this time the truck was rolling along at about a walking pace, with the Suburban about 20 yards in front of us. I opened my door and bailed out just as the truck came to a stop, the air brakes masking the sound of my door opening and closing. I heard Hernández opening his door, but I was already moving back past the drive axles on my side of the Freightliner.

The vehicle in the back was an identical black Suburban and two guys got out, one from the driver's side and one from the passenger's side, both were holding handguns. This is where my logic fell apart, I thought that the guys in the front would focus on the driver while the guys in the back would both come up the right side, my side, of the vehicle. They obviously didn't like this plan since one came up on each side of the trailer. I had to do something quickly or else Hernández would have a guy behind him as well as two in front of him.

Crouching down I could see the guy on the other side of the truck from about the waist down just after he walked forward of the double axles at the rear of the trailer. I knelt down under the trailer and shot this guy once in the pelvic girdle with the shotgun from about 15 feet away. Without waiting to see the damage, I swiveled to the left and shot the other guy in the groin as well from about 10 feet away as he was bringing his pistol up to shoot me. Although this probably shredded the internal organs in their groins, even if I had hit their femoral arteries the damage would not be instantly fatal and these guys could still be effective stationary threats. That being the case, I jacked in another round and shot the second guy in the head as he lay on the ground before swiveling back to the right and shooting the first guy on the other side of the trailer in the head as well.

You may ask why I bothered to shoot these two in the pelvic girdle first, it had nothing to do with being cruel or sadistic. The reason you shoot a threat in the pelvis is if there is a chance that they may be wearing body armor. If they are, it won't be covering their groins. If you shatter the pelvic girdle with the first shot, they will be incapable of supporting and balancing their torsos. This leads to a much easier head shot when they drop to the ground in a heap.

My little Honcho shotgun was now almost empty and only held two more rounds, so I laid it down under the trailer and pulled my old Colt from my waistband in the back and ran up to the front of the rig on the passenger's side to see if Hernández needed any help.

He didn't. Apparently, these hijackers were fairly impressed with themselves and their success to date. They had been leaning back against the Suburban as the rig rolled to a stop waiting for the guys in the other Suburban at the rear to do their jobs. As Hernández climbed out of the truck they stood up and came walking toward him, each with a gun in his hand. About this time, back at the trailer on my side of the rig, I shot the guy coming up behind Hernández which caused the guys in the front to pause for a fraction of a second before making the mistake of bringing their guns up. Before they could line up on Hernández, he double tapped them both in the chest. They were both dead about the time they hit the ground.

While Hernández dialed 911 and told them what had happened, I moved the Suburban at the front of our rig off the road while touching as little as possible, then dragged the bodies to the side of the road as well. The rear Suburban was not an issue as they had pulled off the road behind the rig. We'd taken photos of the crime scene on our phones before doing this in an effort to show the cops the scene as it originally occurred, but it seemed like a bad idea to leave a Suburban and dead bodies in the middle of a dark road late at night. While waiting for the cops to show up we had a coffee from the Thermos in the cab and called Hector to let him know what had happened and where it had happened. At least he'd know what sheriff's department to call if we didn't touch base again tomorrow.

Eventually we could hear the sirens and see the flashing lights reflecting off of the trees along the side of the road to the north as two ambulances and two Brown County sheriff's SUVs blew down the road from Nashville.

I'd collected all of the weapons, ours and theirs, and laid them out on the side of the road about 10' in front of the truck. Hernández and I were just leaning against the cab on the driver's side when the cops and the EMT's arrived. As you would expect, the deputies pulled in with their headlights on us and the guys took cover behind their opened doors with their weapons trained on us. We were told to turn around, lace our fingers behind our heads, kneel on the ground and cross our ankles. We were then handcuffed and taken to different vehicles to be interrogated separately while the EMT's did their due diligence and pronounced the four hijackers dead from gunshot wounds.

We went through what had happened with the deputies. By this time, I think that they started to figure out what had gone down. They rearranged the handcuffs so that our hands were now in front of us so that we could access the photos on our phones and illustrate what had occurred as we gave them a rundown on the events.

These Kentucky deputies were pros though, they never uncuffed us, they kept us separated in different vehicles and once the crime scene investigators showed up, they drove us to the Brown County Sheriff's Department building in Nashville to take our depositions. They then called Hector to make sure that we were who we said we were.

By this time, the sun was coming up. We'd been cleared of any wrongdoing but were told that our presence may be required in court so not to make any plans for an international vacation in the near future. After everything was said and done, and all the paperwork was completed, the deputies loaded us back into one of their SUVs to take us back to the rig. On the way back we got the guys to stop by the McDonald's drive-thru which was about a quarter mile from their shop. We bought everybody breakfast and coffee before heading back to the rig.

The crime scene had been cleaned up by this time, the SUVs towed away, and the deceased taken to the morgue. The guys then gave us back our weapons and we shook their hands before they drove off leaving Hernández and I standing on the side of the road with our rig.

"Well, I don't think whoever's behind all of this will be in a hurry to try that again any time soon. What do you say we just get back on the road, deliver all this booze and get back to La Veta?" I queried Hernández.

"I believe that you may now have an ulterior motive to get back. Could it be that you are missing a little Caribbean-Hispanic lady?" said Hernández with a sly look on his face.

"She's not that little, now get in the truck."

He just laughed.

CHAPTER 15

BY FRIDAY WE'D DELIVERED ALL of the booze to the locations in Wichita, Tulsa and Denver. Hernández drove us out to DIA so that we could retrieve his truck from the long-term parking lot. I had to drive his truck back to Walsenburg since he was the only one who could drive the rig.

We convoyed back to Walsenburg and got to the Azteca yard about 4:00 in the afternoon. After we got our kit out of the truck and filled out all of the required paperwork, Hernández' drove us to my place in La Veta. It had been an interesting week and I'd gotten to know Hernández pretty well.

"Thanks for the memories," I told him. "Now go home and get some sleep, you've done all the driving for a week."

"I think I will. It's been interesting, but I'm beat. I'll see you around amigo. Take care."

And with that Hernández drove off in his Raptor truck and I hauled my stuff inside the house. I always believe in taking care of business first, so I unloaded my rolling bag in the mud room by the back door, separated my whites and colors and started doing my laundry. While the first load was washing, I went upstairs to put the rolling bag away and got out my cleaning kit from the closet and went back downstairs. I got a beer out of the refrigerator and took it into the living room where I had laid out the Honcho pump gun. In between doing laundry and drinking beer I cleaned and oiled the pump gun then disassembled, cleaned and oiled the old Gold Cup as well, even though I hadn't had to use it.

Once I had finished with the guns, I grabbed the cleaning kit, the pump gun and the Colt and went upstairs to put them away before jumping in the shower to clean up myself as well. Wrapping the towel around my hips I went back down the stairs to see how the laundry was going. I jerked to a stop in surprise as I walked into the kitchen.

Kassy was in the kitchen and had dumped out my rucksack on the kitchen table and was separating the 'smalls'; the underwear, handkerchiefs and socks from the from the rest of the stuff I'd crammed in there during the past week.

"You forgot to wash this stuff. Lucky for you I came along. I kind of like that look. Is it a casual dress sort of day?" She was leering inappropriately.

Now keep in mind that I was almost butt naked with only a towel wrapped around my hips while she was attired in old cut-off jeans, a t-shirt and flip flip-flops. An involuntary physical response, at least from my side, started to raise its ugly head, read into that what you will.

"I think I'd better go back upstairs for a minute," I informed her.

As I retreated upstairs all I heard was giggling coming out of the kitchen. Paybacks can be, and often are, totally out of proportion to the initial act. I think General Patton said that.

I grabbed a quick shave and put on some cargo shorts and an old DEA t-shirt before returning to the kitchen. Kassy had folded the previously washed laundry and had laid it out on the kitchen table and was sitting there drinking one of my beers. I grabbed the folded laundry off the table so that I could put it where it belonged upstairs and told Kassy to grab me a beer and meet me on the porch swing.

Going out on the front porch I found Kassy swinging on the swing. She handed me a beer as I sat down in mid-swing. I opened it and took a big pull before I asked her if she was now going into the 'breaking & entering' business?

"It's not B&E if the front door is open," she informed me.

"I take it that you've researched this issue in the past then?"

"A girl likes to have career options. Now that we have that out of the way, why don't you tell me what happened while you and Hernández were out on the road. The late-night phone call early Tuesday morning had Papa in a tizzy. He wouldn't tell me what was going on."

"Maybe there is a reason he didn't tell you; did you stop to think about that?" I asked.

"I know that you and Hernández went out trolling for truck hijackers. I assume that you found them. Correct?" The Inquisition had begun.

"Correct."

"Since you and Hernández managed to deliver the load, I would assume that the hijacking was not successful. Correct?"

"Correct."

"So said hijackers are now behind bars waiting for the legal process to take place and our loads should no longer be in jeopardy. Correct?"

"Incorrect."

"The hijackers got away?"

"Incorrect."

"You are not making any sense. Either the hijackers were apprehended, or they were not, which is it?"

"Kassy are you actually a true blonde?"

"I'm a Caribbean-Hispanic girl, the chances of me being blonde are slim to none. What does my hair color have to do with anything?"

"Well, you are acting like a blonde. If the jackers were not apprehended and they did not escape, what do you think happened to them? We were hauling a load worth almost half a million dollars. What lengths do you think a criminal enterprise would go to for a load that valuable?"

It finally started to dawn on her what I was saying. She sat up straighter, stopped swinging, grabbed my hand and told me to tell her what happened. At this point I figured that she would badger it out of Hector eventually, so I could save him the hassle and just tell her now.

"Hernández and I were on the road in the middle of Kentucky late at night last Monday when two black Chevy Suburban's came up behind us on a remote stretch of road. One eventually passed us and blocked the road while the other came up behind us as Hernández pulled off the road. I jumped out and went toward the back while Hernández got out and went toward the front. There were two armed guys in each Suburban, the ones in the back got out and were coming up the sides of the trailer, one on each side. The other two were coming toward Hernández from the front. As you know, they didn't get the load."

"You shot them?" She looked a bit horrified at the thought.

"Well, I only shot two of them. Hernández shot the other two."

"And they are dead?"

"Deader than doornails and presently taking up space in the Brown County morgue."

She sat back and stared off into space for a while as she sipped her beer. I don't think that she ever thought that this truck jacking had anything but financial consequences, the truth was starting to dawn on her. Sadly, I thought that she may be regretting hanging out and holding hands with a guy that actually shot and killed people. Her next words would likely determine the potential of any future relationship between us.

You could say that I was pleasantly surprised when she hopped up off the porch swing, held out her hand to pull me up as well and simply said, "Oh well, live by the sword, die by the sword. Where are you taking me to dinner?"

We walked over to the Mission Deli Mesa Steak House, where I had first met her and Hector. We both had the salsa and chips for starters followed by a steak. During the meal Kassy was dying for a detailed description of the failed hijacking but I let her know that I really didn't want to talk about it. It was just something that needed done, so Hernández and I had done it.

Walking back to the house she said that she had to go home. She grabbed her backpack off the couch in the living room and came back to the porch to give me a chaste kiss on the cheek before she began walking toward her car.

Before she got off the porch, I grabbed her arm and stopped her in her tracks.

"Hey, I should check to see if you really are actually a true blonde or not," I lecherously whispered in her ear.

"Well, I'm led to believe that there is only one definitive way to check out that supposition," she said as took a step back, reached down with one hand and started fooling with the pull tab on the zipper of her cut-offs, running it slowly up and down about an inch.

While I stood mesmerized at the thought of that zipper tab hitting bottom, and what that might lead to, impure thoughts were erupting once again in the occipital lobe at the back of my head responsible for imagination. She pulled the tab up before dancing off the porch with a peal of laughter and got in her Mustang. She waved as she drove off, still laughing.

I was now of the opinion that I would soon be developing a serious case of what the Hispanics term 'bolas azules' if I kept hanging around with Kassy.

The following day, after the morning workout routine and run, I drove over to the shop to see what damage old Miguel and Antonio had visited on the shop while I was away. I was suitably surprised to see that the building was still standing. Walking over to the taqueria side I found Kassy and Coco behind the counter. It was too early for the other younger girls, the waitress and hostess, to arrive. They'd be in before the lunch rush.

I ordered a coffee and a couple of donuts to take to my office. Kassy had turned around to the coffee machine to get my order ready while Coco looked me in the eye with a mischievous grin on her impish face and asked, "So tell me, Mr. King, what is your opinion regarding those pesky zipper tabs on cut-off shorts?"

Hearing this, Kassy just hung her head while placing both hands on the counter by the coffee machine and said, "Coco, that was supposed to be just between you and me."

"Well, I'm young, impetuous and I can't keep my mouth shut and I still want to know his opinion regarding zipper access on cut-offs," declared our resident Colombian miscreant.

Two could play this game. "Well, young Coco-Loco, when you're 'going for the gusto' as they say, zippers are preferred. First, they are much quicker to operate and provide faster access to the naughty bits than those buttons found on cut-offs made from old Levis 501's, for example. Secondly, they are much quieter to manipulate in a public setting such as a dark movie theater than Velcro. What do you think?"

Coco just turned beet red and for the first time since I had known her and did not have some snarky comeback.

As I turned to walk over to the office, I heard Kassy say, "King one, Coco zero."

Miguel and Antonio finally showed up for work and came into the office. It seemed that the word-of-mouth advertising was starting to bear fruit and that the gun shop side of the business was picking up. We had an order for a couple of Remington 870 Wingmasters come in, apparently in anticipation of duck season and ammo orders were coming in steadily. The orders for the two Ruger Mini-14's and the two little Ruger SR22, .22 semi-automatic pistols had come in, but one of the guys who had ordered an SR22 had to renege due to an unexpected medical issue. I decided to buy it for the shop and perhaps the guy would be able to afford it later.

That done, I called Hector and asked him if he was at home, and if he was could I come over at lunch to discuss the hijacking issue with him. He suggested that we meet at the shop for lunch instead as we may want Kassy in on the discussion. We decided to meet here at 1:00.

Hector arrived and he, Kassy, Miguel and I had a lunch of Caribbean shrimp tacos and iced tea. Shrimp tacos didn't sound too appetizing to me but were surprisingly good. After lunch we all retired to my office in the corner of the shop and got down to business.

"Okay, after the incident in Kentucky we can be fairly certain that John Greene is instrumental in the hijackings as he was the only dispatcher that had access to information concerning the load that we were carrying and the route. What are you going to do about him, Hector?" I asked.

"At the moment we are watching him and trying to figure out who he was feeding this information to. I don't think that he believes he is under suspicion, but we are not giving him access to information concerning high value loads at the moment."

"That good because we may have a different scenario in play than we originally thought. You said that Greene and Sax hired on within 6 months of each other and shortly after Greene was hired the hijackings started. What if they are both in on it? It makes sense as this would give them much better coverage concerning the high value loads and their routing. Furthermore, if one was on vacation, which is exactly the situation we just had when Sax was away and Greene was on duty, they would still have coverage."

Everyone thought about this for a minute before agreeing that this could be the case. Hector then asked me how I would deal with this hypothetical scenario.

I'd given it some thought and asked Hector if he had any clients in-state that shipped high value loads.

"The only high-tech manufacturing company we service is Ursa Major Technologies out of Berthoud. They are a propulsion outfit that works on aerospace, space launch and hypersonic projects," replied Hector.

"Where do they usually ship to?"

"They don't ship big loads often, but when they do they ship all over the country."

"Do they ever ship interstate?"

"Occasionally they'll ship components to the Peterson Space Force Base in Colorado Springs."

This was perfect. I laid out my plan to trap Sax if he was in fact a co-conspirator with Greene. If he wasn't, no harm, no foul.

Any propulsion component coming out of Ursa Major Technologies would be of huge interest to their competitors, the dollar value could be astronomical on the black market and industrial espionage was always a concern to high tech companies with military connections. What we needed was to get Greene away from his keyboard for a while before feeding Sax the details for a quickly arranged shipment from Ursa Major in Berthoud to Peterson Field in Colorado Springs. Although the most direct route would be straight down I-25 to Colorado Springs, due to the supposed hazardous nature of the cargo the load would be shipped on a safer rural route south on I-25 from Berthoud to the interchange with 52 south of Frederick. The route would then be east on 52 to 79, about 12 miles east of Hudson. South on 79 to Bennett before jumping on I-70 going east to Limon. At Limon the load would be routed on 24 straight to Peterson Field.

"I can see a few problems with this," said Kassy. "First, you would need to have an actual load booked from Ursa Major Technologies. Second, they would have to agree to using their load as bait. Third, the insurance required for such a scheme would be outrageous," she correctly pointed out.

"Kassy, you are absolutely correct in everything which you just pointed out, but you are thinking like a businesswoman, not a devious gringo ex-DEA agent. We don't actually need a load; we just need whoever is behind the hijackings to think that we have a high value load waiting at the Ursa Major facility in Berthoud. We'll ask them to crate up some junk in suitably marked crates and we will openly load these onto a flatbed trailer in the event that there are people watching the facility. We'll then drag this junk all over eastern Colorado under the pretense that the load is hazardous and wait for someone to hijack it. If nobody does, then Sax is in the clear. On the other hand, if the load is jacked, we will know that Sax is involved along with Greene."

Hector said it was a good plan and to make it happen. We'd need to bring Hernández onboard so that he could get Greene out of the way and then to drive the rig. We didn't want to put any of the real drivers at risk.

It took about a week to get the management at Ursa Major onboard as well as to get Greene booked into a Diversity, Inclusion and Equity course in Denver, which was required for any company receiving government contracts these days. Occasionally this woke nonsense comes in handy.

The Wednesday after the meeting in my office, Hernández drove a flatbed rig up to Berthoud, to the Ursa Major Technologies facility which sat just to the west of I-25 and strapped down three large wooden crates of various sizes onto the flatbed trailer. The crates had all the appropriate 'hazardous' stickers on display and anyone watching would have thought that they were the real deal.

Hernández followed the briefed route religiously and sure enough, about 3:00 in the afternoon two pickups ran him off the road between Limon and Simla. Hernández peacefully gave up the load and the hijackers took the rig and the load and left Hernández standing beside the road.

At this point Hernández pulled out his concealed phone and called Hector, who alerted the Highway Patrol. The hijacked rig and both pickups were pulled over just east of Peyton and all four of the hijackers were arrested. The State Troopers gave Hernández a lift back to Colorado Springs where Miguel was waiting to pick him up and bring him home. Another driver would pick up the tractor trailer rig in Peyton later.

This little operation yielded a couple of benefits. First, we now knew that both Greene and Sax were in on the hijackings. Secondly, when the State Troopers interrogated the hijackers, it was revealed that the organization behind the hijackings was an offshoot of the Dixie Mafia based in Biloxi, Mississippi. The FBI was now taking an interest in them so they shouldn't be a problem in the future.

CHAPTER 16

TO SUMMARIZE, THE HIJACKING RING had been broken up, we'd identified our moles and handed them over to the cops so that they could be prosecuted, and the Azteca Trucking Lines were back in business without the constant threat of having a lucrative load hijacked. I could now start concentrating on the gun shop since my consulting days, and sadly the money from them, were now a thing of the past.

The following week Antonio told me that the old VW Bug was finished and ready for delivery so one afternoon we took his truck and trailer down to his cousin's shop in Trinidad to pick it up.

His cousins had done a phenomenal job on the old Beetle. The little 1,500cc engine purred like a sewing machine and the interior was like it had just come out of the factory. The seats had been done in blue denim and everything else inside was eggshell white, including the headliner. The exterior was a work of art. Everything on the car had been straightened or replaced and the bumpers had been re-chromed. The paint job was magnificent. The base color was a charcoal grey, but flowing back from the front to the rear was a billowing American flag. The flag waved along the top and down both sides which contrasted nicely with the charcoal grey background, which really set the red, white and blue off nicely.

The guys had also sourced a set of Borrani wire wheels for it, which really made the whole car pop. I thanked Antonio's cousins and paid the bill before Antonio and I got it on his trailer and secured. We covered it with a car cover and secured that as well, we couldn't have anybody seeing it until 'the Day'.

We got back to my place, unloaded the Bug and rolled it into the detached garage behind my house before putting the car cover back over it. It would reside here until we were ready for it. I locked the garage door on the way out since I didn't trust Coco not to come snooping around.

Going back through the house, I grabbed two beers and met Antonio out on the porch swing, and we just shot the breeze and drank beer until he decided to go home. I thanked him for his troubles and let him know that I owed him one now.

The next day I received a phone call from Dennis telling me that Coco's paperwork was ready and I told him that his shotgun was ready as well. I'd drop him a text on WhatsApp once I figured out when I could get up there. Walking over to the taqueria side of the shop I asked Kassy if I could speak to her for a moment and we walked out the front door to get some privacy and enjoy the sun.

"When is Coco's birthday and what's the plan?" I asked her.

"Her birthday is a week from this Friday. We'll close at noon on Friday and decorate the taqueria and hold her birthday party here starting about 6:00 so that people can get off work and clean up before coming to the party. Why do you ask?"

"I wanted to double check as I don't want to miss the party. The problem is that I need to get to Denver that Friday to fill out some paperwork for the ATF concerning my FFL for the shop here," I explained.

"You are speaking Greek, Mr. Fisher. Could you please translate what you just said?"

"Sorry. I need to go up to Denver next Friday to meet with the Alcohol, Tobacco and Firearms people concerning the renewal of my Federal Firearms License," I lied. "I'll probably be a little late getting back, but I'll definitely try to be here."

"You had better get back in time for the party or I guarantee you that you will never get to see that little zipper tab on my shorts in anything but the full up position in the future," she informed me with a smile.

"That is what we call an idle threat, Ms. Archuleta. I am sure that I had no chance of seeing that little tab in anything but the full up position regardless what I did or did not do next Friday."

"A smart man would hedge his bets and be at the party."

"I have never been accused of being a smart man, but I will definitely try my best to be here. If I am not here right at 6:00, make some excuse for me because I will be there at some point."

"Kiss me and you have a deal." This is known as blackmail.

"What? Here in front of everybody, in the middle of the day?"

"The choice is yours, cowboy, now step up to the plate or walk back to the dugout. I'm waiting."

Sometimes you just have to take one for the team. I grabbed her around the waist, pulled her to me and gave her a great big kiss. Needless to say, she took advantage of the situation and did some of that Gallic stuff where she shoved her tongue between my teeth for a second before she pulled away and ran back inside laughing.

As I made my way back through the courtroom divider gate and to my office, I heard Coco say, "King one, Kassy two." If she was this way at 16, she'd be seriously obnoxious by the time she got into her early 20's.

I texted Dennis and said I'd be driving to Denver early the following Friday. I suggested that we meet up at the In-N-Out Burger joint near the Park Meadows Mall where County Line Road crosses I-25 at 10:00 in the morning. A few minutes later I received a 'thumbs up' emoji from him in return.

Okay, that was sorted out. I then went into the shop proper to find Antonio. Since his cousins had done such a good job on Coco's Bug I wanted to find out if they could work their magic on my old '65 Dodge pickup.

"Dude, that would have to be magic! That has got to be the ugliest pickup ever built. What possibly possessed you to buy that thing anyhow?" was Antonio's response to my query.

I explained to him that it was so ugly that it eventually grew on you. Furthermore, it was mechanically perfect and was more or less a 'sleeper', it just needed the body straightened out and some decent wheels and tires.

"It grows on you like mold on a potato," he replied. "Let me call them up and see if they will even consider pulling it into their shop. They have a reputation to uphold, you know. Let me get back to you on this."

Okay, that was another thing sorted out. Moving right along I called Hector from the comfort of my own office and explained to him that since I had lost my consulting gig at Azteca Trucking Lines and the fact that the gun shop was still getting on its feet, I needed to find another job so that I could keep food in the fridge and keep up my half of the deal made with his daughter concerning the 'Kassy's and the Caribbean King's Taqueria and Gun Shop' enterprise.

"She didn't tell you?" was his confusing reply.

"Didn't tell me what?"

"That I put you on the books as the Security Director for the Azteca Trucking Lines."

"It seems to have skipped her mind. Do I have your permission to spank your daughter?"

"You may do so at your own peril." He was laughing now.

"Okay, just so I can budget myself, what is my salary as Security Director?"

"Considering what you may have saved the company regarding the recent conclusion of the hijacking issue and out of the goodness of my own heart, I figured $250,000 per year would be reasonable compensation. You'll also get medical and dental, and two weeks' paid vacation a year. Is that okay with you?"

"Hector, that is more than okay! Thank you very much. I need to hang up now and go paddle your daughter."

Walking back through our odd courtroom divider I went directly behind the taqueria counter and confronted the shapely owner of the establishment.

"Kassandra, did you perhaps forget to tell me something important recently?" I asked sweetly.

Putting the tip of the index finger of her right hand under her chin while looking up at the ceiling in a contemplative pose, she thought for a moment before saying, "Not that I can remember offhand."

While everybody watched, both customers and employees, I grabbed her hand and pulled her behind me back around her counter and into the dining area proper. While doing this I grabbed a big wooden spoon off the counter with my free hand. Sitting down at an empty table I drug her across my lap while she squealed with laughter.

"I just spoke to your father, and he told me about the security gig with Azteca. He seemed surprised that I had not heard about it from you. He then gave me permission to paddle you. I want you to know that this is going to hurt me more than it will you." I just said the last part because I had been told that parents often tell their kids that before paddling their butts.

Looking down at that magnificent backside, clad in well-worn 505 Levis, I had second thoughts about damaging the goods, but dammit she'd be a better person for it and, let's face it, she deserved it.

I got in three or four good whacks before she jumped up rubbing her backside and told me, in between bouts of laughter, that paybacks were on the way. If you remember correctly from the 'casual towel day', I should have informed her that this was in fact payback. The patrons in the shop at the time seemed to be on my side as they gave me a standing ovation. Kassy shook her finger at them but was laughing so hard she couldn't speak. I chased her around the taqueria with the spoon for a few minutes to get my exercise before I tossed the spoon back onto the counter and made my way to my office. The patrons were still giving me a standing ovation, so at the gate through the courtroom divider I stopped and took a bow before continuing to the office.

That was fun, I may need to do that again but I'd hate to bruise the fruit if you catch my drift.

CHAPTER 17

COCO'S BIG DAY HAD FINALLY arrived. Over beers the previous evening I had informed Antonio of my nefarious plan. I would be driving to Denver early tomorrow to 'do some paperwork' and would be back later after the party had started. When he saw me walk in, he needed to make some excuse and walk the 5 blocks back to my house and drive the Bug over to the shop and park it out in front. He'd leave the keys in it and just walk back in and enjoy the festivities, no one the wiser.

The next morning, I got up bright and early and took off for Denver while everyone else worked until noon before Kassy took Coco back to their house and the locals started the decorating and cooking as required.

I got up to Denver on time and met Dennis at the agreed on In-N-Out Burger joint where we had lunch and afterwards, in the parking lot, I handed over his Honcho shotgun and he handed over an envelope with Coco's paperwork in it. Promising to visit La Veta soon, Dennis drove off while I cruised over to the Park Meadows Mall to do some shopping.

I picked up some new 505 Levis for me, these have zippers as opposed to the buttons on 501's. A much more workable fly in my opinion if you remember the previous zipper dissertation with Coco. I also got some more socks and underwear before heading over to the Nordstrom store to get a little something for Kassy, and to be honest, myself. I'd seen the ad in their catalog and the model had the same general coloring and body shape as Kassy and I knew that it would look incredible on her. Granted, a guy selecting clothes for a woman is a recipe for disaster, but I was willing to give it a shot and take the risk.

The dress in question was the Cowl Slip Midi Dress in the wine color from Astr the Label. It had a cross strap back and a leg baring slit up one leg to mid-thigh. It was as sexy as could be. The problem would be the size. I had to threaten Coco with bodily harm before she would tell me Kassy's dress size about two weeks ago. I was told a size 6, if Coco got it wrong, I was going to put Nair hair remover in her shampoo. I had them gift wrap it before I headed back out to my truck.

I then drove over to Bowers Tactical on Yosemite Street to see if there was anything that I wanted, which was essentially everything, but I settled on a Sig Sauer, a Colt and a CZ t-shirt. It was now about 3:30 in the afternoon and I needed to get back on the road if I was going to make it to the party before it was over and having my ass kicked by everyone in the town of La Veta.

I blew the cobwebs out of that 5.7 liter Eagle Hemi engine in my ugly old pickup on the way home and managed to pull up in front of the shop right at 7:30pm. Grabbing Coco's paperwork and Kassy's gift I jumped out and went in the front door to a 16 year old's birthday party gone wild. There was a DJ rig set up in the back of the dining area by the kitchen and the tables had been pushed up against the walls and the courtroom divider. All the tables were full of parents eating Mexican dishes from the kitchen while the floor in the middle was full of kids dancing to the DJ with balloons and confetti all over the dance floor. It seemed that everyone was having a good time, but when I tried to talk to Coco, Kassy or Hector I was given the cold shoulder. At some point in my excommunication, I went back out to my truck to get Coco's paperwork and Kassy's gift and put both in the lowest drawer in the office desk before venturing out again. Never show up late to a

Hispanic girl's 16th birthday party. Apparently, this is a serious breach of social etiquette. I was well and truly ostracized until the party was over about 9:30 in the evening.

I had noticed Antonio leaving just after I had come in, so the worm was about to turn. I put on my most obsequious expression and asked everyone to come into the office so that I could apologize appropriately. Once they were all in the office; Coco and Kassy sat on the couch in front of the desk with their arms folded across their chests while Hector took a seat in the X-back chair to the left of the couch. None of them looked very happy with me. I said I was sorry for being late and the floodgates of acrimony opened wide. Kassy asked me how I could be so unfeeling as to disrespect Coco on her 16th birthday, and not even be thoughtful enough to bring a present. Coco was in tears and Hector said I was a typical bastardo ingrato, which I found out later roughly translates to 'ungrateful bastard'. While they were beating me down, I reached down into the desk drawer by my right leg and pulled out the envelope with Coco's new paperwork inside. I laid it on the desk, and everyone got quiet.

"Perhaps you should take a look at this before you continue with your vilification." I pushed the envelope toward Kassy, who was now looking confused. She tentatively took the envelope and opened the clasp. As she took the documents out of the envelope and examined them one by one, the look of amazement on her face kept growing and growing. She would look at me with that 'deer in headlights' look after she inspected each document. She was stunned, astounded and astonished all at the same time and just stared at me with those big beautiful brown eyes while she passed the documents one by one to Hector. After Hector had taken a look at them all, he asked if they were real.

"Those are authentic documents issued by the U.S. Citizenship and Immigration Services, the Social Security Administration, or the Colombian government," I answered. "Well, except for the little one, that was issued by the Colorado Department of Motor Vehicles."

Kassy was still in shock as Hector passed the documents back to her and she handed them over to Coco. Coco looked at all the documents in amazement and just kept going through them over and over before she eventually started to cry.

"Coco, what you have in your hands is a certified copy of your original Colombian birth certificate, the documentation for a green card, the actual green card, a social security card and a driver's license valid as of today. You are now a lawful permanent resident of the United States of America, and you can legally operate a motor vehicle even though you haven't even taken a driver's test. You and Kassy will need to work on that last item."

Coco suddenly jumped up and came flying right over the top of the desk to hug me. She ended up sitting on my lap while crying on my shoulder as she hugged me so hard that I thought she'd crack a rib. You couldn't really blame the kid; she'd been in limbo for a few years. This was a big day for her.

Kassy, showing a serious lack of restraint in front of her father simply came over, grabbed my head in both hands, turned me toward her and gave me a long, drawn out kiss while she cried as well. Hector simply said that perhaps I was not such an imbécil inútil, or useless half-wit, after all.

Once everyone had calmed down, I told them that I was not quite finished. Reaching back into the drawer I pulled out Kassy's present and set it on the desk. I told her that this was for being such a good big sister to Coco. She reached for the box and took her time unwrapping it. When she finally opened the box, she lifted out the dress and got a huge smile on her face. She stood up and held it against herself and said she loved it. I suggested that she shouldn't wear it while walking down busy streets as she was sure to cause a number of fender benders when any male driver between the ages of 16 and 60 rubbernecked her.

"Okay, I still have not given Coco a proper birthday gift, have I? If you will all follow me out the front door, I will try to remedy that." I got up and walked out the front door with everyone behind me. Walking up to the restored VW Beetle I opened the driver's door and pulled the keys out of the ignition. Turning around I tossed them to Coco.

"Well, you have a driver's license, so it only seemed proper to get you something to drive. I suggest you let Kassy teach you how drive it before you give it a shot on your own. It is pretty cool, isn't it?"

Coco and Kassy were all over the Bug like the white on rice. Both were giggling like schoolgirls, which in Coco's case was exactly what she was. All in all, it appeared that Coco's birthday party was now a resounding success and I was no longer in purgatory.

I locked up the shop, the cleanup could wait until tomorrow. Standing on the front step with Hector while the girls were giving the Bug a test drive, he told me that I'd done a good thing and that he was happy that he'd brought me to La Veta. High praise indeed from Hector.

Sadly, I went home without seeing Kassy in her new dress, but it was something to look forward to in the future.

CHAPTER 18

I WOULD HAVE TO SAY that my time in La Veta had been interesting and satisfying up to this point, but I was ready to dial it back a little and concentrate on getting the gun shop on a better financial footing, figuring out just what my duties as the Security Director for the Azteca Trucking Lines actually entailed, finally getting my old Dodge truck a facelift and perhaps spending more time with Kassy and maybe figuring out what was going on in that pretty little head of hers.

In an effort to accomplish these goals I drove to the shop the morning after Coco's birthday party to make a plan. The first thing that I saw when I drove up to the shop was Coco's new VW parked alongside of the building in what was usually assumed to be my reserved parking spot. I did not see the little red Mustang, so I figured that the girls had arrived together in the Bug and that hopefully Kassy was giving Coco driving lessons and not the other way around. I also noticed a number of other vehicles parked along High Street in front of the taqueria.

It seems that the participants in last night's fandango had decided to help with the clean-up, which was a very considerate thing for them to do. As I walked in Coco ran over and gave me a big hug, the little heathen was starting to grow on me. She grabbed my hand and led me over to a table and sat me down before going back behind the counter where Kassy was working. They brought me a big plate of sopapillas and a coffee Americano grande, they knew me well. Kassy went back behind the counter and got herself a coffee before coming back to sit with me. When she reached for one of my sopapillas I slapped her hand. You don't steal a man's sopapillas.

It became fairly obvious that the townsfolk had been made aware of Coco's new paperwork and many came by and told me that it was a nice thing that I had done. I suggested that since Coco now had papers that we could ship her out of town as soon as possible. This got me a few chuckles and a slap on the back of the head from Coco once she heard what I had been suggesting.

Kassy wasn't saying a word, she just continued to sip her coffee while looking at me over the rim of her cup. This was fine with me; I could think of many worse ways to spend a Saturday morning than spending it drinking coffee with what I considered to be a tantalizing woman. Eventually though, the silence got deafening.

"What?" I asked her.

"Nothing, I was just thinking that you are not the man I thought you were when you first came to town. It is surprising to me that you have such a big heart and actually consider others before yourself, not the egoísta bastardo I would have expected from a cowboy, law enforcement, macho type.

"In an effort to dissuade you from thinking that I am anything other than what I am, I would like to inform you that although I may have an enlarged heart, it is of the coal black variety. I am not a macho, cowboy type, horses have hated me since I was a child. Furthermore, according to the Webster's dictionary definition a 'macho' person is one who exhibits machismo, which is an exaggerated masculinity or an exaggerated sense of power or strength, I try to avoid this. On the other hand, another definition of macho is being excessively virile. I would like to admit to this except that I haven't been given the opportunity to express my excessive virility since I have been in town. Sad but true."

"Finally, has it ever occurred to you that perhaps this is all a front and that I am simply trying to get in your pants?" A lot of truth is said in jest.

She considered this for a moment as she took another sip of coffee while trying to hide that gorgeous smile behind the lip of her coffee cup before responding.

"Let me address the points that you have mentioned one by one. First, regarding your heart, your actions speak louder than words. You cannot run from who you are. Secondly, you must exercise patience while in the quest to express your virility. You do realize that the Good Book tells us that patience is longsuffering and is a fruit of the Spirit. Sometimes it is the quest, not the conquest, which is important. As far as getting in my pants, I would like to point out that I am wearing a skirt at the moment so that argument is null and void. That said, if I was wearing pants, I would simply say that I already have one ass in my pants, why would I want two?" and in a fit of laughter she jumped up and ran behind the counter before I could grab her and discipline her with the wooden spoon again.

From behind me I heard an imp say, "King one, Kassy three."

I just hung my head in defeat and told the imp to keep her scorekeeping to herself.

Grabbing my coffee and the remaining sopapillas, I retreated to my side of the shop. Miguel and Antonio showed up and we huddled up at the display counter to discuss business. We were slowly but surely building up a clientele from further afield. The word seemed to be getting around that we were the go-to shop, not so much from a firearm shopping perspective but from a 'let's go discuss our requirements at the taqueria, listen to what they recommend, go through the catalogs and see what fits the bill and let them order it' point of view. We were now getting customers from as far away as Trinidad, Pueblo, Westcliffe and Alamosa.

Antonio was diligently pursuing his online gunsmithing course and would be certified shortly. He'd need a workshop and tools to be able to provide this service to our customers. I'd discussed this with Hector and we had come up with a plan that seemed to be a win for everyone involved.

There was only one other house on the cul-de-sac off Cherry Street where I lived and it had recently come up for sale. It was only a little place, about 1,500 square feet, but it had a nice little garage behind it that would make a perfect gunsmithing shop for Antonio.

Since business was picking up and the fact that I was now gainfully employed by the Azteca Trucking Lines full time, I suggested that we start paying Antonio a reasonable salary if he would agree to become the resident gunsmith as well as his other duties at the shop. Hector would buy the place across the cul-de-sac from my house and he would sell it to Antonio on very favorable terms.

This would not only give us the gunsmithing capability we desperately needed, but it would also allow Antonio to move out of his parents' house while giving him a base of operations to seduce a certain Alejandra Contreras from Cuchara who he had been seeing lately.

Young Antonio was beside himself with gratitude. I am not sure if that was because he could finally move out of his parents' house or that he could now develop a serious strategy concerning Ms. Contreras' virtue, either way it was a win-win situation, except perhaps for Ms. Contreras' virtue. We'd have to let young Antonio sort that one out for himself.

Moving right along in the list of tasks which I had set for myself today, I asked Antonio if his cousins in Trinidad had come to their senses and agreed to give my old Dodge truck a makeover. He said that they would do it under one condition, which was that they had full artistic license on the project. They said that if the gringo loco insisted on bringing them the ugliest pickup ever built as a project, his choice of vehicles showed a certain lack of judgement and they did not want this lack of judgement to interfere with their artistic creativity.

I thought about this for a second before coming to the conclusion that they really couldn't make it any uglier, so I agreed. Antonio said that he'd collect it this Wednesday and take it down to Trinidad. Turning to Miguel, Antonio asked if he could have Wednesday off as he would be busy moving into his new house as well.

I'd have to come up with another vehicle, but it was time to get the old Dodge D100 pickup prettied up a bit. I said my goodbyes, walked over to the taqueria counter and reiterated to Heckle and Jeckle that paybacks were often embarrassing and painful to those on the receiving end before walking outside, getting in my truck and driving over to Hector's place to discuss the definition of my new position within the company.

Arriving at Hector's house I knocked on the front door. After a few moments Hector answered the door dressed in old jeans, a long sleeved Western snap-button shirt rolled halfway up his forearms and barefoot.

"Hello, King, what brings you out here on a Saturday?"

"I just wanted to give you an update on the gun shop and to discuss exactly what my responsibilities will entail as your new Security Director for the Azteca Trucking Lines," I replied.

I sat down on one end of the main couch facing the kitchen while he got us a cup of coffee before he sat down on the other end of the couch. I let him know that the gun shop was slowly but surely coming along and that we were now getting clients from all the counties surrounding Huerfano County. The sale of ammunition was constant but could be expected to rise during the various hunting seasons in the fall. I then let him know that Antonio was extremely grateful for the opportunity to move out of his parents' house and the upcoming courting of Ms. Contreras. Hector could expect him to express his gratitude in the near future.

Getting down to business I asked Hector what he expected out of me as his new security director. The truck jacking business had been put to bed, Kassy had hired two new dispatchers and everything seemed to be moving along nicely again.

Hector leaned back and said, "Your job will basically be oversight. You'll need to show up at the office about once a week just to show your face and mingle with the employees in Walsenburg, but you'll also need to occasionally ride along with the drivers to see if you can spot any lapses in our security procedures or things that need to be changed to improve security. You'll need to go through our Preventive Maintenance policies and procedures to ensure we are doing our due diligence regarding our equipment and you'll be expected to go with Kassy when she is meeting potential clients to present our security procedures and policies if they ask.

"The role is very free format and I'll let you set it up the way that you want. What we want to avoid is a repeat of this whole truck hijacking and dishonest employees' issue which we just came through."

I thought about this for a second, then said, "Hector, this is very generous of you and I really appreciate it. I like it here in La Veta and I really would not be able to stay if my only income was generated by the gun shop as it now stands."

Hector laughed. "I could have an ulterior motive. Since you have been here and the taqueria and gun shop have opened, Kassy and Coco have had something to occupy themselves with and I can finally relax in my own home. Do you have any idea as to the disruptive abilities of two young women living in one house?"

"Glad I could help you out with that, but don't get the idea that they're moving in with me!"

Hector got pensive for a moment then told me, "King, that was an extremely selfless thing that you did for young Coco and at the time you must have organized it you really did not know her well at all. Can I ask you why you did it?

I kind of knew that at some point this question would come up. People are not geared toward 'random acts of kindness' anymore, which is sad. The old Golden Rule, treat others as you would like to be treated, is something I held dear.

"Hector, the world has become a much less kind or trusting place in the past few decades. People seem to only think of themselves and never give a thought to others who are much less fortunate. As adults we can deal with this and fend for ourselves, although this does not excuse ignoring those less fortunate. Kids do not have the experience or tools to deal with poverty, loneliness, abuse, much less the situation that Coco was in when Kassy found her in Trinidad.

"I only did what I thought was the right thing to do. I always follow my moral compass. From my work with the DEA, I had friends in the other federal agencies including ICE. Once Kassy told me Coco's story and the fact that she was a ghost with no chance of a normal life, I decided to do something about it. So, I did. That's really all there is to it.

Hector looked at me with a grin and said, "Nonsense! Not only did you give her an identity, you got her a driver's license and a car as well!"

"Hector, as you previously mentioned, perhaps I also have an ulterior motive. If she has a car and a license maybe she'll leave La Veta and I can also get some peace. You realize that she is constantly trying to hook me up with your daughter, don't you?"

"Admit it, King, you like the little scamp, Coco, not Kassy. She is entertaining and she does grow on you after a while. Furthermore, from what I am led to believe, you may be showing some interest in Kassy in any case. You could do a whole lot worse than my daughter, Mr. Fisher. Granted, she could drive any sane man crazy if she decides to, but your mental health is not my concern. Let's have some lunch."

CHAPTER 19

AFTER LEAVING HECTOR'S PLACE, I got in my truck and headed back into town. I stopped by the Cliff Brice Foodstore to do some grocery shopping then went home to put everything away before returning to the gun shop to waste the rest of the afternoon drinking coffee and observing Kassy as she shimmied and swayed around the taqueria. I can assure you that there are many worse ways to burn daylight.

Sunday rolled around and I was up early to do my calisthenics routine before hitting the road for another 6-mile run. These runs were getting easier, but I was still a wreck when I got back home. Keep in mind that La Veta sits at about 7,000 feet so 6 miles at that altitude is a pretty strenuous undertaking.

Recovering on the porch swing, I saw Coco's Beetle pull into the cul-de-sac. Coco was driving and Kassy was riding shotgun. They pulled in front of my house and jumped out. It was apparent from their attire that they had just come from the yoga studio. Kassy had on those incredibly sexy little yoga shorts and a sports bra barely concealed by an old Jose Cuervo tequila tank top. Coco was dressed in some Bohemian looking harem pants and a tie-dyed t-shirt. They just came up on the porch like they owned the place and sat down on either side of me.

"What's up, Kingman?" asked Coco the Clown.

"I am trying to recover from my latest 6-mile run."

"Well, that explains the flushed look and the sweaty clothes. Sitting that close to Kassy can't be helping things either." More wisdom from the Clown.

At this point Kassy interjected and told Coco to "zip your lip".

"Oh, we're back to zippers again. If you two would like to be alone for this conversation I'll be running along as I now have wheels and a license."

16-year-old girls talk non-stop and would drive normal people around the bend. "Why don't you stick around, you might learn something," I suggested.

That shut her up for a second, so I asked the two girls what they were going to do the rest of the day. They were going to pack a picnic and go up to Martin Lake to eat lunch and lay in the sun. They thought that they would stop by and ask if I would like to tag along.

Martin Lake sits in the Lathrop State Park and is about 12 miles as the crow flies from my place and is typical of man-made reservoirs found in the west. They generally do not have much of a beach and whatever beach they have will be more gravel than sand, but you work with what you have.

I would have declined the invitation if it had been anyone else, but looking at Kassy in that yoga attire made me wonder what she would look like in a swimsuit, either a one or a two piece, I wasn't picky. I am sure that the view would be mouthwatering in either case. That said, if my imagination got the better of me out at the lake and I embarrassed myself due to a 'totally involuntary physical response' to such an outstanding view, I would never live it down. This was a typical risk versus reward situation. I decided to live dangerously and told them to pick me up on the way there.

An hour later the Bug returned, and Kassy got in the back while I rode shotgun with Coco driving, remember I had decided to live dangerously. Kassy must have been one heck of a driving instructor since Coco was handling that 4-speed manual transmission like Richard Petty would have. The kid was a natural. We got up to the parking lot beside the lake around noon and carried our gear down to the little beach just to the west of the parking area.

I unfolded the three cheap little Walmart lounge chairs we'd stowed under the hood and set them up in a row with the cooler at my end of the row. I had on a pair of Hawaiian motif board shorts, so I just took off my t-shirt, grabbed a beer out of the cooler, sat down and waited for the show to begin.

Coco was a budding little hottie, but still really just a kid. She simply dropped her shorts, ripped off her t-shirt and ran into the water in a Speedo one-piece. If there would have been any teenaged boys around, they would have been swarming around us like flies.

Now keep in mind that there was a subtle dance going on between Kassy and myself and that I had never seen her in a swimsuit, which regardless of what people say is just a half step up from lingerie This was about to get interesting.

Kassy was wearing what was essentially an oversized t-shirt, which they formally refer to as cover-up. Kassy was obviously trying to figure out how to remove the cover-up in the most ladylike manner possible. I was enjoying her discomfort. Eventually she sat down on the middle lounge chair, pulled her arms in through the arm holes like a turtle pulling its legs back into its shell. Now she somehow had to get that shirt over her head without lifting her arms and stretching out that sexy torso. I guess she admitted to herself that she was acting like a child and just pushed it over her head before folding it and standing up. She placed the folded shirt on the chair then ran into the lake to join Coco.

I am fairly certain that my heart had stopped, I know that I stopped breathing as the view was simply breathtaking, no pun intended.

Kassy was not wearing a meant-to-be sexy swimsuit. Granted, it was a two piece, and showed a lot of skin, but it was just a normal mid-rise bikini bottom with a standard halter top, all in an island flower motif. On Kassy it was simply stunning. On her it was not the cut of the swimsuit that made it sexy, it was simply her making the swimsuit look sexy, if that makes any sense. I could feel my 'totally involuntary physical response' responding to the view, I'd either require more beer or I would need to shove the remaining ice in the cooler down my board shorts.

The girls finally came out of the water to lounge, so I took the opportunity to get into the water to cool off, if you know what I mean. Spring fed reservoirs in Colorado stay cold throughout the summer, which is exactly what I needed at the moment.

Needless to say, this was not the end of my torment. As I got out of the water, I noticed Kassy putting sunscreen on Coco's shoulders. I then had to camouflage the fact that I was sneaking peeks at Kassy rubbing oil all over her own arms, legs and six pack stomach afterwards. The 'involuntary physical response' was beginning to make a comeback.

She then laid down on her front, with that amazing backside pointing skyward and asked if I would mind putting lotion on her back. The Inquisition could not have devised a more diabolical torture. While rubbing lotion on her back, especially as I neared the waistband of her bikini bottom, I forced myself to name the capital of every state in the union in my head, or anything else that would keep my mind off the task at hand.

When the job was done, I quickly grabbed another beer and put on my Oakley's. At least now she couldn't be absolutely certain that I was staring at her. The thing is, I really didn't think that she realized the effect she was having on me. The girl just did not seem to realize how devastatingly attractive she was, which of course just made the whole thing even worse.

We finally ate the ham and cheese sandwiches that the girls had prepared earlier, then we all got in the water to cool off again before packing everything up around 4:00 and heading back to my place to drop me off. Coco made us all sit on towels so that we wouldn't damage the new seats with our damp swimming attire.

As I climbed out of the Bug, Coco whispered, "Well done! I was worried that you were going to blow a gasket back there for a while." She had a huge grin on her face. I leaned back down and told her, "You're not the only one who was worried about that happening."

The following Wednesday after I almost had an aneurysm at the lake, Antonio showed up at my house early in the morning with his truck and trailer while I was doing my calisthenics. I'd forgotten that he was going to take the old Dodge down to his cousin's shop in Trinidad for a makeover today. We got it up on the trailer and tied it down and off he went. I was supposed to go to the Walsenburg office today to go over some maintenance reports but now I didn't have a vehicle. I knew Kassy was also going to Walsenburg today so I gave her a call.

"Hey, you want to go on a date today?" I asked when she picked up the phone.

It was quiet for a moment before she asked, "Are you serious?"

"Sort of," I said. I then explained my present sans vehicle situation. I needed a ride to Walsenburg, and I knew that she was headed that way at some point today.

"So, you are really not interested in dating me?" she asked somewhat annoyed.

"Not true, mon chérie. I think that the rulebook says that I am required to date you before I move on to ravishing you. I'll need that dating scouts' badge before we move on with our budding relationship," I explained.

"You just want me for my car."

"Not true, I want you for your body, but if the car is available today, I'll take that as well."

"Okay, I'll pick you up in an hour. You do remember that you promised me a lunch at the New Century Asian restaurant in Walsenburg for getting your PowerPoint presentation sorted out awhile back, don't you?"

"It's a date then. See you in an hour."

She drove up in her Mustang in one hour exactly. She had on the same black pinstripe pencil skirt and white blouse that she had worn the day we had moved into the shop in town. It still looked great on her.

"Thanks, Kassy. Antonio took my old truck down to Trinidad this morning for a makeover. I'd forgotten about it and hadn't arranged for another set of wheels. I'll borrow a company truck before coming home this evening."

"Yeah, I'm sure that you wouldn't want to be seen driving around with me, would you? What does 'mon chérie' mean anyhow?" Women can be so thin skinned at times.

"I believe the direct translation from the French would be 'my cherished'. Over the years, going back until at least the 18th century, when using the term 'Mon chérie' in reference to a particular person, the translation would be 'my love'. Anything else I can help you with?" I explained as I looked at her with a lascivious grin.

"You are impossible!" she exclaimed while looking straight ahead trying not to smile.

We arrived at the office in Walsenburg and went our separate ways with the understanding that we would meet up for lunch at 1:00 in the afternoon, when I would honor my debt and take her to lunch at the New Century restaurant.

After reviewing maintenance records until I couldn't see straight, I walked down to the front desk and asked Candy if she could organize a company truck for me for the next couple of weeks or so. She said she'd do it and not to forget that I had a lunch date with Kassy at 1:00. There was obviously a grapevine communications network in play at the Azteca office which I was not privy to.

I called Kassy and told her to meet me outside the front entrance at 1:00, I'd be the handsome guy with the flattop haircut in a company pickup. She giggled and said she'd be there.

I drove up in my new company truck right at 1:00. Kassy came out the door and was looking all over, then at her watch as if she was annoyed. Since I was the only company truck in front of the building, I was curious as to what she was doing. Anyhow, once I tooted the horn, she gave me a wave then came over and hopped in the truck.

"What the heck were you looking around for? This is the only company truck in front of the building," I asked.

"I was looking for a company truck driven by a handsome guy with a flattop hairdo, but I didn't see one. Guess you'll have to do," she let me know while once again trying not to smile. Everyone is a comedian these days. I turned left onto Second out of the Azteca gate and then a right on Sproull. I hung a right on Spruce then a left on Walsen and we were in front of the New Century Chinese Restaurant.

Once inside Kassy ordered the cashew shrimp while I ordered the orange chicken. To drink we had jasmine tea. It was a nice change of pace from the Mexican food prevalent in La Veta and my own home cooking. We sat at one of the smaller tables and just had a good lunch while we gossiped and talked about things at the taqueria and gun shop.

On the way back to the office Kassy said that this had been a nice little date.

"Well, you know, as I've previously mentioned, I could be doing this just to get in your pants," I reminded her.

"You are not a very observant man, Mr. Fisher. If you were, you would have once again noticed that I am not wearing pants," she replied.

"I was speaking metaphorically."

"I am a successful business woman, Mr. Fisher; I do not deal in metaphors. In the spirit of this discussion, let us suppose that I was wearing pants as we speak. Would you still want to get in them?"

"In the spirit of our ongoing friendship I would plead the 5th Amendment self-incrimination clause and decline to answer that question as the answer may incriminate me."

"Good answer. Besides, I don't think that metaphorically speaking we'd actually both be able fit in my pants comfortably so best just to avoid the issue entirely."

Dropping Kassy off at the front of the building, I pulled the company truck into a spot reserved for such vehicles and followed her into the building. I had some more work to do regarding the maintenance program and would be spending the next few hours in the garage and machine shop on the southwest corner of the Azteca lot. I thanked Kassy for a delightful lunch and told her that I'd see her back in La Veta.

Pulling back into La Veta around 6:00, I was minding my own business when I happened to glance over at the Paradise Coffee Shop on the east side of Main Street and saw Coco and some white boy getting into her new vehicle. They had been holding hands before they had to split up to get in the car and I managed to get a photo of the lovely couple on my phone before they got into the car. I had her now! Payback was going to be a lot of fun.

Getting home, the first thing I did was call Kassy to enlist her help. When she picked up the phone, I told her what I had seen and asked her if she knew anything about Coco's new beau. She said that she didn't, but she'd begin the interrogation as soon as Coco got home. I asked her not to, we needed to plan our campaign. I suggested that we hold off until we got a chance to discuss strategy. She agreed to a planning session at the taqueria the following day.

CHAPTER 20

THE FOLLOWING MORNING, WE MET up at the taqueria and after she'd sorted out her crew and I had sorted out mine, we sat at one of her tables to concoct a devious plan to harass Coco about her first true love. We couldn't agree on a plan and just decided to play it by ear.

Coco knew something was up, and although she didn't know that she was the star attraction, she couldn't keep away. She sauntered up to the table behind Kassy and asked what we were up to. This was too good of a lead-in to let it pass us by.

Turning toward Coco, Kassy asked, "Isn't it about time you had a boyfriend? You've got a car; school is out for the summer, and you could go park by any of the lakes around here at night and watch the submarine races. You do know what the submarine races are don't you?" asked Kassy with a contemptuous smirk on her face.

This put Coco on the defensive, which is where we wanted her. "Of course I know what the submarine races are. It's when a guy and a girl drive out to the lake late at night and go 'parking'. Everybody knows that!" she exclaimed.

My turn. "And what happens in this car when this guy and girl are out at the lake parking late at night? We all know that there are no submarines in these lakes, so there is no possibility of anyone watching submarine races. There must be something else going on in the car."

Coco was turning a shade of maroon now. Colombians blush maroon, not red or crimson. "I guess they make out."

Continuing my interrogation, "You guess? You don't know? Do they keep their clothes on when they are 'making out'?"

"How would I know what they do? I guess some do and some don't. What's gotten into you guys?" We had her right where we wanted her.

Kassy took the lead at this point. "And you, do you keep your clothes on or off? We have it on good authority that your car was seen pulled over at the Walsenburg Reservoir late last night and that you had a boy in the car. I know for a fact that you came home very late last night."

"I think someone is pulling your chain. I don't have a boyfriend and Juanita and I were at the movies in Walsenburg last night, that's why I was home late."

While Coco was defending herself, I had calmly taken out my phone and opened the photo of her and her beau at the Paradise Coffee Shop yesterday afternoon. I laid the phone on the table and pushed it over to Kassy and Coco.

"How do you explain this then? This was taken yesterday afternoon and as you can see, you and this boy are holding hands. This can, and usually does, lead to inappropriate behavior in cars while parked by the lake late at night. Perhaps we should ask Juanita if she was with you last night."

And then the dam broke. "Okay, okay! His name is Tim Wilson. His family moved into town this summer and I met him at the country club when Juanita and I went there for lunch one day. His father works for the Forest Service. We didn't do anything out at the lake but kiss!"

"He's white, a gringo? With a vanilla name like Tim Wilson, he must be! You could be a race traitor. What is Hector going to say?" I implored.

"Moron, you're a gringo does that make Kassy a race traitor?" A reasonable comeback on her part.

"You are comparing apples to oranges, young lady. Kassy and I rarely, if ever hold hands or kiss, and we haven't been to the submarine races yet."

At this point Kassy lost the plot, looked at me and said, "Yet implies there is still hope, Mr. Fisher."

"We are too mature to go parking by the lake at night and I seriously doubt that we could get comfortable in either my truck or your Mustang. Perhaps we can figure out a more age-appropriate venue later, but you are getting off topic here, Ms. Archuleta."

At this point we all cracked up with laughter. We'd had little Coco going for a while.

Before she got away Scot free, I asked her what it was worth to her to keep me from telling Hector that she was being frisky with a white boy?

"If you promise not to say anything to Hector about frisky white boys, submarine races and parking by the lake, then I promise that I will not grab one of your guns from the counter over there and shoot you in the butt. Do you understand what I am telling you, King?"

Never, ever try to blackmail a 16-year-old Colombian girl. They simply do not know how the game is played and have fiery tempers even at that age. On to other things.

Things got fairly routine in La Veta for a few weeks. Once a week Kassy and I would carpool to the Azteca office in Walsenburg to do our chores there, in either her car or my company truck since my personal truck was still not finished yet. Other than that, I looked after my half of the shop and Kassy looked after hers.

The next 'big event' was that Hector had bought the house across the cul-de-sac from me and then resold it to Antonio under very reasonable terms. We all pitched in and helped him move out of his parents' house, then lo and behold we had to help Ms. Alejandra Contreras move out of her parents' house and into Antonio's new house as well. I mentioned to Antonio that both he and Alejandra were Catholic and that this arrangement could be construed as living in sin. He just said that I was jealous. I then explained that the whole idea of buying the house was to provide a gunsmithing service, not to chase Alejandra around scantily clad in an effort to make more little Antonio's and

Alejandra's. He said he could manage both tasks at the same time. He was that rare type of man who could actually multi-task.

Eventually Antonio's cousins called him and told him that they had done all they could to make my old Dodge presentable and that I should come and get it. So, the next Saturday he drove me down to Trinidad to collect my truck. When we got there my truck was under a cover and the réprobos, reprobates in English, were giving me grief from the second I got out of Antonio's truck. They reaffirmed that my truck was absolutely the ugliest vehicle that they had ever worked on and that they had exhausted every trick they knew just to get it into the semi-presentable shape that it was now in. On and on they went until finally they strolled over to the truck and pulled the cover off.

These guys had worked magic, no doubt about it. What they had done was nothing short of spectacular. The 5.7-liter Eagle Hemi was still under the hood, and it was still driving that Passon Performance 5-speed manual transmission. The crossmember which I had installed was still there as was the Chrysler 8-3/4" rear end. They'd trashed my suspension, and even got rid of my old Hurst shifter!

My truck now sported a Fatman Stage III front suspension while the rear suspension was provided by a No Limit Fat Bar system which incorporated large long bars and QA1 coil over shocks. They'd also lowered the front end a couple of inches to give it a more aggressive stance as well.

The truck now rolled on Billet Specialties Bullet wheels; 18" x 8" up front and 20" x 10" in back. These were mounted with Goodyear rubber; 245/45R18's in front with big 265/50R20's in the rear.

Aesthetically you couldn't even tell it was the same truck. Everything had been straightened and the gaps between the panels had been uniformly tightened up. The truck had been painted a solid black cherry color with real hand painted hot pink pinstriping. Originally there were two ridges in the middle of the hood running from just behind the front of the hood back toward the firewall. The boys had kept the ridges but had cut a series of 9 louvers just outboard of each ridge. The inside edge of each louver was aligned with the respective ridge in the center of the hood, but the 9 louvers got larger with each set of 3 as they went from front to rear; a set of 3 x 4" louvers followed by a set of 3 x 5" louvers then a set of 3 x 6" louvers. The lip of each louver was also outlined in hot pink.

The runners for the original wood bed had been rebuilt and powder coated in silver while the wood had been replaced by smoothly sanded and varnished mahogany planks.

The interior had been painted to match the exterior and the bench seat had been removed and replaced by two Recaro Classic Pole Position seats. The headliner was crimson fabric and my old shifter had been replaced by a custom job made out of welded-up chromed chain with an 8-ball shift knob.

The entire truck was a work of art. I dreaded seeing the bill but was pleasantly surprised when I saw the 50% discount. When I asked what the discount was for, they told me that they had heard what I'd done for Coco and getting Antonio out of his parent's house had probably saved his sanity, so we were good. I paid the bill, shook their hands, got in and fired my new truck up. Antonio followed me back to La Veta and our cul-de-sac. He waved as he went in to annoy Alejandra while I parked my truck out front and called Kassy.

"Hey! You want to go watch the submarine races tonight?" I asked her.

"Are you ever going to grow up?" was her snarky response.

"Probably not, but I just got back from Trinidad with Antonio. We picked up my new truck and it is hot; I need a hot chick in it while I show it off."

"The term 'chick' is no longer politically correct, Mr. Fisher."

"I know, that's why I still use it. If you can weasel out of Coco what her and Tim's plans are for the evening, I bet we can surprise them at the submarine races. You in or out?"

"Pick me up at 9:00, we'll grab a late dinner then go annoy the children."

"You're on. Wear something sexy." I hung up before she could reply.

I drove over to Hector's place and picked up Kassy, who was waiting on the front porch. She was dressed in old 505 Levis, a pink t-shirt and a pair of old school Converse high-tops were on her feet. Not what I had in mind when I said sexy, but let's face it, Kassy would look sexy even if she dressed up like an Amish farmgirl. She walked over to the truck and let out a whistle of appreciation, obviously the girl had a fine taste in old trucks that have undergone a major facelift. When she opened the door, she noticed that the old bench seat was gone and two Recaro racing seats had been installed. I told her that her seat had been specifically sized to accommodate the dimensions of the perfect female posterior on a 5'9" tall, 125lb supermodel. She got in the truck and declared the seat a perfect fit. She'd get no argument from me.

We drove into town and had dinner at Legends on Main while we made our plans. After dinner we would cruise all the known parking spots at all the nearby lakes until we found the American flag motif VW Beetle. Since Coco hadn't seen the new improved '65 Dodge D100 truck, we should be able to sneak up on them. The plan was to pull up directly behind the Bug with the lights off and then switch on the lights and hit the horn, hopefully scaring the bejesus out of Coco and Tim and likely preserving Coco's virtue while giving young Tim a heart attack.

As adults we should have had better things to do with our evening. Actually, I could think of a thing or two I'd like to do while I had Ms. Archuleta as a captive audience in my new truck, but entertainment was at a premium in La Veta and Coco needed some payback for being extraordinarily disrespectful to her elders, specifically Kassy and me.

Around 10:00 we decided to begin our quest at the Walsenburg Reservoir. Since this was the closest body of water to town suitable for submarine races, we didn't really expect to find them there and we didn't. Moving further afield, we drove over to Lathrop State Park to search both Martin Lake, where we had gone swimming and I had some issues with involuntary physical responses, and Horseshoe Lake which is the other body of water in the park. Martin Lake brought back some fond memories of Kassy in her bikini and there were a few couples out for the submarine races, but we didn't see the Bug with the American flag graphics.

Moving westward to Horseshoe Lake we resumed our search and finally found the Bug all the way at the north end of the lake at the parking area, near the boat ramp located there. We saw the VW as I drove past, so we kept going for a while before turning off the lights and heading back. By the time we got back to the parking lot, Coco had actually driven down the boat ramp as far as she could before parking and getting down to business, which was perfect for us as they couldn't get past us after we had parked behind them. With my lights still out, I slowly drove through the parking lot and then just shut off the engine and coasted up behind them before stopping about 10' away to get a lot of light on the subject when I hit the switch.

Looking over at Kassy, who had a very mischievous look on her face, I started counting down from 5. When I said 'one', I switched on the headlights on high beam and hit the horn. Kassy was already at the driver's side window knocking on it and yelling 'get out of the car' before I could get out of the truck and over to the passenger's side. Tim got out tucking in his shirt which was a bad sign. Perhaps we were too late to save Coco's virtue. I told him to get over to the other side of the car. He had never met me and didn't know who I was and was about to wet himself. Over on the driver's side, Coco had got out of the car scared to death thinking that some bad people had come up on them in the middle of the night and that bad things were about to happen. Once she saw that it was Kassy and I, she went from scared stiff to ballistic in a heartbeat. She was yelling and screaming at the top of her lungs and gesticulating as only Hispanics can do, but Kassy and I were laughing so hard we couldn't even speak to try and calm the girl down.

Coco finally ran out of steam but was still muttering unprintable things in Spanish. Finally, Tim, who had stood silently by watching the show asked her, "Do you know these people?"

"For my sins, yes. The miserable thing with the pink t-shirt is my aunt. The gilipollas she is with is her wannabe boyfriend. Meet Kassy and King."

In an effort to defend myself I told Tim that I was not a gilipollas, which could mean anything from jerk, idiot, or moron to dork or even dickhead. Furthermore, I was also not Kassy's wannabe boyfriend as I was justifiably afraid of her father, Hector. As Coco was Hector's niece, I suggested that perhaps Tim should be justifiably afraid of Hector as well.

"Do not listen to him, Tim, he's just trying to get back at me for making fun of the way he chases Kassy."

"I beg to differ, young Coco; I believe it is Kassy who is chasing me, but you are getting off topic here. What was going on in that car? The windows are steamed up and Tim was tucking his shirt in when he stepped out of the car. I hope that we are not too late to salvage your virtue."

"I don't want my virtue salvaged!" Coco screamed. The rest of us just went silent with looks of astonishment on our faces as we all, Tim included, stared at Coco. Coco finally realized what she had just said and tried to walk it back.

"Wait, that is not what I meant to say, but you guys have me flustered. There was nothing wrong going on in my car, we were just getting to know one another, what's wrong with that?"

"And that caused the windows to steam up?" Kassy was at bat now.

The kids didn't seem to have a suitable response to Kassy's question and looked suitably chastised. Kassy and I really had to struggle not to laugh at the lovebirds. After some more mental abuse from the adults, we bid the kids a good night and got back in my truck. As we backed up the boat ramp, I hung my head out the window and yelled, "Kassy and King one, Coco and Tim zero!"

While driving back to Hector's place to drop Kassy off, she asked if it was her chasing me or was it me chasing her?

"Do you think that either would be wise? We are supposedly business partners and we both are gainfully employed by Azteca Trucking and should be acting like adults. The old adage is that you should never get your paycheck and your 'sugar', if you know what I mean, from the same place. Correct?" I asked.

"You are a very infuriating man, Mr. Fisher. Whoever came up with that old adage had their head up their butt. Who was it anyhow?"

"At the moment I am thinking it was the Marquis de Sade."

She gave me a devilish grin, "Ahh, perhaps there is hope even yet."

We got back to her place, and before she got out of the truck, she gave me a somewhat less than chaste kiss on the lips. Her tongue kept trying to get between my teeth and my teeth kept trying to let it get by. My self-control was slipping, I'd need to work on that. As she climbed down from the truck, I asked her how that Recaro seat fit after sitting in it for a while? She said it still fit like a glove.

On the way back to town I was pensive. I was hopelessly enamored by Ms. Archuleta but I had to keep in mind that my whole existence at this point depended on Hector. If I let anything happen between Kassy and I and it turned out to be just a fling, or worse yet, a one night stand, then I'd have to leave La Veta and start up again somewhere else. Forget the fact that Hector would likely castrate me and I'd have to wander the earth as a eunuch forever more. I was not joking when I told Kassy that it is a very, very bad idea to get your sexual gratification and your paycheck from the same place, historically this never ends well. This type of thinking, while logical and rational, did nothing to address the fact that Kassy just turned my crank. At some point I'd have to either fish or cut bait. I'd need to give this some more thought, but right now I needed a cold shower.

The following Monday I picked up Kassy at her house to do our weekly penance at the Azteca offices in Walsenburg, as now that I had my truck back it was my turn to be the carpool driver. She was waiting for me on the porch wearing a sleeveless lime green bodycon mini dress with a crewneck that would have halted traffic at the Indianapolis 500. It wasn't doing my involuntary physical response issues any good either. As she hopped in the truck and put her laptop bag and purse in the footwell I told her the dress looked fantastic on her.

"You don't think that it makes my hips look too big?" she asked while running her hands along her hips.

"Don't you guys have any mirrors in that house? Your hips look just fine. Of course, I don't have my glasses on so a closer visual inspection may be required later."

"King, you don't wear glasses."

"Would you quit raining on my parade and just go with the flow here?"

She just laughed and opened the little vent window to get some air blowing on her. Needless to say, her riotous mane was blowing wildly all over the truck until she grabbed a scrunchie out of her purse and tamed it. I liked the look.

I dropped her off at the front door before parking my truck in my newly assigned space. Rank has its privileges. Walking in the front door I said hello to Candy, Coco's office spy. As I walked by the reception desk to go upstairs Candy sly said, "Ms. Archuleta is looking pretty hot in that mini-dress today, don't you think?" Without missing a step, I told her that Ms. Archuleta looked good enough to eat in that dress.

"Some people would say that could be taken as a Freudian slip," said Candy.

"Some people would be right," I replied as Candy turned beet red.

When lunchtime rolled around, I picked Kassy up in front of the office and we went to the Subway at 3rd and Main for a sandwich. While we ate, we just chatted about current events and relived the incident at the lake last Saturday when we embarrassed young Coco so bad that Coco still wasn't talking to Kassy. Dropping Kassy off in front of the office again, I parked the truck and was walking by the reception desk for the second time that day when young Candy informed me that she had informed Ms. Archuleta regarding my Freudian slip and Ms. Archuleta had asked her to inform me that I could only read the menu but could not order. These women were ganging up on me now.

I met Kassy at the front door for the third time that day at 4:00 in the afternoon when we decided to call it a day. On the way back to Hector's place to drop her off I asked her what she meant about 'reading the menu and not ordering'? Apparently, it all came down to commitment, unless you were committed to a meal there was absolutely no reason to order and reading the menu was as good as it got.

"Very philosophical. What happens if the diner only wants a starter or dessert?"

"Not happening, cowboy, here in Huerfano County you either order the whole meal or you go hungry. Now pay attention to your driving and quit looking at my legs," she instructed with a mischievous grin.

CHAPTER 21

IT WAS GETTING ALONG TOWARD mid-summer now and things in La Veta had settled into a rhythm. Kassy and I would go to work in Walsenburg once a week, usually on a Monday, then work at the taqueria and gun shop the rest of the week through Saturday.

Hector did whatever Hector wanted to do, and Coco worked at the taqueria from Monday to Saturday. We now had a pesky gringo teenaged male making a regular appearance at the taqueria as well. Tim wasn't such a bad kid, but I was keeping my eye on him. It wasn't that I was worried about Coco's virtue any longer, but I wanted to recruit Tim as a spy and feed me stuff on Coco that I could use to annoy her. It was a work in progress.

Antonio had finally finished his gunsmithing courses and now certified. This was bringing in a significant amount of business for my side of the shop. It seemed that many folks had firearms that needed some work done to them, but due to the lack of a gunsmith anywhere near La Veta, they just put them in their gun cabinets hoping that the situation would change. Antonio had more work than he could handle so on weekends I'd walk across the cul-de-sac after my morning workouts and runs and help him out as best I could. As per our deal, he was schooling me in the fine art of gunsmithing.

I saw Hernández every now and then when I was in Walsenburg, but he seemed to be staying busy managing the trucking firm up there and rarely had a chance to get down to La Veta. When he did, Hector would usually give me a call and I'd run over to Hector's place and we'd all just touch base concerning the trucking operations and security and do some shooting in the back yard.

One Wednesday at the taqueria, after the lunch rush had subsided, Kassy said that she wanted to organize a 'beach party' back at Martin Lake before the end of the summer. I told her to knock herself out, but she'd likely have to reserve the little beach to do that. I suggested that perhaps a cookout and some volleyball would be a nice touch as opposed to just laying out and drinking beer. I told her to let me know how the planning progressed and I'd help her out as needed. I was already dreading the return of the involuntary physical responses in public, but a team of wild horses wouldn't have kept me away.

The gun shop was now in the black, not by much but we were at least making some money as opposed to slowly losing money. Antonio's gunsmithing plus the word-of-mouth advertising was allowing us to turn the corner. The taqueria had been a success from the time Kassy had opened the doors. She liked her professional job with Azteca trucking, but she really loved running her own business.

Toward the end of June Kassy came by my office and told me that she had managed to reserve the 'beach' at Marin Lake at the end of the month on a Saturday. She informed me that Miguel, Antonio and I would be responsible for the cookout and volleyball portion of the festivities, and we should begin making plans and arrangements now.

I huddled up with Antonio and Miguel and told them about the 'beach party' and what our roles in it would be. Miguel said he wasn't getting in the water but would happily drink beer and watch the girls. I put him in charge of getting all the grocery supplies required for a cookout together and assigned him the grilling duties. Turning to Antonio, I told him that we needed two good steel barrels and a welding shop since we'd need to fabricate some grills for Miguel to supervise. Antonio said that he'd sort that out, but that I should be on hand when the grills were fabricated. I took it upon myself to order a good quality volleyball net and some volleyballs online and have them delivered to my house.

A few days later Antonio called me and asked me to meet him at the Spearmint Heavy Duty Tow Truck Company located at Moore and Locust. He'd found two barrels and some angle iron and the guys at Spearmint were willing to weld everything up if I'd get there and show them what I wanted.

I got to the tow truck yard and took a look at what we had. I asked the guys if they could cut both barrels in half lengthwise down the sides while I drove over to the La Veta County Store and got some Easy-Off Oven Cleaner, some dishwashing soap and some sponges and scrubbing pads.

When I got back, the barrels had been cut in half lengthwise and Antonio had cooled them down with the hose. We spent the next hour scrubbing each of the four sections spotlessly clean before moving on to the next part of the project which was making two cradles out of angle iron to hold a barrel half each. After this was completed, we had to somehow make hinges for each barrel so that the top could be closed. I was stumped, but the tow truck guys found some pipe and rebar and we made one long hinge along the backside of each barrel. The final touch was to make the actual grills out of expanded metal and fit them so that they sat about 2 inches down inside the lower barrel half leaving plenty of room for charcoal in the bottom and to fabricate handles where necessary.

Once the grills were completed, we put them in the back of my truck, on old blankets so as not to mess up the mahogany boards in the bed, and I drove them home while Antonio paid the tow truck guys.

A few days later the volleyball net and volleyballs arrived curtesy of UPS. Now all the gun shop crew was responsible for was the chow. I called Miguel up and he said to quit hassling him. He said he'd be ready on time.

The big Saturday arrived and while the girls went up to the lake to stake out the claim on the beach area, the guys started loading up the supplies and equipment. Miguel showed up at my house with his pickup loaded with coolers containing all the food, beer, ice and grilling supplies. The ice was required to keep everything cold but may be required to do double duty regarding those pesky involuntary physical responses which were sure to arise, pun intended.

Antonio helped me get the grills and the volleyball kit in the back of my truck then hopped in and we followed Miguel up to the lake.

When we arrived, we noticed that the girls had already laid out the volleyball courts in the sand and lined up the beach chairs in front of it facing the lake. They were eating sopapillas and drinking coffee out of Thermos bottles when we arrived. At this point they were all still in shorts and not scantily clad; there was Kassy and Coco, Alejandra, the other young girls from the Taqueria and Miguel's wife Gabriela. I also noticed that Tim was there with two of his buddies. I put them to work immediately getting the grills set up and the volleyball net put up as well. While this was going on I asked Kassy where Hector was? She said he'd be there later in the day.

It was starting to warm up now and time for the girls to drop their laundry so that they could cool down in the water. The guys, except for Miguel in his jeans, had board shorts on so we didn't have any laundry to drop and just stood around eagerly awaiting the show. Coco and her young co-workers were youthfully uninhibited and just dropped their shorts, pulled their t-shirts over their heads and ran for the water. Tim and his buddies just gawked. I couldn't really blame them as I noticed that Coco had decided to ditch the Speedo one piece from the previous outing at the lake and now had on a proper bikini. Her partners in crime were similarly attired. I was sure that this was planned.

Alejandra and Kassy were a little reluctant at this point as Antonio and I were staring at them expectantly. They finally removed their t-shirts and bashfully removed their cut-offs, folded them up and placed them on the lounge chairs before standing up in all their glory and letting our eyes feast on them. The view was as expected.

Alejandra was a couple of inches shorter than Kassy, but slightly more curvaceous. She was a classical Hispanic knock-out. They had both opted for the same style of swimwear, but in different colors; Alejandro in a black floral pattern on white while Kassy's was a white floral pattern on black. The swimwear on display, which also managed to display a lot of Alejandra and Kassy, were simple halter top triangle Brazilian bikinis. I turned to ask Antonio if he was having any involuntary physical reactions to what had been unveiled? He informed me that only the Pope, and maybe not even him, could avoid having a reaction to the flesh on display. Good, at least I wasn't alone in my torment, misery loves company.

Eventually everyone got in the water to splash around a bit while Miguel and Gabriela got the grills going and set everything out on some folding tables we'd brought out as well. The adults finally retired to the lounge chairs to drink some beer while the kid's played volleyball until the burgers and hotdogs were ready.

By this time Hector had arrived to watch the proceedings. After everyone else had had enough to eat, I sat Gabriela, Miguel and Hector down and served them while making sure that they were comfortable. Antonio and Alejandra cleaned up after everyone, and after a suitable digestive period the volleyball games began in earnest. First it was the adults versus the kids. The adults lost likely because Antonio and I were too busy concentrating on Alejandro's and Kassy's backsides in those little Brazilian bikinis, but maybe not since I noticed young Tim and his friends were having similar problems with their female team mates on the other side of the net. Then myself, Kassy, Coco, Tim and one of his buddies faced off against Alejandra, Antonio, Hector and Coco's two coworkers. We lost as Tim and Coco were too busy playing grabass to actually take the game seriously. Finally, it was Kassy and Alejandra versus Antonio and me. We lost miserably as we just couldn't keep our eyes off of the physical attributes of our opponents and their serves just either passed us by or bounced off our foreheads.

A good day was had by all. Miguel overserved himself with beer, so I drove him home in his truck while Antonio followed in mine with Gabriela. Everybody got to where they needed to go. Alejandra and Antonio went into his house to study each other's body geography, and Kassy and I just sat on my porch swing as we watched the sun go down. We did some of that light kissing stuff before Kassy decided that she had to go home.

On the way to her Mustang, she asked if there had been enough ice at the cookout to cover all the issues? I told her there was not enough ice at the North Pole to cover those issues. She laughed and drove off. The term 'minx' came to mind.

CHAPTER 22

THE FOLLOWING TUESDAY, AFTER GOING to the office on Monday with Kassy, I had gotten to the taqueria early just to read the Rocky Mountain News while drinking coffee and having a few sopapillas hot out of the oven. Kassy and Coco were there getting things ready for the day's business. Since Miguel and Antonio hadn't arrived yet either there were just the three of us in the shop.

We were all just going about our business when suddenly the front door was flung open, and two unusual characters burst in. They were almost comical in appearance as they had 'Old Mexico' written all over them, from the extra-long, pointy toed Trival cowboy boots they wore, to the bell bottomed jeans cinched with belts with silver conchos. They also wore the short sleeved guayabera shirts which really marked them as being from out of town. What was not comical in the least were the guns they were holding, which appeared to be Glock 19's.

One was tall and thin, about 6'2" while the other one was built like a fireplug and went about 5'9". Both were trying to sprout mustaches but were failing miserably. Mentally I had already named the taller one Cisco and the shorter one Pancho after the characters in the '50's TV series 'The Cisco Kid'.

The girls were behind the counter when the duo rushed in and Cisco told his sidekick to, "Conseguir a la chica!". I was later told that this meant 'grab the girl' but at the moment a translation wasn't necessary as Pancho went past me to go behind the counter while the bean pole kept his gun on me. I don't think that they actually knew who I was, or that I owned the gun shop on the other side of the courtroom divider. This ignorance would cost them big time in a few minutes.

As Pancho went behind the counter to grab Coco, Kassy rushed at him to keep him from getting his hands on her, she had obviously understood what the other guy had said. The fireplug slapped Kassy viciously in the face, knocking her to the ground and ensuring that he was not long for this world. Coco was obviously in shock and staring at the thin man holding a gun on me.

Pancho stepped over Kassy, who was moaning on the floor, and grabbed Coco to bring her around into the dining area. As he was frog marching her toward the front door, the Cisco character was lecturing her in English.

"You should have never applied for a copy of your original birth certificate Xocoyotl, we watch for that sort of thing. When you then applied for a driver's license, we had your address. Not very smart on your part. You are my property, and I am taking you back as per the original agreement."

As Coco went by, she looked at me with fear in her eyes and simply said, "He killed my mom." I was shattered, it was because of me that these guys had found her and now they were taking her back and likely selling her into the sex trade as originally intended. If they got her out of town, I knew that they would continue where they left off and 'break her in' before selling her off in Denver. I had to do something quickly but I didn't have a gun anywhere near me.

I just sat meekly while Cisco held his gun on me as he backed toward the door following Coco and his partner. As soon as they were out the door and it was swinging closed, I sprinted toward my office and hurtled the courtroom divider. Remember that LaRue PredatAR 5.56 rifle that old Joaquin said that I'd never sell here in Huerfano County? Well, he was right, I'd never sold it so I had been experimenting with it. Last weekend I'd installed an Eotech

XPS-2 holographic sight on it with the singe 1-minute-of-angle red dot. I'd taken it up to the old airfield north of town and sighted it in for 100 yards but hadn't had time to clean it yet so it was still laying on the table beside my desk in a soft case.

Grabbing the case, I unzipped it and slammed in one of the two loaded mags that I kept in the case and racked the bolt before running back out of the office. I hurdled the courtroom barrier again and pulled the front door open just enough to get my left foot in the opening. As I swept the front door open with my left foot, I brought the rifle up to my right shoulder.

These clowns had parked their Dodge Durango SUV out in front of the shop on High Street as opposed to parking it in the driveway, this meant that they had to cross about 20 yards of lawn before they got to their vehicle. Coco and Pancho were about 5 yards from their truck at this point. Since Pancho was grasping Coco's neck in his right hand and pushing her along, he was just off to the side of her left shoulder. Also, since Coco was only about 5'6" tall and Pancho was about 5'9", his head was slightly above the level of her left shoulder as well.

I had been shooting 5.56mm Black Hills 77 grain boat tailed hollow points out at the old airfield and had sighted the rifle in at 100 yards. At 15 yards I'd be hitting low by around ½ an inch since the bullet would not yet have risen through my line of sight at that distance. I figured that if I held it just above the center of the back of his head that Coco would be okay while Pancho most definitely wouldn't be.

Shortly after raising the rifle to my shoulder, I squeezed the trigger and Pancho's head exploded, with most of it ending up on the passenger's side of that Durango SUV. The rest of Pancho fell forward dragging Coco down as well. This was a good thing as it kept Coco down and out of the way of any more flying lead.

Cisco had the reflexes of a cat. As soon as he heard my shot, he whipped around and fired off a round. It hit me on the inside of my left thigh, but it was a through-and-through wound which didn't hit my femur or any arteries. I was still standing.

I brought the rifle around and settled the aiming dot on Cisco's head, while he was in a Weaver stance and pointing his Glock at me with a proper 'thumbs forward' grip. At this point he got arrogant and cocky and said, "It looks like we have a Mex…" He didn't get to finish the sentence as about that time my second round hit him in the mouth and blew most of his teeth out of the back of his head. There is a time for talking and a time for shooting, Cisco had gotten his timing wrong.

At this point I collapsed onto the concrete slab outside of the front door. Even though that 9mm went through me instead of hitting something solid, it still hurt like crazy. Kassy had come up behind me and grabbed me as I fell.

"What was he trying to say?" I asked her.

"I think that he was trying to tell you that you were in a Mexican stand-off."

"Do I look Mexican?" I asked.

"No, you do not, but then again, nobody is perfect."

Kassy unbuckled my belt and pulled it through the loops to use it as a tourniquet on my leg.

"I think that you are using this situation to take advantage of me, Ms. Archuleta."

"That would be no fun. You will need to be in perfect health before I do take advantage of you, otherwise you may not survive the ordeal," she said with a grin.

After Coco had finishing kicking the crap out of the two corpses littering the lawn while berating them in colorful Spanish, Kassy asked her to clean the bits and pieces of Pancho out of her hair and then call 911 and explain what had happened. La Veta does not have a police department per se, but a Marshal's Office. Soon the marshals showed up accompanied by an ambulance. After they carted me off to the La Veta Clinic on Oak Street, the marshals took down the statements from Kassy and Coco and did a cursory crime scene investigation before declaring it a 'righteous shoot'. Needless to say, Coco did not reveal exactly why she had been targeted but just left it as the random targeting of an attractive teen girl for nefarious purposes. She ensured that the adjective 'attractive' was included in the official report.

Once I was stabilized at the clinic in La Veta, an ambulance took me to the Spanish Peaks Regional Health Center in Walsenburg to be stitched up properly. I lasted just over a day there before I called Kassy to come get me.

Once I got back to my house, it was almost as bad as the hospital with a never-ending supply of concerned citizens and well-wishers. I almost didn't have any time to myself. Kassy and Coco took it upon themselves to nurse me back to health, Hector showed up every day and Antonio and Alejandra checked in on me each evening. Miguel would show up every now and then with tequila and beer to ensure that I was getting a well-balanced diet.

I was sitting on the porch swing with Kassy one evening after the gunfight at the taqueria, after everyone else had gone home when she said, "That bullet came close to the family jewels as they say, are you sure that they are okay?" She said this with a naughty smirk on her face.

"Would you like to check?" Two can play this game.

"Not at the moment, but there may come a time when that is required."

Minx is a term referring to a flirtatious, mischievous, yet still classy woman. This fit Kassy to a tee. Kassy obviously wasn't going to heed the doctor's orders not to get me too worked up or excited while I was healing.

CHAPTER 23

AT THIS POINT I DECIDED to grow a set of cojones and ask Kassy out on a proper date. This was a veritable minefield on a variety of levels. First, it would take our platonic relationship to a new level when the old level was frustrating enough. Second, as mentioned previously, if the relationship went belly up and we parted ways acrimoniously I would be leaving Huerfano County in a hurry with no other career prospects on the horizon. Finally, depending on how Hector viewed the breakup, I might be running for my life.

But the decision was made so now I had to figure out a proper venue for the date. I was 35 and she was 29, we were not into the clubbing scene and the number of acceptable venues in this part of the country were few and far between. Research was required.

I finally decided that if she did decide that a date with myself would not damage her reputation to sorely, that I would take her to the Tuscanos Brazilian Grill in Colorado Springs and then the Whiskey Baron for some country and western dancing and a few drinks afterwards. When I had worked up the required amount of courage that allows one to accept rejection, I popped the question to her.

We were sitting at a table drinking coffee in the taqueria on a Tuesday morning before her crew and mine had made an appearance. She was reading the Denver Post when I put my coffee cup on the table and asked her to put the paper down for a second. When she had, I made my play.

"Kassy, we've been skirting the issue for the past few months, and I think perhaps that we need to consider taking our relationship up a notch," I told her.

She took a moment to fold the Post up and place it on the table before she leaned forward, rested her elbows on the table and rested her chin on her hands and asked, "So what do you propose, no pun intended. Usually there is a ring involved in proposals."

"I think that would be rushing things at this point. Would you like to go on a date?" Okay, the cat was out of the bag.

"With you?" This was not going the way that I had intended.

"Of course, with me! Do you think that I am in the habit of asking girls out for other guys?"

"I was just clarifying the situation. Yes, Mr. Fisher, I would be delighted to accompany you on a date." There was a big smile on her face now, and one on mine as well.

"Did you have a date set for this date or were you simply waiting to see what my reaction would be before actually making plans?"

"I'm way ahead of you, Ms. Archuleta. I'll pick you up at 6:00 next Saturday evening at your place then we will drive to Colorado Springs for a dinner at Tucanos Bar and Grill before heading over to the Whiskey Baron Dance Hall & Saloon for some dancing and drinks. I suggest that you pack some dancing duds as the venues are somewhat different plus, I'd like to see you in that dress I bought you in Denver. This is what is known as an ulterior motive."

"Well, well! I see that you are way ahead of me, but I'll be ready and waiting at 6:00, don't be late." Her smile had grown magnificently by this point. I'm not sure why I was considering a rejection as she seemed to have been waiting for this moment. Women are hard to figure out.

About this time Coco waltzed in the front door, took one look at Kassy and said, "Did he?" Kassy said that he did, so they retired to the kitchen to discuss what this means in the overall scheme of things. I went over to the gun side of the shop with visions of Kassy in that cowl slip midi dress dancing in my head.

Needless to say, by lunchtime the entire town knew that I had asked Kassy out on a date. Everywhere I went guys were giving me a thumbs up and the women were giggling at me. If this date went sideways, I'd never be able to hold my head up in La Veta again.

The big day rocked up and I was ready. I'd cleaned the new and improved Dodge D100 inside and out and had put a coat of wax on it. I'd wear fairly new 505 Levis with a light blue broadcloth button-down shirt, covered by a black sport coat and my Timberline boots to Tucanos Bar and Grill, but would lose the sport coat on the way to the Whiskey Baron Dance Hall & Saloon and change out the Timberlines for my rarely worn pair of Tony Lama gray bull hide cowboy boots.

Around 5:00 I shaved, showered and even put on some Aqua Velva to make me smell good. I then took a shot of tequila from a bottle that Miguel had left behind for liquid courage and got in my truck to go pick up Kassy. I felt like a teenager on his first date, I was that out of practice.

I got to Hector's place and knocked on the door. Hector opened the door and told me to come on in and have a drink while Kassy finished getting ready. When I got to the living room, I found Miguel and Coco were already sitting on the couch. Hector got me a whiskey and water and we all just made light conversation until we heard Kassy's door open on her side of the upstairs walkway. I damn near dropped my drink.

Kassy was wearing that wine-colored cowl slip midi dress that I had bought for her in Denver on Coco's birthday. She'd chosen to wear some burgundy espadrille platform wedges to set off the dress and she'd let her hair go curly and island girl wild. She had accessorized with a little black clutch purse and a black lace choker necklace. She came down the stairs and into the living room and pirouetted in front of us.

I have never seen a more desirable woman in my life. I was in awe.

"Shall we go?" she asked me.

I grabbed her backpack with her dancing attire in it and said that the reservation was for 7:30 so we should probably leave now. The peanut gallery escorted us to the door. As I ushered Kassy over the threshold Coco advised me to be very careful as something as hot as Kassy was tonight could cause first degree burns from a distance. Miguel just said that he'd pray for me again.

I went around and opened Kassy's door and handed her up into the form fitting seat before going around to my side, firing the truck up and driving out of sight of the spectators.

I told Kassy that she looked exquisite this evening, she said that was exactly what she wanted to hear. I said that I must have gotten the size correct as the dress seemed to be a doing a good job of exposing what it was supposed to reveal and obscuring the view of what it was supposed to hide. She told me that it is a rare thing when a man who is not romantically involved with a woman can get her dress size correct on the first try. I told her that I may have had some help. She said that she was going to kill Coco.

The rest of the way to Colorado Springs went by in a blur as we just chatted about current events and told each other a little more about ourselves. I had gotten on I-25 north out of Walsenburg and took it all the way to Colorado Springs before getting off on 24 and following it east until we got on 21 north to Tucanos, which was located in the Cinema Point shopping area.

As we were seated, I explained the culinary adventure of the Brazilian churrascaria steakhouse buffet style known as rodizio where waiters bring out large cuts of various roasted meats on long skewers to the diners' tables and carve off portions on request. Separate buffet tables offered appetizers, salads and desserts. I told her that I hoped that she was hungry.

Kassy was over-dressed for a churrascaria, but I didn't hear any of the males in place complaining. That slit up to mid-thigh was drawing a lot of attention. If Kassy felt uncomfortable being over-dressed, she didn't show it. We had stuffed ourselves even before we shared a banana split at the end so

Kassy decided that she would change into her dancing attire in the Tucanos ladies' room and then we would need to walk around and do some window shopping in the various shops built around the huge parking lot to work off the meal before we went dancing.

I went out to the truck, changed my boots, took off my sport coat and put it behind the seat, then got her backpack and brought it back to our table. Kassy took it and went to the ladies' room with every male eye in the place tracking her. I was enjoying this immensely. A few minutes later she came back out dressed in the same outfit she had worn when I first met her stranded beside the road; snug, well-worn Wrangler jeans with a V-necked Boho blouse tucked into the jeans over brown laced up roper boots. I noticed that those same male eyes that had been tracking her in the cowl slip midi dress were now tracking her in her form fitting jeans.

After doing some window shopping and walking off our meal, we got back in the truck and got back on 21 before driving north to Barnes Road and heading west. Taking a southwest dogleg on Austin Bluffs Parkway to North Academy Boulevard, I hung a right and followed it to Vickers Drive. The Whiskey Baron Dance Hall & Saloon was about 100 yards east on the south side of Vickers. It was after 9:00 when we rolled up to the dance hall and things seemed to be getting busy. We got a table near the dance floor and ordered a beer apiece and just listened to the live band at the front of the dance floor for a while. Eventually Kassy asked me if I was going to ask her to dance.

Now this is where it gets tricky. I had grown up in Idaho doing line dancing, the two-step, the western swing and waltzes so I was in a comfortable environment, but I didn't know if Kassy could even dance to country and western music! Well, we took it slow on a few waltzes and then turned the heat up. Not only could Kassy dance, but she could dance better than I could! Once we had that figured out, we just went to town and danced just about every dance unless we needed to cool down a bit and rehydrate with a beer. She was a phenomenal dancer, and I wasn't too bad if I say so myself. At times people would clear the dance floor just to watch us.

I'm guessing that after her frat boy ran himself off the road and she came back to La Veta, that she hadn't had a chance to get out much and she was just letting herself go. It was fun to watch and unbelievably sexy.

We closed down the joint at two in the morning, Kassy and I had danced the night away. I had limited myself to a beer an hour since I was driving, but Kassy may have overserved herself slightly. I walked her to the truck and she was snoring softly before we even got back on I-25 and headed south.

Now I had a problem. I could take Kassy back to Hector's and try to get her in the house very early in the morning and risk getting shot. If I didn't get shot as a burglar, I'd have to explain the condition Kassy was in to Hector and then possibly get shot. I decided to take Kassy to my place and deal with the issue in the morning. We pulled in front of my place around 4:00 in the morning and I got out and helped Kassy up the steps to the porch. When we got to the front door, Kassy leaned against the house while I got out my keys and opened the door. I followed her up the stairs and into the guest room at the front of the house where she fell onto the bed and began that girl's snoring thing again.

Now temptation raised its ugly head. Should I undress her down to her underthings and cover her with a duvet or should I just get her stretched out on the bed and then cover her with the duvet? The undressing option was very appealing until I got a good mental picture of her waking up scantily clad and then beating me like a drum for taking such liberties.

I got her boots off and arranged her as comfortably as I could. I then covered her with a duvet before retiring to my room, undressing to my shorts before getting into bed and going to sleep. It had been a long, enjoyable evening.

I was up about 8:00 the next morning feeling bright-eyed and bushy-tailed. I checked on Kassy, who was still asleep before going down to the kitchen to prepare a breakfast of scrambled eggs, sausage, toast and coffee. While preparing breakfast I heard the shower going in the full bath upstairs between the bedrooms, so I knew Kassy was up and running. I got the breakfast laid on the table and grabbed a coffee while waiting for Kassy to come down for breakfast.

She finally walked into the kitchen wearing the old bathrobe that usually hung on the back of my bathroom door.

"The smell of sausage and eggs cooking woke me up, so I thought I'd take a shower before coming down. It smells divine, I could get used to this."

Taking a good hard look at her in that bathrobe and having a fairly reasonable idea as to what was underneath it, I told her that I could get used to it as well.

"You do remember the 'reading the menu but not ordering' thing, don't you?" she asked as she took a seat at the table.

"That went in one ear and out the other. Sometimes a man just has to eat," I replied.

"Sometimes a girl has to eat as well, and this is one of those times. Are you going to feed me breakfast or what?"

So, we had a relaxing breakfast while we talked about the previous evening and the fun we'd had. She apologized for over-serving herself, but said that she hadn't been out dancing in years, let alone stayed out after midnight. She also informed me that for a gringo I danced pretty well. I told her that she was an exceptional dancer and that if she hadn't changed into jeans before hitting the dance floor and had worn her slit-to-the-thigh midi dress that she would have caused more heart attacks in that saloon than Colorado Springs had seen in a month.

"You think so? There were some other nice looking girls there as you well know."

"Kassy, perhaps I am a bit biased, but I think that you passed 'nice looking' a few miles back. Every guy in the joint was trying to get a peek at you without their dates knowing about it. They were failing miserably."

"Really, I didn't notice. I was having too much fun. We should do that again some time."

I told her to just let me know when she had recovered from her first time out in a while, and we'd schedule a repeat performance. We finished our breakfast and had another cup of coffee before we cleaned up the kitchen. Kassy went back upstairs to put back on her dancing clothes before we headed back to her place.

As we were standing on the porch while I locked the front door, I heard catcalls and whistling coming from Antonio's place. He and Alejandra were out on their porch drinking coffee when we came out. They obviously misread the situation and thought we'd spent the night together and Kassy was now red as a beet.

"Just ignore them," I told her. "I'll fire the miscreant later if he tells anybody that he saw you coming out of my place at 10:00 in the morning."

"Why, are you embarrassed about it?"

"Not at all, but the number of jealous men of Hispanic ethnicity in this town who would stop speaking to me, or worse beat me like a piñata, would go up exponentially. It would also be bad for business," I replied with a straight face. She punched me in the shoulder, Antonio and Alejandra started up with the whistling and catcalls again and we got in the truck and I took her home.

Arriving back at Hector's house was fraught with danger as well. I had kept his daughter out all night, he would no doubt hear from the grapevine that she had overnighted at my place and of course Coco would be there to fan the flames. We arrived and Kassy got out and collected her backpack from the footwell on her side and started up the steps to the porch. I dutifully followed. Before we'd even reached the front door Hector opened it and walked outside to confront us with Coco right behind him.

"It's a little late in the morning to be bringing my daughter home, don't you think?"

"We closed the dance hall in Colorado Springs down at 2:00 in the morning and we did not want to wake you up, Papa," Kassy told him.

"So where did you spend the night, young lady?" Hector was on a roll, but I couldn't tell if he was serious or not.

"I spent the night at King's house, in the guest bedroom. I had one too many beers while we danced and King figured that you would shoot anyone prowling around the house at 4:00 in the morning, which is when we got back to La Veta." Coco was giving me a thumbs up behind Hector's back at this point.

"So, tell me, daughter, did this gringo try to have his way with you while you were less than in control of your faculties?"

"Papa, I don't think this gringo would try to have his way with me even if I paid him to do so. Now get out of my way so that I can go change and freshen up." With this, Kassy pushed by Hector and Coco to go up to her room leaving just Hector, Coco and I on the porch.

Coco was looking at me like I was from a different planet. "You didn't even try?" she asked.

"Coco, go back in the house," instructed Hector.

When she had, he turned to me and said, "You didn't even try? Are you a maricón? Do you realize how many hijos de puta have tried and failed to get in her pants? I have shot some of them for that. You are either a saint or have enormous self-control, which is it?"

"Hector, I find your daughter dangerously attractive, but I believe in the old adage that you never get your carnal gratification and your paycheck from the same source. So, although I am very smitten by your daughter, she is off limits to me. What would you do if we had a relationship that went sour, or worse ended up being a one night stand? The social stigma in a small town like this would be brutal and the only way to mitigate the disgrace to both you and Kassy would be for me to leave La Veta and everything that I have worked for here."

Kassy's room had a window which overlooked the front porch and she had obviously been eavesdropping. "Papa, would you please try to talk some sense into that hombre estúpido!"

In an effort to get away from prying ears, Hector and I walked down to my truck and leaned against the bed to continue the education of the 'stupid man'.

"Do not interrupt me in what I about to say, comprendes?" I told him that I understood.

"Good, now do you honestly think that I brought you down here simply to sort out my hijacking problem? Of course not! I had what you white people call 'ulterior motives'. I knew from the days when you were chasing me, back when I was known as Juan Cortez, or the Jackrabbit, that you were a principled man with a functioning moral compass. Men like this are very hard to find these days.

"True, I needed your help fixing the hijacking issue, but I needed you to go into business with my daughter to give her something to do besides hang around here taking care of me and doing the books at my trucking company. You really didn't surprise me much when you and Hernández shot those pendejos who were hijacking my trucks, but you certainly surprised me when you did such a nice thing for Coco. You were not responsible for Coco and you had no familial ties to her, you simply did it either out of the goodness of your heart or simply because it was the right thing to do.

I started to interject to suggest that I was not a saint, but Hector held up his hand and said, "Guarde silencio." Which actually translates as 'Keep silent', but is a polite way of telling someone to shut up. So, I did.

"Then, when you shot those two assholes who tried to steal Coco, and let's face it you shot the fat one not only because he was kidnapping Coco, but also because he had the poor judgement to slap Kassy, I knew I had picked the right man.

"Now if Kassy had shown no interest in you at this point, we would have carried on with our business arrangements as they were, but for some unknown reason you seemed to have lit Kassy's fuse, so I carried on with my plans.

"You see, King, Kassy has had no life since she came back to La Veta after that idiot frat boy splattered himself all over the highway, she took it hard as they were engaged at the time. I personally thought that the frat boy was a waste of skin, but when Kassy makes up her mind you may as well sit down and see how it plays out.

"Now I have been watching you two and so has Miguel, Antonio, Alejandra, Hernández, Coco, Candy and others and they tell me that you are good for my daughter. That being the case, I am asking you to relax, date my daughter and show her that she is in fact a desirable woman and that there is a life outside La Veta if she wants it. What do you say?"

I pondered what he had said for a moment just to give my answer the gravitas it required, then answered, "I could probably do that," with a stupid grin on my face.

Hector shook his finger in my face and instructed, "You will treat her with respect and court her properly. I will not have my daughter accused of any inappropriate behavior. I will still shoot you in the ass if your treat her in any way disrespectful. Entiendes?"

I told him that I understood entirely. I also said that I would be going home now as he would need to explain to Kassy that we had had this conversation and I didn't want to be there to watch the fireworks.

CHAPTER 24

THEN THE SUMMER TOOK A turn for the worse, Antonio and Alejandra decided to get married. Now don't get me wrong, I was happy for the couple, but weddings have a ripple effect for every other unmarried couple in the region. The unmarried girls start to think that perhaps they are running out of time to snare a suitable guy and they begin to prowl in earnest. If you are somewhat less than a catch as a male, this is a good thing. If you are a reasonably handsome guy with no noticeable defects, all the unwanted attention is a pain in the butt and frightening. If the girls already have their claws into a suitable victim, then the question of commitment arises, usually instigated by the girl's mother. You start to hear the mothers asking the daughters why should the man buy the cow when he is getting the milk for free? This of course causes much 'weeping and gnashing of teeth' among the men who were quite happy getting the milk for free. Let's be honest here, the girls seemed to be okay with supplying the dairy product for free as well. Everybody was happy up until some couple decides to tie the knot without thinking of the ramifications felt by the community as a whole.

In my case, I wasn't getting any free milk so that was not an issue for me, but I could see where this commitment thing was gaining traction. I would likely have been more committed if I was receiving free dairy products. This presented a Catch-22 scenario for the girls; either keep Mama happy by pursuing matrimonial bondage and committing before they were actually ready to commit, or keep themselves and their admirers happy by offering, free of charge, a certain dairy product for the ongoing attention as well as the emotional and financial support of said admirers until they were. This is why I say the summer took a turn for the worse.

Kassy was selected as the maid-of-honor and one of Antonio's old army buddies was the best man, so I didn't have to stress about getting shanghaied into that role. As this was going to be mostly a Hispanic shindig, the scope of the wedding would be breathtaking.

Kassy would come to my house after closing down the taqueria and Alejandra would walk across the cul-de-sac so that they could huddle up to plan the wedding. Antonio and I would sit out on the porch swing drinking beer while waiting to be asked our opinion concerning some aspect of the wedding.

"Antonio, you realize that once you go through with this wedding thing that life as you know it will cease to exist. Sitting on the porch drinking beer will be a thing of the past, watching football in your underwear, gone. Anything that made you an ex-pararescue stud buzzard will be relegated to history and you'll probably have to start wearing an apron," I explained to him.

"Possibly, but at least I'm getting some sugar out of the deal while you date an island girl centerfold contestant and all you get out of the deal is a set of bolas azules," Antonio countered.

"My colorful huevos are the price I must pay to ensure that we are both committed to each other without the lure of premarital sex, which is a sin I remind you. A year's chastity is a small price to pay for a life of bliss. We are a little older than you children and do not require physical stimulation to show our admiration for each other."

At this, Antonio spewed out the of beer which he had just imbibed. "She has you wrapped around her little finger. Face it, amigo, if Kassy would say it is okay, you'd run in there now, kick Alejandra out and have your way with the girl!"

"Truer words were never spoken," I admitted.

At this point Kassy and Alejandra came out to discuss who to invite to the wedding. I offered my opinion that it would be simpler and more financially responsible to just elope, but that opinion got knocked in the head about the time I voiced it. It seemed to me that the only people in the county what were not going to be invited were those individuals who were presently incarcerated.

Kassy followed Alejandra back into the house, but turned before going through the door and said, "Are they really blue? That must be painful. You boys shouldn't be having this type of discussion while the living room window is open behind the swing. That said Antonio, I did appreciate the 'island girl centerfold contestant' comment," she laughed as she continued on into the house.

"I think that you are going to have your hands full if you make it through your year of chastity, compadre," offered Antonio.

The year in question was Kassy's idea, which I thought seriously sucked. Her thinking was that if we could keep our hands off of each other for a year while we dated, that it would show a serious commitment on both parts and that the relationship was not based on some shallow need for sex. I tried to explain to her that my need was not shallow, but that it was essential for my physical and mental wellbeing, but that got me nowhere. I did get her to agree that I got credit for 'time served', that is that the clock started ticking from the day I saw her stranded on the side of the road. Even with that, I still had a long row to hoe.

The girls finally had the wedding planned and the date was set for the last Saturday in July. The ceremony itself would take place at Christ the King Catholic Church on Main Steet in La Veta. The church itself was fairly small so only the immediate families of those about to be sold into matrimonial bondage would attend the actual service. The reception would be held at the clubhouse at the Grandote Peaks Golf Club south of town.

The hen's party was held at some undisclosed location in Colorado Springs and sadly no photos or video of the event were ever revealed to me. The guys took Antonio up to the Snooty Fox Gentlemen's Club in Colorado Springs for his bachelor's party, again no photos or video were allowed. I inadvertently got some video on my handheld Go Pro camera which I would use to blackmail Antonio in the future. You wouldn't think that a guy with only one foot could team pole dance so energetically. Alejandro would be impressed, or maybe not.

Since I was not related to either one of the principals in the wedding and the fact that the church only had limited seating, I was not invited to the main event itself. That being the case, Miguel and I retired to the clubhouse at the Grandote Peaks Golf Club to ensure that everything was ready to go there and to have a few pre-reception beers to get us in the spirit of things. Miguel insisted on a few shots of tequila to set the mood as well.

Everybody had gone home to change after the wedding so when I saw Kassy again, she had on a very elegant black lace above-the-knee length cocktail dress. I was obviously not fully into the spirit of things as I found myself wondering what one wore under a little dress like that since there were no visible panty lines showing. I guess I'd find out in about another 8 months. It is a fine line for the girls to walk, you don't want to upstage the bride, but you still want to get plenty of attention. Kassy had mine.

The dinner went well, and all the proper toasts were made and then the party started in earnest. The girls had opted for a DJ as opposed to a live band to get some variety in the music, and the people started dancing almost as soon as the dinner was over, the tables were cleared and everyone was lubed up enough not to feel too shy about tripping the light fantastic in front of strangers.

I had danced with Alejandra and Coco and was working my way over toward Kassy when the DJ started to play some of the music from the Dirty Dancing and the Flashdance soundtracks. I looked over toward Kassy, who gave me a nod and mouthed, 'Let's do it'.

Now both of us were good dancers, as we found out at the Whisky Baron Saloon, but this was 'dirty dancing' and I hadn't done this since forever. It was time to knock the rust off.

We warmed up with 'What a Feeling' by Irene Cara from the Flashdance soundtrack and Kassy got in the groove. That little black lace number she had on was likely showing off more than she anticipated while we danced, but the crowd was loving it. We then moved it up a notch with 'Gloria' by Laura Branigan from the same soundtrack. After a short break, we got back up when 'Hungry Eyes' from the Dirty Dancing soundtrack played, which was good for the full body contact dancing, but the 'involuntary physical responses' threatened to disrupt the action. Kassy thought this was funny, me, not so much. This segued right into 'Manhunt' from Flashdance, where we could show off some of the moves that were coming back to us. This led to 'Romeo' by Donna Summer from Flashdance as well. We were sweating a bit now but having a lot of fun. We sat back down for a breather when I noticed Alejandra speaking to the DJ and pointing at us. I knew something nefarious was afoot.

The DJ then asked for the dance floor to be cleared as he had a special request, but before he played the request, he asked that a Ms. Archuleta and a Mr. Fisher please move to the center of the dance floor. Kassy had a gleam in her eye that suggested that things were about to get interesting. We got up and moved to the center of the floor and faced each other while we waited for the music to begin. It was 'Hungry Eyes' by Eric Carmen from the 'Dirty Dancing' soundtrack.

We got off to a bad start as we had no idea what the music would be, so I asked the DJ to start over again. Kassy put her arms around my neck while I held her hips. The music began and we were ready, and we nailed it. I really didn't want the song to end, but eventually it did. I kept my eyes on Kassy as our foreheads touched. The crowd went wild, but it was almost as if we were the only ones in the room.

Eventually the night came to an end, and everyone went home. I walked Kassy over to Hector's truck and told her that this was probably the best night of my life.

"Probably?"

"Okay, up to this point it's been the highlight, but I'm hoping that we can move it to second place in about 8 months or so."

"We'll see about that, big boy. Thank you for a wonderful evening, Mr. Fisher. You are a fairly proficient dancer, but I believe that a little practice may be in order if you know what I mean?" she said with a wink.

And with that, her, Hector and Coco went off to their place and I went home to mine. You shouldn't wish your life away, but I was hoping that the next 8 months would go by in a blur. Picture a kid waiting all year for Christmas.

CHAPTER 25

THE WEEK AFTER ANTONIO AND Alejandra got hitched, I had driven over to Hector's place to discuss some security concerns that I had with the Azteca standard operating procedures. As I pulled into the driveway, I noticed a black Ford Excursion leaving just as I arrived. Hector was standing in the open front door with a puzzled look on his face when I got up on the porch. I asked him what the problem was but instead of answering me he gestured that I should go inside. Closing the door, he poured us each a cup of coffee before we sat down on one of the couches in the living room.

At this point Hector told me what had just happened. Apparently the two gentlemen who had just left had insinuated that they were private investigators from Mexico who had been hired to look into the estate of one Ernesto Gallardo. Señor Gallardo was a known criminal and smuggler who had been killed in a shoot-out with a rival gang in Santa Ana a few months ago. It seemed that Señor Gallardo may have hidden some of his ill-gotten gains and these men had been employed to look into the matter.

Hector had pleaded ignorance and had even graciously invited the men into his house for refreshments as they discussed the issue. The two men seemed to be especially interested in a jewelry box. Since Ernesto had been a known associate of Hector back in his Caribbean smuggling days, they decided to pay him a visit to determine if Hector had received anything from Ernest recently, or if he knew anything about the jewelry box. Hector assured the gentleman that he'd been out of the game for years now and had not heard from Ernesto since he'd gone straight. The men seemed to take him at his word, but Hector obviously did not take them at theirs.

"They showed me some fake badges from an investigative service in San Miguel de Allende. I am familiar with this service, and they do not issue badges but wallets with appropriate ID cards behind plastic windows. I got the impression that these were not very nice men and there is more to the story behind the jewelry box.

"The interesting thing is that I did receive a package from Mexico a few days ago but I have yet to open it, it's still out in my truck. These payasos may be watching the house now so we will just let it stay there for a while. Let's have some lunch before you leave. I'll open the package tonight after it is dark and see what is in it. I'll give you a call this evening if it is anything interesting."

That evening, Hector called and said that what he had found in the package was interesting and asked me to come over to his house in the morning to take a look at it. After checking in at the taqueria cum gun shop the next morning, I drove over to Hector's house. Hector answered the door with a grin on his face, he was more animated than I had seen him in a long time. After grabbing the required coffees, we went into the living room and sat on the couch again. Placed in the middle of the coffee table was an ornate jewelry box carved out of ebony wood and inlaid with mother-of-pearl. Without saying a word, Hector opened the box and laid out the contents on the coffee table. There was a set of car keys, an index card with a set of latitude and longitude coordinates on it, a photo of a Mexican license plate, a clipping from the El Universal newspaper in Mexico City dated August 7, 2019 and a folded piece of paper.

Opening the folded piece of paper, Hector put on his reading glasses and proceeded to translate the Spanish written on it to me:

'Juan Cortez, I managed to rob the robbers, but their associates have caught up with me in the end. I am sending you this so that perhaps you can make some use of it. It has been a good run my friend, but I intend to go down fighting on my own terms before I will allow this Riviera Maya bunch of pelotudos to take me alive. They are a vicious gang of cabróns and I'm afraid that it would not have been very pleasant for me if they managed to capture me alive. I am sending you this jewelry box before I get to Santa Ana for what looks to be the final showdown. Nobody knows that I have done this, so you should be safe. By the time you have received this package, there is a good chance that I am no longer walking in the Land of the Living. Hopefully someone even as dull as you can figure out what I have given you. Try not to spend it all in one place. Via con Dios amigo. Ernesto.'

Hector then told me that Ernesto had been one of Hector's associates or competitors, depending on the day, back when they were running illicit contraband around the Caribbean. When Hector had started up operations in the United States, Ernesto had relocated to Mexico, and they had both stayed in the game and in touch.

The other items were a mystery at the moment, but I took photos of each item with my phone and told Hector I'd look into it and see what I could come up with. I asked him if he was going to tell Kassy about his visitors and the jewelry box, but he said not at the moment as that would be premature. I agreed, then headed back to my truck to get busy on this mystery from the comfort of my own home.

Looking up the coordinates on Google Earth was relatively straight forward. 29°10'19.29" N by 110°53'38.06" W put you in a junkyard just outside of San Pedro el Saucito northeast of Hermosillo going through the mountains. The photo of the license plate did not yield much by itself, just that it was from Estado de Mexico. Looking into the set of keys was an exercise in futility. From the shape of the key bows, I could tell that it was from a '70s Ford/Lincoln/Mercury, but other than that the keys were of no help. I now turned my attention to the clipping from the English version of the El Universal newspaper.

'During the morning of August 6, 2019, two people, one wielding a firearm, broke into the Casa de Moneda branch in Mexico City. After throwing a security guard to the ground and taking his gun, one of the robbers then went to the vault, which was unaccountably open, and filled a backpack with 1,567 gold coins. The coins, known as "centenarios," have a face value of 50 pesos, but trade for 31,500 pesos ($2,141) apiece, according to the Mexican bank Banorte. This makes the total value of the heist at least $3.3 million US dollars. The bandits have not been apprehended at this time. '

From what I was getting out of the items left in the jewelry box, it seemed that the Riviera Maya gang had originally hit the Casa de Moneda branch in Mexico City and managed to get away scot-free with the centenarios. Sometime afterwards, Ernesto and his crew managed to rob the robbers, but must have gotten themselves identified when they did it. The Riviera Maya gang was actually a ruthless outfit that had relocated from Romania to Mexico in the past and apparently did not take kindly to having their stolen loot stolen. They had pursued Ernesto and his bunch north toward the town of Santa Ana in the state of Sonora.

It seems that as Ernesto was getting pursued, he had passed through Hermosilla on the way to his demise in Santa Ana and dropped off the golden coins at the junkyard identified by the geographic coordinates. I assumed that the keys and the license plate would come into play to identify the actual location of the treasure once you were on the ground in the junkyard.

I called Hector and gave him my take on the situation. He suggested that I come over to his place the following Saturday for lunch and we'd have a chat about this treasure that had apparently fallen into our laps. He'd also invite Hernández over as whatever we decided to do, we'd need a few more people involved and a few more eyes on any harebrained scheme we would come up with to go fetch the gold.

I drove over to the gun shop-slash-taco stand to see how things were going there before taking Kassy to dinner at Legends on Main. I ogled Kassy's form and figure while working up an appetite. When her, Maria, Coco and the girls had the place cleaned up and ready for the next day, Kassy went into the ladies' room to change out of her jeans, which I thought were just fine, and into something more appropriate for dinner. She came out wearing a mid-calf length bohemian looking peasant dress with a squared necked, in floral print material. Very conservative until you thought about what was lurking under the surface. Still waters run deep as they say.

We got to Legends around 7:30 in the evening. We both decided on the special, which was nachos or quesadillas for starters, green chili corn chowder soup, meatloaf, mashed potatoes and gravy for me and the stir-fried turmeric shrimp with shallots and chilis over pasta for her. I had the strawberry rhubarb pie for dessert while she opted for the bourbon apple pie. A meal fit for a king, again no pun intended. During the meal we just chatted and enjoyed ourselves. Although I hated my enforced chastity while showing commitment and all that, but a platonic relationship does lend itself to good company and casual conversation while simultaneously driving you nuts.

CHAPTER 26

THE FOLLOWING SATURDAY, AFTER MY morning workout and a stop at the shop to make sure that it hadn't burned to the ground overnight, I drove over to Hector's place and saw Hernández' black F-150 Ford Raptor parked out front. I knocked on the door and heard Hector yell to come in, so I did. Hector and Hernández were sitting on the couch facing back into the living room and they had the contents of the jewelry box scattered out on the coffee table again. After I had shaken hands with Hernández and we'd caught up with each other for a bit, Hector asked me to run through my assumptions and conclusions concerning the scenario surrounding the jewelry box. I laid it out exactly as I had done previously for Hector over the phone last week, then handed the floor back to Hector.

Hector smiled then said, "We should really check this out. If the coins are in that junkyard, it is a cool three million dollars plus change. If it isn't then we'll only be out the cost of a Sonoran vacation."

Hernández, being the thoughtful guy that he was, mentioned to Hector that there were obviously other people looking for the loot as well, and they didn't seem to be very nice people.

"True, but if we can get in and out quickly, we should be okay," Hector said.

I thought that I should inject some caution as well. I postulated that if we did get tagged going after the gold and somehow managed to get the coins back here, that we ran the risk of dragging some very unscrupulous characters in behind us and putting a lot of people we were fond of at risk.

Hector wasn't about to let it go. I could tell that part of it was the lure of an easy three million dollars, part of it seemed to be avenging his old buddy Ernesto and part of it was just having one, perhaps his last, exhilarating adventure.

"Okay, we'll need to do a risk versus reward exercise at some point, but before we can do that, we need to come up with a reasonable plan to make the assessment," said Hector.

So, we started brainstorming a plan. Getting down to Hermosillo wasn't an issue, we could simply fly from Denver to Phoenix to Hermosilla. Renting a car at the airport and accommodation in Hermosilla also did not present any problem.

The problems would arise once we were actually in the junkyard outside of San Pedro el Saucito. If we did manage to locate the coins, 1,567 gold centenarios weighed approximately 117 pounds. We'd have to get them out of the junkyard unobserved and then get them back through Customs at the US border without getting caught. The smart thing to do would be to melt them down and recast them so that they could not be identified as the coins from the robbery, but that still left the issue of smuggling 117 pounds of gold into the U.S. Also, the value of the coins was not due to their weight in gold, but due to the fact that they were actually rare gold centenarios. Melting them down would significantly devalue them. Furthermore, the time it would take to recast the gold was more time the Riviera Maya bunch had a chance to hit our crew on their home turf in Mexico.

We decided to give it some thought overnight and to reconvene the next day. I went back to my place and gave the issue some serious thought but couldn't figure out a foolproof way to get the gold across the border in a timely manner, if we did in fact find it. One thing I did realize is that flying into a foreign country with weapons was out of the question. I am sure that

Hector's connections in Mexico could provide weapons, but if we did have to shoot our way out of Mexico and we got hung up by the Federales in the process, we'd be spending many miserable years behind bars in a Mexican prison. It would be better to just rely on a quick in-and-out plan and avoid any gunplay with the Riviera Maya boys.

The next day was Sunday, so when we huddled up in Hector's living room again once he, Kassy and Coco got back from Mass. Kassy was hanging out in the kitchen, but instantly knew that something nefarious was in the breeze and came over to find out what it was. Hector had a case of sloping shoulders and had me explain the situation to Kassy. She liked the idea of an easy three million dollars, but she wasn't so keen on us going down to Mexico and playing 'five fingered discount, ten toed getaway' with the Riviera gangs' loot. I interjected that the money did not really belong to the ex-Romanian crew, but she simply said that I was obfuscating the issue. I thought that this was a pretty big word for Caribbean-Hispanic cover girl and I told her so. She grabbed me by the ear like Chinese women do when they are disciplining their offspring and told me that I wasn't paying attention.

Hector sprang to my defense, "Kassy, let go of his ear. How do you expect him to warm to you if you are pulling on his ear? Women do not act that way toward those they are attempting to ensnare. At the moment we are simply trying to see if it is even feasible to take a run at this gold, only that."

"I am not trying to ensnare King; I think we are past that now. We are in the verifying commitment phase which seems to be wearing on the man," she said this while giving me a wink. She apparently had no idea how mentally and physically painful this commitment phase was to a healthy, virile young man like myself.

"Furthermore, Papa, I know you well. You have been itching for a reason to go on another little caper since you gave up the game a few years ago. I know for a fact that you men will attempt this even if your plan has holes in it like a Swiss cheese. You guys come up with your best plan and then I will take a look at it from a business woman's perspective and then tell you if you can go execute it or not. Do I make myself clear?"

"Si, mi hija," Hector replied as he capitulated to Kassy.

As she walked back into the kitchen to make us some lunch as a proper daughter should, Hernández remarked to Hector that Kassy seemed to take after his bossy, domineering side of the family. Hector agreed with this assessment but said that at least she had gotten her mother's looks. Yolanda must have been an exceptionally attractive woman if Kassy still looked as hot as she did even after mixing in Hectors DNA. After contemplating this revelation, while waiting for lunch to be served from the disciplinarian in the kitchen, we came up with a plan. It did have holes in it, but what plan doesn't? We briefed Kassy on the plan later that afternoon after lunch. After thinking about it for a while, she gave us her blessing with the understanding that we would remain in contact with her and Miquel throughout the entire venture.

At this point, we needed to put some pieces in place, book the flights and hotels and purchase four Rothco canvas cargo bags to carry the loot. Since there was a good chance that we were being watched, Hector and I needed to figure out a way to get to Denver without anybody knowing we had left. It was decided that Hector would go to work in Walsenburg on the day in question, park his truck in his designated spot and then wait for Antonio and I to pick him up in Antonio's Dodge Ram 4-door pickup. I would drop off my luggage at Antonio's the night before, then just walk across the cul-de-sac in the morning and get in his truck on the day of departure. My truck would remain parked in front of my house as a red herring while we were gone.

We decided to pull the trigger a week from the coming Tuesday to give us time to get the rest of the pieces in place. The flight bookings were easy enough since American Airlines Flight 1379 left Denver international Airport on the day in question at 12:12 in the afternoon and arrived at Aeropuerto International de Hermosilla at 3:16pm the same day after a 51 minute layover in Phoenix.

We would book into the Holiday Inn off Boulevard Luis Donaldo Colosio Murrieta as it was in the center of town, it was on the way to the junkyard, and it had a Mariscos El Charco restaurant within walking distance. The rest of the logistics would be handled by Hernández and would be planned and put in place before Hector and I flew out.

The Sunday before the escapade in Mexico was due to commence, Kassy and I were sitting on my porch swing sharing a beer. She was inappropriately attired for a 'commitment evening' in some black Nike tennis shorts and a white Lotto tank top. I still thought that she had no idea how good she looked in anything and those long, ochre toned legs were getting a lot of my attention.

"King, is this little soiree you boys are planning going to be very dangerous?"

I didn't want to worry her, but I felt that I had to be honest with her as her father would be front and center. "If everything goes according to plan, we should be in and out before anyone even knows we're there. That said, if they get wind of what we're planning to do, it could go south on us very quickly and we'll need to get back across the border as fast as possible."

"Promise me that if things do not go well that you will forget about the gold and get Papa and yourself out of there as fast as you can. We really do not need the gold, but Papa may need the adventure at this stage of his life. Do not let him lose sight of what is important and it would be nice if you could bring yourself back across the border in one piece as well."

"I'll do my best, chica, but you know Hector is a stubborn old man when he gets the bit in his mouth. I think it runs in the family."

Downing what was left in the beer bottle, Kassy placed it down beside the swing on the porch then rolled over and straddled my hips with her hands on my shoulders.

"That's all that I ask, Mr. Fisher, and for your information stubbornness is an Archuleta family trait. You will now kiss me wantonly and with vigor so that you remember what you are coming back for. This commitment thing has an end date and I am sure that you will want to be there for it."

So, I kissed her wantonly and with vigor until the sun went down and she said that she had to go home and feed Hector. As she disentangled herself from me, straddling someone while he is sitting on a porch swing takes a certain amount of balance, dexterity and finesse, she asked me if I thought that would hold me until I got back from Mexico.

"No, it will not. That was nothing but flirtatious teasing. I need a meal not a snack," I informed her.

"Is a five-course meal worth waiting for?" she asked.

"Of course, it is, but what about a starter?"

"Patience, Mr. Fisher, we still need to assess your commitment here."

"A lot of good my commitment will be if I have a heart attack due to high blood pressure before the commitment period is satisfied," I retorted.

"I highly recommend yoga to control your blood pressure, Señor King. How do you think I'm keeping mine down?" she replied with a wink and an alluring swing of her hips as she headed out to her Mustang.

This was teasing pure and simple. I began to wonder if commitment had anything at all to do with what was going on, it seemed to me to be torture or death by teasing. I was convinced that it was a Mexican or Caribbean thing as no self-respecting Caucasian would do this to their intended significant other. I was looking forward to getting some payback with interest at the end of the commitment period.

CHAPTER 27

THE EVENING BEFORE HECTOR AND I WERE TO FLY OUT, I took Kassy to dinner again at Legends and afterwards we once again ended up on my porch swing. Needless to say, Kassy was still worried about our upcoming adventure and wanted to spend some quality commitment time with me before things kicked off. If things went totally down the drain, Kassy stood to not only lose her platonic love interest but her father as well. I tried to play things down and told her that the plan was solid and there was a good chance that the gold wasn't even in the junkyard and we were going off on a wild goose chase. This did little to alleviate her concerns, but it was the best I could offer at the moment.

Before she left that evening, she gave me another one of those blood boiling, toe curling, Caribbean-Hispanic island girl kisses before driving off to spend some time with Hector at home. With nothing better to do, I rechecked and repacked my old military duffle bag on the kitchen table before wandering across the cul-de-sac to throw it in the back of Antonio's Dodge Ram. All I could do now was get a good night's sleep and get ready to start the ball rolling tomorrow morning.

Around 6:00 Tuesday morning I had a cup of coffee, rinsed out the pot and the cup, locked my front door and walked over to Antonio's house and got in the passenger's side of the truck while I waited for him to come out. We were on the road to Walsenburg at 7:00 and at the Azteca Trucking Lines offices in Walsenburg just before 8:00. Hector was waiting for us inside the lobby and walked out with his duffle bag when he saw Antonio's truck pull up in front. He tossed his bag in the bed with mine and off we went to Denver to catch our flight out to Phoenix just after noon.

Hector was in the back seat so I had to turn halfway around to talk to him, but we rehashed the plan with Antonio offering his input as well. Antonio dropped us off in front of the Jeppesen Terminal around 10:00 in the morning and after getting our boarding passes at the American Airlines counter in the West Terminal we got to stand in line for a while before passing through security and then taking the train to Concourse A to catch our flight.

It was a short flight to Phoenix then about an hour layover until we boarded the flight to Hermosillo. We arrived at our destination about a quarter past 3:00 in the afternoon. After passing through Customs, we rented a Jeep Renegade at the Avis counter, loaded up our duffle bags and drove out of the airport and onto the Boulevard Jesus Garcia Morales heading into the heart of hot, dry and dusty Hermosillo.

Turning south on Boulevard Antonio Quiroga we drove for about a quarter of a mile before taking a left on Boulevard Luis Donaldo Colosio Murrieta and made our way to the Holiday Inn Express.

Hector got out and went inside to get us checked into our rooms to avoid any language issues. When he came out and got back in the Renegade, I drove to the parking lot on the east side of the building. We grabbed our duffle bags and made our way to our adjoining rooms on the third floor. We decided to clean up a bit and relax before meeting in the lobby at 6:00 to go grab a bite to eat at the Mariscos El Charo restaurant, which was about a 300 yard walk to the east. We both ordered the steak fajitas and washed them down with a couple of Negro Modelo beers. As we ate, we decided to get up around 7:00 in the morning and grab a snack and a coffee at the Starbucks on the south side of the hotel parking lot before driving over to San Pedro el Saucito to scout out the junkyard. If no threats were detected we'd go into the yard and drive around as if we were looking for something in particular while we zeroed in on the coordinates which Ernesto had given Hector. After that, we'd play it by ear.

The next morning, after checking out of the hotel and throwing our bags in the rental Renegade, we each had a couple of donuts and a grande Americano apiece at the Starbucks next to the hotel before we headed out to scout the junkyard. Hector drove and doubled back the way we had come in from the airport before getting us back on Boulevard Jesus Garcia Morales heading east toward the mountains on that side of the city. Sonora State Highway 100 changed names from Boulevard Jesus Garcia Morales to Boulevard Luis Encinas J. somewhere along the way before we got off of it and headed northeast on Boulevard Ablelardo L. until it headed due east and became Eusebio Francisco Kino. These Mexican roads seem to change names randomly just to confuse the unwary. Eusebio Francisco Kino became Internacional A. Nogales at some point and headed north just after it became Sonora State Highway 15 as it cleared the southernmost point of the mountains east of the city. We stayed on 15 until the interchange with Highway 14 which took us northeast toward San Pedro el Saucito. The junkyard was located about a mile along Highway 14 on the righthand side of the highway.

Getting off of the highway, we drove past the front gate of the junkyard but couldn't see much as the gate only led into a courtyard with a large shop building at the far end. We kept going and took the next right which took us unimpeded into the junkyard itself. I failed to see the logic of having a front gate if you could simply drive into the junkyard by taking the next available right, but maybe it was a Mexican thing.

I had downloaded the GPS Coordinates app onto my iPhone, which showed exactly where the phone was located at any given time so we'd use this to find the coordinates supplied by Ernesto. As Hector drove around the junkyard, which had a grid-like pattern of dirt roads built into it, I kept my eye on my phone until we were finally just west of the given coordinates. The actual coordinates seemed to be under one of the few trees growing in the yard.

We climbed out of the Jeep and while watching the coordinates on the phone we were directed to an old beat to crap 1978 Mercury Zephyr sedan that at one time had been beige. This was a good sign as you'll remember that the old set of keys which Ernesto had included in the jewelry box were for a '70s Ford/Lincoln/Mercury. Things were looking good at this point. They began to look even better when we discovered that the license plate on the back of the car, which could not be seen from out in the yard as the back of the car was backed in toward the tree's trunk, read MCN-15-18, which matched the photo that had been included in the jewelry box.

We now had to search the car without drawing attention to ourselves. While Hector walked back to the large shop building near the front gate to enquire about the old Zephyr, I took out my pocket sized can of WD-40 and shot a healthy dose into the front and rear door locks as well as the trunk lock. Needless to say, the car had either been locked up when it was dumped in the yard or when the gold centenarios had been hidden in the car. After letting the WD-40 do its thing for a minute or so, I tried the old keys in the trunk lock. One fit and the trunk lid lifted with a screech. There was absolutely nothing in the trunk, not even an old spare tire. I then moved on to the front door on the passenger's side. The door opened surprisingly quietly, but there really was nowhere you could hide 117 pounds of gold coins in the front of a 1978 Zephyr. The only place which I could think of to hide anything anywhere else in the old Zephyr was under the rear seat. I got the rear door on the passenger's side open without too much trouble and was just about to pull the bottom of the rear seat up when I heard Hector and another man talking and coming my way, not a good time to be making a discovery.

I waited until they walked up to the car and acted like I had been giving it a good inspection. I found out later, as they were conversing in Spanish at the moment, that Hector was asking about the cost for the old Zephyr and was telling the yard hand that he had a similar Zephyr at home and needed a parts car so that he could make one functional Zephyr out of the two. The yard hand asked the obvious question, which was why would anyone would actually want a functional Zephyr? Hector told him that it had sentimental value as the car had belonged to his daughter who had recently passed away due to breast cancer. I made a mental note to offer Kassy a free amateur breast inspection when we got back to La Veta to forestall her imminent demise.

Anyhow, the yard hand said that Hector could have it for 500 US dollars if he would tow it out of the yard. Hector thought about it for a minute and then said he'd think about it, but would need to look over the car thoroughly. The junkman said that was fine and just to come by the office and tell him what his decision was when we were finished before he started walking back toward the large shop building, which was also apparently the office.

When he was out of sight, I explained to Hector that there was nothing in the trunk and nowhere to hide 117 pounds of gold coins in the front seats, which only left the rear seat pan. I hadn't had a chance to look there as I heard him and the junkman coming toward the car. Hector being Hector, asked me what I was waiting for.

I opened the rear passenger door again, grabbed the bottom of the rear seat and gave it a yank, the whole seat popped up and out so I pulled it out of the car and handed it to Hector. The springs and stuffing had been carefully removed from under the rear seat leaving only the cheap vinyl covering to create more space above the seat pans. Lying in the seat pans, one on each side of the driveshaft tunnel, were two well-worn canvas bags. I grabbed the one nearest me and backed out of the car before setting it on the ground in front of Hector. Hector unbuckled the strap at the neck of the bag, took a look inside and just grinned like the proverbial Cheshire Cat.

Each bag contained gold centenarios, a little over 55 pounds per bag. We were apparently the new owners of the "Casa de Moneda" loot. We now had to get it from the old Zephyr to our Renegade without drawing attention to ourselves. Hector walked over to the Jeep and backed it up beside the Zephyr. When he had done this, I reached in and grabbed the four Rothco canvas cargo bags that I had purchased back in Colorado strictly for this purpose. While Hector leaned against the front of the Jeep drinking a bottle of water and keeping an eye on things, I quickly transferred the gold coins from the two worn out canvas bags they were originally in to the four new bags and placed them on the rear floorboards of the Renegade and covered them with the old canvas bags.

That done, we locked the old Zephyr back up before heading out of the junkyard. On the way out we stopped by the office and Hector went in and told the man that he would need to think on it some more, but he would be back in touch within the next few days to let him know what he had decided. While Hector was in the workshop cum office, I noticed that there were two men standing just inside the workshop, in the shadows, who seemed to be taking an inordinate amount of interest in me and the Jeep.

When Hector climbed back into the driver's seat, I pointed out the two men who seemed curious about us. It occurred to us that perhaps the Riviera Maya bunch may have known about the junkyard, but not about the Zephyr. The smart move would be to execute our extraction plan immediately and not go back to Hermosilla since we had only booked for one night in the Holiday Inn and we had our duffle bags with us. With that decided we began the long drive to Nogales. We had nothing to defend ourselves with so we needed to get moving as soon as possible and hope that we could get out of the area without any problems.

We got back on Sonora State Highway 15 and began our northward trek to Nogales where we were to meet up with Hernández. I had already called Hernández and told him of the change in plan. Hector took us to Los Chinos, about 50 miles north of San Pedro el Saucito, where we stopped for fuel and lunch. I then took over the driving duties and brought us to Magdalena de Kino. Hector took the wheel back and drove the final leg to Nogales where we were to meet Hernández at the Carlisle Wire & Cable manufacturing facility the following morning.

We needed a place to lie low through the night and without knowing how much the opposition actually knew about us, we couldn't afford to check into a place using our passports. Pulling into Motel 32 just off of the Boulevard Luis Donaldo Colosio, less than a mile south of the Carlisle plant, Hector got out and essentially bribed the girl behind the counter with two $50 bills to rent us two rooms for the evening without identification. Corruption can be a good thing.

That evening we walked over to the Toscanos Restaurant, about a quarter of a mile from the motel on Nacozari de Barcia street, where we had scallopinos di brolo and a few beers for dinner before heading back to the motel to get some shut eye.

The next morning bright and early, Hector and I didn't bother checking out of the motel and drove to the loading docks at the Carlisle plant to meet up with Hernández, who just happened to be picking up a load of high temperature PTFE resin and fluoropolymer insulated wires and cables to be delivered to a client in California. Pulling in beside the passenger's door of the Azteca rig we got out, shook hands with Hernández and discussed the plan from that point on. Hector and Hernández then climbed up into the sleeper compartment and lifted up the mattress. Pressing some hidden latches Hector pulled the lid off a compartment hidden below the mattress pan.

"Do all Azteca trucks come equipped with this feature?" I asked.

"Once a smuggler always a smuggler. Now quit jacking your jaw and hand me up those canvas bags," Hector replied.

I handed all four of the bags of coins up to Hector, who passed them to Hernández, who stored them in the hidden compartment before relatching the lid and replacing the mattress. This should be sufficient to get across the border as the Border Patrol and ICE were looking for drugs or illegal immigrants, not gold. Also, gold doesn't have a scent so there was no worry about the sniffer dogs.

Hernández would cross the border and pass through Customs at the big US Customs and Border Protection Nogales Station and then proceed to California to deliver his load of specialty cables and wires to the customer in Silicon Valley near San Jose. After that he would pick up a load of electronic equipment to be delivered to Hewlett Packard Enterprises in Colorado Springs before heading back to the Azteca yard in Walsenburg.

Hernández would give Hector and I a lift to just before the border crossing and we would walk through the border crossing to the Shell station on the other side after clearing Customs and Immigration. We would just have to leave the rented Renegade at the Carlisle plant and let nature take its course. Hernández would pick us up there once he had cleared Customs and take us to the Enterprise Rent-A-Car offices on West Ellis Street. We'd rent a car and drive back to Pueblo to turn our car into the Enterprise shop there while Hernández continued on to San Jose. Antonio would meet us in Pueblo and take us back to La Veta.

Even if the guys watching us from the shadows of the workshop at the junkyard took down the details of the rented Renegade, or took photos on their phones, it would take them awhile to find the rented Jeep and would not know what type of vehicle we were now driving. Hector had wisely used an old alias from his dope running days when we rented the Jeep at the Hermosilla airport. The address for that alias was a Denny's restaurant in St. Louis, Missouri so they shouldn't be able to track us down in La Veta.

On the way back to Pueblo, Hector and I had a chance just to relax and chat about anything we wanted to. I was driving the first leg from Nogales north to Tucson then east on I-10 to San Simon, Arizona, where we would fuel up, grab a bite to eat and change drivers. This was a stretch of about 200 miles which gave us about 4 hours to discuss whatever was on our minds.

Looking at Hector I started the ball rolling by asking why we just did what we did? He really didn't need the money, although three million dollars would come in handy, and there was the risk that the Riviera Maya crew might still come after us if they had tagged us in the junkyard. Granted, they obviously didn't know about the old Zephyr, but perhaps they did know about the junkyard and those two guys in the shadows were just hanging around to see who turned up and showed some interest in the yard.

Pondering the question for a moment, Hector replied, "King, there is no rational excuse for going after that gold. The irrational motivation is that I am in my sixties now and have been bored ever since I quit running dope. I didn't sell dope because it was lucrative, which it was, I did it for the thrill, the adrenaline rush of doing something illegal and getting away with it time and time again.

"You are correct, I do not need the money, but do you think that you can honestly tell me that the gun shop and the position you hold at my trucking company are keeping your juices flowing? Tell me you don't sometimes miss jumping out of airplanes or breaking down doors. We simply did this selfishly to get back in the saddle and enjoy the spice of life for a few days."

"I'll give you that, Hector," I agreed. "But you must realize that there could be some blowback from the Riviera Maya crew and now that you have a home and a family, they have a location and leverage where they can come at you. Don't forget that you now have Kassy and Coco to consider as well."

"This is why I referred to this as selfish, we did it to validate our existence knowing full well that if things did not go exactly as we planned, the response from the opposition could be devastating. We will need to keep our eyes open for a while when we get back home."

Hector was silent for a few minutes, then said, "The more I think about it, the best thing that we can do now is to contact the bank in Mexico City which was robbed and give them the coins back. We've scratched out adventurous itches, we don't actually need the money and once the money is back with the bank there is really no reason for those cockeyed Riviera Mayans to come after us unless it is simply to assuage their egos and save some face after being bested by an old Mexican guy and a sexually frustrated gringo."

I agreed with Hector that giving the money back to the bank seemed like a good idea all the way around, but I was curious who this sexually frustrated gringo was he had mentioned. Hector laughed so hard I thought he'd throw up a lung.

"I know exactly what she is doing to you, amigo, she told me! I agree with her entirely, if you can hold it together until she is ready to give herself to you, then you will have proven to yourself and to her that she is something valuable to you and by doing so you will have also proven that you are someone valuable to her. There are many cultures in the past that have required this commitment before a physical relationship is allowed to blossom, and I think that it was a very wise tradition. Do you see how many marriages end up in divorce these days? Nothing worthwhile ever comes easy, the same goes for women. I could only take her mother Yolanda out to dinner, or for walks in the park, or out where there were other people for a year before she agreed to become intimate. In the long run it was well worth it. I sympathize with you, but it is something you must do if you desire my daughter. If it makes you feel any more hopeful, the year is a flexible time period but it is totally determined by the woman in question.

I suggested that if this was a tradition in his culture that the women in question should be required to dress in sackcloth and ashes, or perhaps a burka during this flexible period to avoid teasing and overstressing the male counterpart. Perhaps the Arabs were on to something here. Hector said that he had suggested something similar to Kassy, who had replied, "Where is the fun in that?" I could picture her grinning as she said it.

We pulled into the Chevron station in San Simon to fuel up, stretch our legs and to get some coffee and snacks since there was no restaurant in San Simon. We'd have to get to Deming, New Mexico before we could stop for a decent meal. Deming was about 100 miles from San Simon, so that gave us roughly 2 hours where we could either continue contemplating life in general or we could travel in silence and I could take a nap. We opted for the silence and nap alternative.

When we arrived in Deming around 6:00 in the evening, Hector got off on the West Cedar Street exit and crossed South Gold Avenue and hung a right into the Denny's parking lot a block and a half after crossing Gold Avenue. We were both tired of traveling and were hungry. We ordered the chicken fried steak dinner and iced teas. I had the caramel apple pie crisp for dessert while Hector chose the New York style cheesecake. We washed the dessert down with a coffee before hitting the head and climbing back into our rented Impala. I took over the driving duties for the short 60-mile trip to Las Cruces where we had decided to spend the night after a long day on the road which had started in Mexico.

Once in Las Cruces we exited onto East University Avenue and pulled into the Ramada Inn about 300 yards to the east of I-10. Hector got out and got us a couple of rooms on the west side while I parked the car and grabbed our duffle bags and followed him into the hotel. After getting our card keys we made our way to our respective rooms, made plans to meet in the lobby at 7:00 the next morning and bid each other good night. I was beat from traveling all day in the car, so I just showered up, brushed my fangs and crawled into bed after leaving a request for a wake-up call at 6:00.

After hanging up the wake-up call the next morning, I did the usual morning ablutions before packing all of my kit back up in the duffle bag and heading down to the lobby. Hector was already there so we sorted out the bill before climbing back in the rented Impala and driving to the International House of Pancakes next door for breakfast and coffee before getting back on road. We got back on I-10 and followed it southeast for about two and a half miles before we hit the interchange onto I-25 north. It was now a straight shot to Pueblo about 430 miles away as the crow flies. It was going to be a long day's drive.

I was driving again, and we'd decided to make it to Albuquerque before stopping for food and fuel. This would be about a 250-mile drive, or 5 hours if all went well. During this time, we talked about girls, guns and the interesting things we had done in our past. Hector had led a very interesting life and had covered a lot of territory between the Caribbean, Mexico and the States. He should write a book. I, on the other hand, had not traveled as much but had still managed to cram in enough interesting material between growing up in Idaho on a ranch, the Army and the DEA that I could keep up my end of the conversation. This was the first time ever that Hector and I just sat and had a casual conversation. It was enlightening and interesting.

We decided to get through the worst part of central Albuquerque before stopping for lunch, so we took the Alameda Boulevard NE exit and after about a block and a half we pulled into the parking lot for the Tin Can Alley Brewery on the right. We got out and stretched our legs before going into the brewery cum BBQ joint and got seated. Hector ordered the pulled pork slider while I went for the hot link slider. Being adventurous we ordered a pint each of the Sante Fe Pale Ale. The sandwiches and the beers were surprisingly good.

After a pit stop in the men's room we got back on the road, I-25 North again, this time with Hector at the wheel. We were on the last leg of our journey to Pueblo where we would turn in the rental car at Enterprise and Antonio would collect us and take us back to La Veta.

During this final segment of the trip, Hector started pestering me about my plans if and when Kassy ever decided to allow me unfettered access to her, if you know what I mean. This was getting the cart before the horse in my opinion and this line of questioning needed to get nipped in the bud as soon as possible.

"Hector, at the moment we are simply dating. Maybe it will turn into something serious after this year-long period of self-inflicted, non-physical courtship and then again, maybe it won't. If it turns out that we are not compatible then it would be uncomfortable for everyone involved if I decided to remain in La Veta. I'd need to leave for greener pastures and start up again somewhere else.

"There is no way that we could keep working under the same roof of the taco shop and gun store if things didn't work out and La Veta is so small that gossip would kick in immediately concerning the 'breakup' and who was responsible for it. You know how that works in small towns.

"I suggest that we just let things ride and see how it all pans out. I still have about 7 more months of self-flagellation to endure before this even becomes an issue."

Hector pondered my rationale and reasoning for a few minutes before stating that I obviously knew next to nothing about women in general and absolutely nothing about Caribbean-Hispanic thoroughbred women. He had a point. We continued our trip in silence while I ruminated on my lack of knowledge concerning the fairer sex.

We had dinner at McDonalds in Raton, just below the Colorado border before fueling up, changing drivers and beginning the last leg of our journey. It was a little over 125 miles to Pueblo from Raton and Hector thankfully slept most of the way, so that I was not subjected to further interrogation or verbal abuse.

Since we pulled into the Pueblo after business hours, we decided to get some rooms for the night before turning in the car and getting Antonio to pick us up at the Enterprise shop the next morning. There was a Courtyard by Marriott on East 1st Street a few blocks west of the Enterprise Rent-A-Car shop so we pulled in and got a pair of rooms. After cleaning up a bit we walked across 1st Street then about a half block up North Main Street to Dee Tacko for some craft tacos and iced teas. Back at the Marriott we stopped at the hotel Bar & Bistro for a few beers before calling it a day and turning in.

The following morning, we met down at the Bar & Bistro again where we had a breakfast of eggs, bacon and coffee before checking out at 8:00. The Enterprise shop opened at 7:30 and Antonio was going to meet us there at 8:30.

Parking the Impala in one of the returned vehicle parking spots, I went in to sort out the paperwork while Hector carried our bags into the lobby to wait for Antonio and to make sure we hadn't left anything incriminating in the car. About 15 minutes later Antonio's Dodge Ram swung off East 1st Street onto North Bradford Street and then into the Enterprise parking lot before parking in front of the office. Antonio hopped out, came inside and fist bumped Hector and I. We grabbed our duffle bags and threw them in the bed of the Dodge Ram before climbing into the truck, Hector riding shotgun and me stretched out in the back seat. We began the last leg of the trip home.

On the way back to La Veto, Antonio demanded a recounting of the adventure from when he dropped us off at DIA until now. Hector began telling him a highly embellished version of events and I just nodded off.

I woke up when we stopped in front of Hector's place. We all got out to stretch our legs, or in Antonio's case, his leg and a half. This is how he actually refers to his ambulatory equipment so there was nothing rude in me using that description as well. Hector grabbed his bag out of the bed and suggested that we meet up at the taqueria tomorrow morning to figure out how we wanted to play it once Hernández showed up with the gold. We told him we'd see him then. I got in front now and Antonio drove us back to our little cul-de-sac. As we pulled off Cherry Street and into the cul-de-sac, we noticed a little red Mustang parked in front of my place with a spicy looking girl swinging on the porch swing watching us pull into Antonio's driveway.

Antonio waved at Kassy while he informed me that he was very glad that he was now married and beyond that frustrating 'commitment period'. He, like Miguel earlier, said he would light a candle for me. I didn't think that lighting a candle for a non-Catholic would actually do any good, but it couldn't hurt. I thanked him for the lift and the lighting of the candle then grabbed my bag out of the back and walked across the cul-de-sac and up onto my porch under the watchful eye of a world class tease, who was grinning at me while dressed provocatively in worn out, distressed as they say these days, Levis, a red Tecate beer t-shirt and flip-flops.

I dropped my bag on the porch beside the swing and plopped down beside her. After a long, heartfelt Gallic-style soul kiss, Kassy thanked me for bringing Hector back in one piece, she'd already had a call from him, and now she wanted to know what we'd gotten up to down in Mexico and where the treasure was. I walked her through the whole adventure from the time Antonio and I collected Hector at the Azteca office in Walsenburg until we arrived in Pueblo.

"So, there were no bad guys, car chases or gunplay involved at all? Boring. Do you think those two guys that were in the shadows at the junkyard workshop watching you when you left could be a problem?" she asked.

"It's a stretch, but they could be. If they already knew about the gold being in the old Mercury Zephyr, it wouldn't have been there by the time we arrived. If they were aware that the junkyard was of interest but didn't know about the Zephyr, then it makes sense that they would watch the junkyard for strangers showing up and nosing around. That said, after we left the junkyard, we immediately headed north to Nogales and the border to hook up with Hernández. We left the rented Jeep Renegade in a parking lot at the Carlisle plant. Since it had been rented under one of Hector's old dope running aliases tied to an address in St. Louis, it shouldn't be traceable to us here. We rented a new car in Nogales for the drive home so we should be okay," I told her.

"'Should' be okay infers that there is a chance that we may not be okay, correct?"

"That is correct. We'll need to just hang loose for a while and see if there is any blowback."

Changing the subject, I asked her if she wanted to go inside and shower up with me? I'd been on the road for a while and needed to clean up. She contemplated this for a moment then informed me that although the offer definitely had its merits, she needed to preserve her virtue for the duration of the 'commitment period'. I proposed that if we went in and showered together, and only showered, that her virtue would still be intact and we could continue with the commitment torment afterwards. On the other hand, if things got completely out of hand in the shower and her virtue was somehow lost or misplaced, we could simply forget the commitment period and make showering together a daily occurrence.

"Nice try, cowboy, but it is not going to happen just yet. Abstinence makes the heart grow fonder; you know," she informed me.

"I think the actual phrasing is 'absence makes the heart grow fonder'. In this case the result is painfully the same."

"If it makes you feel any better, I will now go home and take a very cold shower. Do you think that you alone are feeling the effects of this commitment period?" she said with a smirk as she got up off the swing to walk to her car.

"Judging by that smirk I would have to say that the pain and suffering is much more pronounced on my side of the fence than it is on your side."

"Possibly," was all she said as she blew me a kiss, got in her Mustang and drove away.

CHAPTER 28

THE FOLLOWING MORNING, AFTER A nice hot shower in comfort of my own home, I dressed in my running gear and did one of my 6-mile runs around the fields to the west of town. The amount of traveling that I'd done over the past few days had knotted me up a bit and it took a few miles to work out the kinks and get back into a rhythm. Arriving back at my house, I took another hot shower before deciding to pull my beautifully reworked, ex-ugly Dodge truck, which I had left out in front of my house as a red herring, behind the house near the garage and gave it a good cleaning both inside and out.

While I was doing this labor of love, I had a chance to think about the situation which we now found ourselves in. True, it seemed like we had pulled it off and made it out of Mexico with around three million dollars of ill-gotten gold coins, but I preferred to think in worst case scenarios. This did not mean that I was a pessimist, but more of a pragmatist. Until we were absolutely certain that we'd gotten away with it, the gold should just stay hidden somewhere in La Veta until we could arrange to get it back to the bank in Mexico.

If this Riviera Maya crew somehow figured out that we'd snuck down to Mexico and relieved them of their ill-gotten gains and came after us, the gold itself would be our only bargaining tool. We'd need to figure out how we were going to play this sooner rather than later.

Putting up my buckets, sponges, rags and chamois cloth, I pulled the Dodge alongside the house on the driveway and went back to the garage to close the door and lock it up. Going back into the house through the back door I noticed that the front door was open and I was sure that I'd closed it after I came back from my run.

Perhaps it was the whole issue with stolen gold and the Riviera Maya boys, but I reached into the pantry cabinet beside the refrigerator and got the little Springfield XD 9mm pistol I kept there for just such occasions. I held it at the low ready position as I walked toward the front door and cleared the living room to the left and then the dining room to the right. Going out the front door I saw the root cause of my angst. Kassy was back on the porch swing looking as delectable as ever in well-worn and snug-fitting 501 Levis, a pink polo shirt and a pair of old school Converse high-top sneakers on her feet.

"What are you doing back here? I thought you were back at home taking cold showers to relieve the hot flashes that you suffer when you imagine showering with me?" I asked.

Looking at the pistol in my hand, "Are we now to the point where you force me at gunpoint into the shower?" This was asked with a wicked little grin on her face.

"Whatever works, Kassy. Another 7 months could well be the end of me. You need to consider the physical deterioration which is occurring in this once magnificent body and the end result by the time spring gets here," I said as I laid the gun down on the living room window sill behind the swing.

"From where I'm sitting the deterioration does not look too debilitating, but to answer your original question, we have been invited to Antonio's and Alejandro's for dinner this evening. We've got about 45 minutes so you need to go shower up, alone again, and then walk over there with me."

"I don't know, Kassy, that's a pretty far walk for a guy in the latter stages of commitment degeneration, but I bet if you jumped in the shower with me this time I would probably liven up and be able to make it over there under my own steam. What do you say?"

She laughed. "If I were to jump in the shower with you beforehand, I guarantee you that you would be able to skip over there unassisted and likely to Trinidad after dinner as well. I'll have to give you an A for effort, but I'm afraid that you will need to shower alone again this afternoon."

"You realize that you qualified your statement by saying 'this afternoon'. I think I may be wearing you down, Ms. Archuleta. We seem to have gone from a timeframe of months to mere afternoons. I am suddenly feeling invigorated."

"You never give up do you? Now go take a shower and let's go eat!"

Dinner at Antonio's and Alejandra's was an enjoyably casual event. Alejandra was a remarkable cook and we had huge beef chimichangas with real pork green chili on top. Refried beans on the side and guacamole and chips for starters. During dinner we just talked about local events, the goings on at the taqueria and the gun shop and just the usual chit chat. After dinner, while Antonio and I got shanghaied into cleaning the dishes, the kitchen and the table, the girls retreated to the living room with some wine to talk girl stuff. Antonio and I retired to his porch swing to drink beer and talk about manly stuff after cleaning up the kitchen.

"So, you still not getting any?" enquired Antonio.

"That is generally considered to be a vulgar question and discourteous to bring up in polite company, but to answer your question, no I'm not."

"Dude, how are you maintaining the strain? That vow of chastity for a year would kill a normal man."

"First, I am not a normal man, and secondly it was not I who invoked this silly Hispanic year of abstinence to prove commitment thing, this is totally on Kassy. That said, I think her resolve is weakening and the duration may be in question." I proceeded to tell him about Kassy's slip of the tongue when she qualified her statement regarding showering together by saying 'this afternoon'.

"Perhaps there is hope yet. Now that we have that out of the way, do you think the Mexican's will be coming after that gold?"

"Which Mexicans ours or theirs?" You have to get a dig in when you can.

"We are Mexican-Americans, idiota. The ones I am referring to are from south of the border and are commonly referred to as simply Mexicans. Do you think they are coming?"

"Think about it, Antonio, if they did somehow get a line on us down in Mexico before we crossed the border, they'll be coming, and they will be very upset. They not only lost over three million dollars, but they lost a lot of face within the criminal community and the cartels down there. We'll need to keep our eyes open for a while and be on the lookout for any strangers coming into town."

Thinking about what I had just said, I told Antonio that we needed to make sure that everybody was tooled up and carrying a weapon while we went about our business; this would include me, him, Hector, Miguel and the girls if they wanted to carry. We'd also need to make sure we had some other weapons with a little more reach handy as well. I'd keep my Honcho shorty pump gun near me but everyone should keep something suitable handy besides just handguns. Better to be paranoid than dead is what I always said.

The girls came out and sat with us on the porch after it got dark. Due to lack of seating, I gave up my place on the swing to Alejandra so that she could sit by Antonio. Which meant that I had to share a great big wicker chair with Kassy, which forced her to sit on my lap. Life was good. Around 9:00 we thanked them for a wonderful dinner and evening and made our way back across the cul-de-sac to my place where I again tried to get Kassy interested in some coed showering, but once again I failed miserably. She planted another one of those toe curling commitment inspiring kisses on me then bid me a fond adieu as she drove off for home leaving a frustrated gringo in her dust.

CHAPTER 29

THE NEXT MORNING, I GOT up early and did my usual workout and run. Arriving back home after the run I showered, shaved and had a quick breakfast of scrambled eggs on toast with coffee before I got in my freshly washed truck and drove over to the taqueria. Kassy and Coco were already there getting things ready for the day's business, so I sauntered over, ordered a cup of coffee and some sopapillas before retiring to my office to go over the paperwork. This was generally a waste of time as Miguel had decided that he ran the shop now and he and Antonio had things well in hand.

Eventually Hector and Antonio showed up so we all ordered coffee and sat at one of the tables on the taqueria side of the courtroom divider to figure out what we wanted to do with the gold and to discuss the possibility of someone coming after it. Coco and Kassy sat with us.

I ran through the situation just as I had with Antonio at his place the prior evening. The gold was still in transit with Hernández, we may have been identified at the Mexican junkyard and if we had been, and they somehow tracked us to La Veta, we could expect a visit from the Riviera Maya crowd.

I suggested that we all tool up and do the concealed carry thing from now until we had gotten rid of the gold. This brought up the obvious question which was - what were we going to do with it?

Hector got involved at this point. He said that although three million dollars would come in handy, it didn't belong to us and the right thing to do was to give it back to the bank in Mexico as long as they didn't ask too many questions. As they would want the money back to balance their books, he really doubted that they would get too curious. Furthermore, by giving back the money there would be no reason for the Riviera Maya crew to come after us unless it was simply an ego and loss of face issue.

Hector said that as far as he was concerned the little adventure down in Mexico and finding the gold was fun and had gotten his juices flowing again, but it was now time to put the whole escapade to rest and get back to our regular routines.

This made sense to everyone who was there, but I reiterated that until the gold was back in the proper hands in Mexico, we were all still at risk if the Mayan mobsters were aware of who ripped off their gold. We would need to be vigilant until Hernández got back and we had made accommodations to get the gold back to the Mexican bank. That said, I told Kassy and Coco that I would provide them with a suitable firearm each in the near future and we would go up to the deserted airfield north of town to practice with them. Everyone else had at least one weapon, usually multiple weapons, from which to choose from.

With that, Hector went home, Coco and Kassy went behind the counter at the taqueria and Antonio and I strolled over through the gate in the courtroom divider and over to our counter.

"Antonio, this Riviera Maya gang sound like they could be bad news. If they come up here things could get pretty interesting. We should be good to go as long as whatever they plan happens at close range, but what if they catch one of us out on the roads outside of town or out at Hector's place? It'd be nice to have a long-range capability as well. How good of a shot are you with a long gun?" I asked.

"Funny you should ask," he said with a grin. "Back when I had two real feet and was jumping out of helicopters and airplanes and such, I was the unit's designated marksman. You being an ex-Army paratrooper, also known colloquially as a meat bomb, unlike myself who was the much more professional Air Force type meat bomb, know that the designated marksmen are trained to provide accurate fire upon the enemy at distances of up to 600 meters with the 5.56 NATO round. After my forced retirement I have steadily trained myself to be able to shoot minute of angle groups out to 800 meters."

Minute of angle (MOA) shooting at 800 yards meant that he could put his rounds in an 8" circle at that distance, which is damn good. Shooting groups that tight at 800 meters, or 875 yards, was very impressive.

"Bullshit!" I replied. "Mexicans simply cannot shoot that well, it is hereditary. I refer you to your ancestor's performance at the Alamo. Granted, you guys finally won, but it took you damn near 13 days to wipe out about 100 Texians and your team had around 1,500 players. The shooting capability of Santa Ana's boys obviously sucked. I think this inability to shoot accurately is simply endemic within the Hispanic community." I had to try and wind Antonio up; he was married now and needed the distraction.

"Once again, I need to educate the pendejo gringo. First, those of us of Mexican ancestry who are here legally are technically termed 'Americans'. Not hyphenated Americans such as 'Mexican-American' which is an outdated categorization of Americans of Hispanic descent. Secondly, Santa Ana was an imbécil who couldn't find his ass with both hands, it is a surprise that it only took him two weeks. Third, I can probably outshoot your fat, pálido culo with a long gun any day of the week. We won't consider short guns as everybody knows how well you shot against Hernández up at Hector's place, although it was probably just a fluke and never to be repeated again."

"That sounded like a challenge, my non-hyphenated friend. This is what I suggest. First, you order two Smith and Wesson Airweights in .38 Special for Coco and Kassy. I think we already have some .38 hollow point ammo in stock for other folks around here. Then, if you remember correctly, we have a Trijicon TA110 3.5x35 ACOG scope somewhere in the shop which we haven't returned yet. Remember the guy who changed his mind and decided that he needed a TA33 3x30 ACOG instead? Why don't you mate that TA110 to the LaRue PredatAR in 5.56 NATO that we keep around here, and we'll take that with us up to the old airfield when we show the girls how to shoot their new toys and you and I will do some shooting down the old runway."

Antonio said he'd get the pistols organized for the ladies and get the Larue rifle sorted out as well. As I started to leave, I said over my shoulder, "That Trijicon scope is calibrated for 75 grain ammo, so make sure you order some of that as well." Antonio just kept looking down and reading something on the counter as he pointed toward the door.

After drinking another coffee with Kassy, I drove over to Hector's place just to touch base. Since it was a nice day, we just sat on his front porch and had a beer in the sun. We knew that we could be in the 'calm before the storm' but there was simply nothing else that we could do until Hernández showed up with the gold or the bad guys showed up looking for it. We'd just keep our eyes peeled and hope for the best.

I got back home and decided to do a load of laundry while I cleaned and oiled both my little Honcho 12 gauge pump gun and my old Colt Gold Cup 1911. I just did it for something to do and because it was something I always did if I thought that some gunplay may be on the horizon.

Throwing the clothes in the dryer, I then decided to make a pot of spaghetti with pesto sauce. While practicing my culinary skills there was a knock at the front door. It was Antonio, so I invited him in for a beer while he set down the soft-sided gun case he was carrying and pulled out the Larue PredatAR rifle that had been orphaned at the shop when old Joaquin informed me that I was running the shop all wrong. He'd attached the Trijican TA110 3.5x35 TA33 to the picatinny rail on top of the rifle and adjusted it for his eye relief. I knew that Larue made a good rifle and that Trijicon was top of the line optics, but I was curious if that 16" barrel was going to allow him to reach out and touch someone at a distance.

"Depends on how far out you're talking about and what you're shooting at or through. The 75 grain boat tail hollow points I've ordered give us a velocity of about 1800 feet per second at 500 yards with a corresponding energy of about 550 foot pounds. If it is a soft target, say a person without body armor on we'd be okay. Shooting through a car door or glass would be a problem. The rifle should be fine up to 300 yards or so in any case," was his reply.

"Well, that's about the only suitable long gun we have available at the moment, so it'll have to do. We'll get it dialed in up at the old airfield. Any idea when the girls .38 Airweights will get here?" I asked.

"Should be here in a day or two out of Denver. I'll let you know."

Antonio packed the rifle back up in its case and went back to his house to have dinner with Alejandra, and I got back to work on the spaghetti. After dinner I cleaned up the dishes and the kitchen and went out on the porch swing to enjoy a beer before bedtime.

CHAPTER 30

THE GIRLS SNUB NOSED .38 Special Smith & Wesson Model 642 'Airweight' 5 shot revolvers showed up on Friday along with the 400 rounds of 75 grain Match Grade Hornady 5.56mm boat tail hollow point ammo that Antonio was supposedly going to outshoot me with. I brought Coco and Kassy into my office and showed them their new revolvers and explained to them that although they were small and light, only 14.4 ounces unloaded, that they would pack a punch at close range. I had to explain that since the weapons were hammerless to avoid them hanging up when being pulled out of pockets, purses or perhaps even bras, that the trigger pull to make them go bang would be slightly greater than a single action revolver, but that we'd practice with them up at the old airfield on Sunday. I told them to take them home, not to load them and just find a good spot to carry them concealed and get used to carrying them there.

As they were going out the door, I told Kassy that I was joking about carrying it in her bra since there didn't seem to be any extra room in there from what I could see. I then told Coco that she still seemed to have plenty of room there so feel free to give it a try. Kassy laughed; Coco flipped me the bird. The kid obviously had no sense of humor.

Antonio, Miguel and I spent about an hour breaking down the boxes of ammo for the Larue rifle and slotting it into ten 30-round magazines in preparation for the shooting contest on Sunday and the detailed sighting in of the rifle for 100 yards to follow. Sunday bright and early, Coco's little Volkswagen showed up at my place shortly followed by Kassy in her red Mustang. We each had a cup of coffee in my kitchen before I grabbed my shooting bag, and we walked across the cul-de-sac to Antonio's place.

The girls got caught up with Alejandra in the kitchen while Antonio and I shot the breeze on his porch for about half an hour before we all piled into Antonio's 4-door pickup and made our way to the old deserted airport just north of town. On the way I asked the girls sitting in back if they had remembered to bring their pistols. Kassy pulled hers out of her purse while Coco, being the smart-ass that she was, actually reached in her shirt and pulled hers out of her bra. Antonio was watching this in the rear view mirror and almost ran off the road. Coco had a smirk on her face until I casually told her that I knew she had some extra room in there, but not to worry since she was still a growing girl. Everyone but Coco laughed.

The old La Veta Cuchara Valley airport is not actually abandoned and is still listed as a usable runway. That said, you'd have to be pretty desperate to land an aircraft there. The old asphalt runway has wide cracks in it, there are no hangars to keep aircraft out of the weather and there are absolutely no services and no fuel. I had been shooting along the runway since I had arrived in the area and had yet to see anyone there except for a few ultralights now and then. Air traffic in the area generally utilized the Spanish Peaks Airfield north of Walsenburg now.

We drove out of town on Highway 12 until we hung a left onto the old Airport Road and pulled up in front of the only remaining building on the west side of the old cracked apron. We all piled out of Antonio's truck, grabbed our gear and walked across the runway to where there were some dilapidated old buildings a couple of hundred yards to the north of the runway. Reaching into my shooting bag I grabbed two official NRA 25 Foot Slow Fire Pistol targets and stapled them to one of the old wooden walls about

10 feet apart. I then took 7 good strides away from the wall and made a line in the dirt with my boot.

Antonio showed Coco how to unlatch the cylinder, swing it out, load the weapon and close it back up so that it was ready to fire. I did the same with Kassy. Once we were happy that they could do this routinely we walked them up to the line I'd made in the dirt, and I told them that we'd shoot from there.

Coco said that this seemed to be a bit ridiculous as we were only about 20 feet from the target. I explained to her and Kassy that statistics showed that the vast majority of self-defense encounters and police involved shootings happened within 7 yards. If the girls could put all 5 rounds, remember that these were 5 shot revolvers, into the black portion of the target three times in a row, that I'd be happy.

I had to explain that these snub nosed pistols were originally referred to as 'belly guns' as people would shove them into the bellies of other people before pulling the trigger. These were top of the line snub guns and could easily shoot accurately out to 10 yards or so. I finally reminded them that these were double action pistols where pulling the trigger performed both the cocking of the weapon and then the firing of the weapon, and that there was no safety built into the gun. Once they put bullets in them, the gun would fire if the trigger was pulled.

Class was now in session. Antonio tutored Coco while I tutored Kassy, which caused some problems. As I had to stand behind Kassy to ensure that she adopted the correct isosceles stance and was leaning slightly into the gun, her backside kept pressing into my crotch. This was distracting to say the least, it was in my case anyhow. I kept asking her to lean over further, but she finally caught on and threatened to shoot me if I ever did that again in public.

Women have a natural tendency to use their weapon as an extension of their index finger, I have never heard a reasonable explanation for this, but it means that you do not want to over-teach them something that they do naturally. Once Antonio and I had shown them a proper stance and how to grip the gun two-handed, we just stood back and watched them shoot. We'd let Coco shot five rounds and then Kassy would shoot five. The first 10 rounds from each girl were all over the place, which was expected as they were new to the weapons and shooting in general. After the next 15 rounds apiece, the girls were keeping them within the white portion of the target. The next set of five had both girls in the black. I now had them load up two more times and shoot. If they kept all ten rounds in the black, I'd call it good and then Antonio and I would have our little shootout.

The girls kept their final ten rounds in the black. I made them swing out the cylinder and make sure the guns were unloaded before I let them high five each other and jump up and down. They were proud of themselves and rightly so.

We walked back to Antonio's truck and picked up the Larue rifle and 4 loaded magazines. I had the girls put their revolvers in their waistbands at the small of their back as I wanted them comfortable with carrying them that way as well as to get used to having a gun on them.

Over the past several months that I had been shooting at the airfield I'd brought out about a dozen hay bales to use as a backstop. The problem with shooting rifles at the airport is that the old runway pointed directly at a house about 1,000 yards off the end of the runway. Granted, that's a long way off, but it wasn't worth the risk. A 5.56 NATO round will easily travel that far.

We loaded 8 hay bales in the back of Antonio's truck and had Kassy stand on a mark I had made in the middle of the runway, just where the taxiway entered the runway off the apron. Using a rangefinder originally built for the golfing community, we rolled down the runway until the rangefinder said Kassy was 600 yards away. We stopped, threw out 8 hay bales and made a wall on the south side of the runway. I stapled 4 of the slow fire pistol targets to the bales; 2 up and 2 down before we got back in the truck and drove back toward Kassy until we were 100 yards from her and then did the same thing with hay bales on the north side of the runway.

Driving back to where Kassy was, we stopped the truck so that the tailgate was directly over the spot where Kassy had been standing. We'd fire from the prone position, from the bed of the truck. The first thing that needed to be resolved was who was the better shot with a long gun, Antonio or me. This was for bragging rights. The second thing that we needed to do was sight the rifle in at 100 yards for Antonio. Each person holds a rifle slightly different and their eye relief from the scope is different. I would not be shooting at the 100 yard targets, that was all on Antonio as he needed to set the gun up for himself.

I pulled my 40 power spotting scope and its tripod out of the truck and set it up on the shady side of the truck while Antonio set up the sand bags he'd be shooting off of in the bed of the truck. When he was ready, the game was on. I told him to fire at will, but only at the two targets on the left, one up one down, on the 600-yard set of bales. The girls were sitting in the back seat on either side of the truck with the doors open and their legs hanging out to watch the show through the back window of the truck.

Antonio fired off a set of five. Four rounds actually found the paper target. This may sound bad, but it was actually pretty good. Keep in mind that the entire target was only 10.5" by 12". Shooting 1 MOA, or minute of angle, at 600 yards would be keeping all your rounds in a 6" circle and he was shooting a rifle and scope set-up which he had never fired before. After adjusting the scope, his second set of 5 rounds were all on the paper and so were his final 5 rounds for that target. He then switched to the bottom target on the left side and sent all 15 rounds into the target.

Antonio changed out the now empty magazine and handed the rifle to me. Now it was my turn, and the heat was on. I had two fliers which didn't even hit the paper out of the 15 rounds I fired at the top target on the right. I managed to keep all 15 rounds on the paper while shooting the bottom target. After grabbing some water out of the cooler in the back of the truck, we walked down to the targets and took them down. Antonio tallied up his score for the bottom target and came up with 188 with two fliers. My score, with 3 fliers, was 183. Antonio had beaten me fair and square. I'd be eating crow for a while now after my previous comments concerning the Alamo and his ancestor's shooting abilities.

Walking back to the truck, I hung my head and admitted that Antonio was the better shot today. The girls high fived Antonio and heckled me relentlessly. Where was the loyalty and support from Kassy? This commitment thing seemed to be a one-way street. This was discrimination pure and simple; the Hispanic community was ganging up on the white boy was all that I could figure. Had they no shame?

Getting serious again, Antonio got on the rifle and I got on the spotting scope so that we could dial in the rifle at exactly 100 yards for Antonio. Once you know that you are spot on at 100 yards, it is easy to adjust to other ranges simply by looking at the ballistics table for the specific ammunition which you are using and that you have thoughtfully taped to the stock of your rifle.

Anyhow, Antonio would fire 3 rounds and I would tell him where they hit. He would make an adjustment on the scope. He'd fire another 3 rounds and we'd go through the same process again. We did this for 15 rounds on the lefthand target before moving on to the righthand target while fine tuning the scope and rifle combination. By the time we were finished Antonio could put 3 rounds in a 3/4" circle at will. This is called shooting ¾ MOA and is very impressive for your first time on a gun, or anytime for that matter.

We drove down to the hay bales at the 600-yard line and threw them in the back of the truck before driving back up the runway to collect the bales at the 100-yard line. Before putting the bales into the back of the truck, I pulled my trusty old Colt Gold Cup out of my waistband, walked back 10 paces away from the bales, spun around and put 4 rounds in the bullseye of the lefthand target then 4 in the bullseye of the righthand target. Holding the gun up I acted like an old gunfighter and blew away the imaginary smoke coming out of the muzzle. Kassy and Antonio were impressed; Coco said I was a showing off, which I was. As I kept trying to tell Kassy, if you've got it, flaunt it.

We loaded the last of the bales into the truck and took them back to the apron end of the runway and unloaded them for later use before we headed back to the taqueria for lunch.

CHAPTER 31

HERNÁNDEZ FINALLY MADE IT BACK to Walsenburg the following Tuesday so Hector and I drove to Walsenburg in my truck to have a chat with him and to collect our ill-gotten gains. Since I had racing seats in my truck now, we borrowed a 4-door Ford F-150 company truck and drove over to Tina's Family Café on Walsen Avenue for lunch. I had the Philly cheese steak sandwich, Hector opted for the roast reef with Swiss sandwich and Hernández had the chicken fajitas. Once we had ordered, Hector brought Hernández up to speed regarding his idea to give the centenarios back to the bank and hopefully preventing any blowback which may be headed our way. He reiterated that we really didn't need the money and now that the fun and excitement of finding and stealing a missing treasure had passed, it was time to do the right thing while keeping everyone safe.

Hernández agreed. When we got back to the office and returned the F-150, Hector and I went to Hernández's office and grabbed the four canvas sacks of gold coins and carried them out to my truck and dumped them unceremoniously in the bed. Getting in, we drove back to my place in La Veta and hid the bags inside some old tires and covered them with tarpaulins in the back corner of the little garage behind my house. We'd let things calm down for a month or so while we figured out how we would return the gold without getting jammed up for having possession of stolen property, which is a felony in the States. Hector would get the Azteca corporate lawyers working on it without letting them know too much.

For the next few weeks, everything carried on normally except for the fact that we were all running around armed with our heads on swivels. Eventually Hector's lawyers told him that they could take possession of any stolen goods, which were not actually stolen by us initially, and return whatever they were to the Mexican Consulate in Denver and let them return it to the rightful owners, no questions asked.

About the time that the lawyers informed Hector of this, the owners of the La Veta Inn on Ryus Avenue called Hector and told him that two strange Hispanic men had booked rooms for a week. They indicated to the owners that they were considering ranchland property in the area. Miguel went over to the Inn and tailed the two gentlemen to Agatha's when they went there for dinner that evening. Miguel ordered dinner as well and charged it back to Hector while he eavesdropped on the men's conversation. They spoke with a Mexico City accent and did not once mention real estate. This combined with the fact that there was no ranchland on the market in Huerfano County at the moment had the alarm bells ringing.

Hector had the men followed while they were in town and the surrounding areas. They would typically get up early and drive off, but they only seemed to visit the smaller towns surrounding La Veta, have lunch, then come back to La Veta to ask a lot of questions concerning people in the town who may have ties to Mexico. After a week, the two men left and Hector had Hernández, myself, Miguel and Antonio meet him at Hector's house one evening to discuss the situation.

"Gentlemen, it looks like the chickens have come home to roost. I am guessing that these two guys were doing some reconnaissance for our friends south of the border and we can expect a visit from them shortly. I really don't know how they found us or which of us may have been identified, but all of us will need to be on our toes for the foreseeable future.

"We are wide open here and as we won't know who the players are until they do something or announce themselves. We will be forced to react as opposed to being proactive. Any suggestions?" asked Hector.

Thinking about it for a minute I replied, "This is the absolute worst scenario possible. We don't know who we are actually dealing with, we don't know when they'll make a move and all we really know is that they want that gold."

"We don't have a lot of options. What I would suggest is just common sense; keep your eyes peeled for any strangers, stay vigilant and keep your weapons with you at all times. Finally, let's stay in touch on a regular basis. By necessity we will be separated most of the time and the only time we will know that someone is in trouble may be when he or she doesn't answer their phone.

"If it is only the gold they want, then we'll just give it to them, but I would imagine that they'll want some payback for making them look like amateurs as well."

Everyone agreed with what I'd said and knew that we were between a rock and a hard place. Giving them the gold and having them just leave would be the best scenario, but we all knew in our hearts that desperadoes like these wouldn't go back across the border without causing some sort of mischief.

A week later, around noon, Antonio got a call from his cousins down in Trinidad, the guys who had rebuilt my truck, who told him that they had been visited by a group of men who obviously knew that they were related to Antonio. The men were asking questions about Hector and King as well as their relationship with the gun shop, the taqueria and the Azteca Trucking Lines.

As the cousins were not aware of the gold or how it was obtained, they could not answer any questions about it.

Antonio asked his cousins to describe, as best they could, the men and their vehicles.

"There were 10 men in total. They were all fairly large men except for the leader who did most of the talking, he is over 6' tall, but thin. The other men are bulked up with gym rat physiques. The boss has some serious acne scarring on his cheeks. They were driving two late model Black Lincoln Navigators with Mexico City plates. Be careful mano, these guys look like they mean business."

Antonio thanked his cousins and immediately called Hector to let him know what his cousins had told him. Hector got off the phone and then called me to give me a heads-up as well. It was time for us to buckle up and get serious, these Mayan peckerheads would be playing for keeps.

It would take the bad guys about an hour and a half or two hours to drive from Trinidad to La Veta depending on if they took I-25 North to Walsenburg and then took 160 toward La Veta or took 12 around the backside of the Spanish Peaks State Wildlife Area directly from Trinidad to La Veta. Everyone was told to be on the lookout for the two Lincoln Navigators.

What happened next was just sheer bad luck. Miguel had left the gun shop and gone home while Antonio had stayed behind to watch after Kassy and Coco as they closed up the taqueria around 8:00 in the evening. Nobody had seen the two Navigators, but everyone was on edge. With no warning whatsoever, the front door of the taqueria flew open and 5 Mexican men burst in with guns drawn and headed straight for Kassy and Coco.

Antonio was in the gun shop office when this happened and jumped up to see what was going on. Just as he got to the office door, he saw two guys go behind the taqueria counter, one grabbed Kassy while the other grabbed Coco. The one that grabbed Kassy got a big surprise when she pulled her little Smith & Wesson Airweight out of her waistband at the back and apparently remembering what I had said concerning belly guns, she shoved it in his belly and fired two rounds. Before she could fire off any more rounds, the guy who had grabbed Coco held onto her with his left hand and backhanded Kassy with his right. She dropped to the floor and another Mexican scooped her up and they made their way to the front door dragging Coco and their now dying compadre, the one Kassy had shot, with them. Two .38's to the gut would be a bad way to go, but in this case, who cared? When you play with fire, sometimes you get burned.

Antonio had grabbed my little Honcho 12-gauge pump gun off of the table where I'd been keeping it lately, but couldn't shoot for fear of hitting one of the girls. As the last Mexican backed through the front door, he told Antonio he was lucky they didn't shoot cripples. Events would later show that this policy was counter-productive in the extreme.

Antonio quickly got on the phone to Hector and told him what had happened. Hector told Antonio to stay where he was and we'd all meet up there as soon as we could. He asked Antonio to call Miguel while he called Hernández and me.

Within an hour we were all in the taqueria looking at the blood trail from the guy Kassy had tagged. We were all quite proud of the lass, but when Antonio told us about the vicious back hand she took, it brought us back down to earth. At this point it became apparent that the consensus was that all these bastards from south of the border had to be put on the other side of the turf for a long dirt nap as soon as possible.

There was nothing we could do except wait for the phone call which we knew was coming and a few minutes later, it did.

Hector answered his phone and put it on speaker while the rest of us got quiet.

"Is this Hector Archuleta?"

"Yes, it is. May I know with whom I am speaking?" asked Hector.

"You may call me Pez Martillo. I believe by now you realize that your daughter and your niece have been taken by me and my crew. You can have them returned unharmed if you would return all of the 1,567 centenarios which you removed from that junkyard in Mexico several weeks ago. Are you interested in making the trade?"

Since it was obvious that Hammerhead, which is what Pez Martillo translated to in English, knew exactly what had occurred down in Mexico, it would be foolish to antagonize him by saying he didn't know what Hammerhead was talking about and it may cause them to abuse Kassy and Coco more than they already had. Hector told him that he would be glad to make the trade but he needed 'proof of life' from Kassy.

Kassy was put on the phone and Hector asked her if she was okay or if she had been abused in any manner.

"Papa, I am okay except for a split lip. Coco is unharmed as well. They have not sexually assaulted either of us if that is what you are worried about. That being said, when are you going to come get us and shoot these hijos de puta?"

"Soon, mi hija, soon," Hector told her.

The phone was passed back to the head honcho of the sons of a bitches that Kassy wanted shot.

"She is a feisty one, isn't she? But back to business. I will trade this hellion and her little friend for exactly 1,567 centenarios at sunrise the day after tomorrow. Are you familiar with the old Macmillan place on La Veta Pass, on the backside of Mount Mestas?"

Hector said he knew the place.

"Good. I need to reiterate that I will accept no less than 1,567 centenarios for this woman and the child. I do not expect you to come alone, but I will only allow you two associates to assist with handling the gold and to recover your daughter and niece. Is that understood?"

"Pez Martillo, Hammerhead, or whatever you choose to call yourself. I fully understand your requirements and I plan to adhere to them exactly as you have described them to me, but what I would like you to know and to fully understand is that if so much as a hair is out of place on my daughter's head, or the little one's head, when I get them back that you and your posse will never make it back across the border alive. Is that understood?"

Hammerhead was laughing when he broke the connection. I seriously doubt if he would have been so amused if he'd seen the look on Hector's face.

We sat down at one of the tables in the dining area and had a counsel of war. The old Macmillan place was an old, abandoned ranch house on the north side of La Veta Pass about a mile and a half off of Highway 160. A dirt road led to the cabin, which sat backed up to the woods in a small open valley of about 5 acres. As these clowns were not from around here, they probably did not realize that you could actually access the cabin by coming in from the north on old 4-wheel-drive trails as well.

It was decided that Antonio and Miguel would leave as soon as possible after getting their gear together. They would need some cold weather gear for the nights as well as enough food and water to last them a few days. After taking the old Jeep trails in from the north they would leave Antonio's truck about a mile from the old cabin and walk the rest of the way to the old Macmillan place. Antonio would take the Larue rifle and a pair of Zeiss SFL 8x40 binoculars so that he and Miguel could provide overwatch of the cabin and let us know what was going on there before the handover. He and Miguel would stay hidden back in the tree line across the meadow from the cabin and not come out in the open. As the tree line was roughly 150 yards from the cabin porch, he could help us out when the shooting started, and we all knew there would be shooting. Since we would be staying in touch by cell phone, they would need to bring some power packs with them as well to recharge their phones. I gave the shorty Honcho pump gun and a box of double ought buckshot loads to Miguel so he could watch Antonio's back while Antonio was watching the cabin. With that, Antonio and Miguel left to get ready and go.

Hector, Hernández and I drove our trucks over to my place and started getting our gear ready as well. I went into the garage at the back of my house and brought all four of the canvas bags containing the centenarios into the house. I then got out my old trauma kit, I'd replenished it after I'd fixed up Miguel in what seemed like years ago at my place in Loveland. We'd need it if things went sideways at the handover.

Sitting down at the kitchen table I got out my old Colt Gold Cup 1911, stripped it down, cleaned and oiled it before putting it all back together. I also popped all the rounds out of the three magazines I had for it, lubed up the spring in each magazine then lightly oiled each round with a rag before loading the three magazines back up. Hernández was doing the same thing at the kitchen table with his Sig Sauer 9mm P226 MK25. Hector came into the kitchen, saw what we were doing then went back out to his truck and got busy on his weapon. Funny enough, I'd never seen Hector shoot. He had an old

Smith & Wesson Mountain Gun in .45 Long Colt, an old school revolver in an old school caliber. I asked him if he could shoot that old relic, he just told me to hide and watch as he flipped out the cylinder and ran a brush through each chamber and the barrel before lightly oiling the same and loading it up.

We had decided to take Hernández's 4-door Ford Raptor pickup to the handover as we needed the extra room for 3 guys and 4 bags of gold coins. I also threw in a box of bottled water as I was sure that everyone would be thirsty both before and after the upcoming showdown.

Eventually Hector racked out on the bed in the guest bedroom upstairs while Hernández laid down on the couch in the living room. I crawled into my own bed. I turned off the light and was asleep before the room got dark. I was the first one up the next morning. Hector was snoring like a freight train in the guest room and Hernández was still asleep on the couch, so I snuck into the kitchen and started making a big pan of scrambled eggs, bacon, toast and coffee. The smell must have woken up my house guests as they stumbled into the kitchen a little while later and we had a decent breakfast.

There wasn't much for us to do until just before sunrise the next day, so we just lounged around trying not to think about what Kassy and Coco might be going through. It would have been counter-productive and there wasn't a damn thing that we could do about it anyhow.

Miguel and Antonio had buried themselves in some scrub oak trees at a point as close to the house as possible on the other side of the little meadow from the house and were giving us hourly updates. The two Lincoln SUVs were at the house and the men seemed to be settling in and occasionally going between the SUV's and the dilapidated house. They had not seen the girls but had the impression that they were being kept in a room upstairs as occasionally a guy would appear at the dormer window overlooking the front porch. Antonio's cousins had said that 10 men paid them a visit, deducting the one that Kassy had gut shot that left 9 people that still needed killing. The odds weren't in our favor, but having Antonio up on that hill with a long gun might even them a bit.

Nothing of interest happened that afternoon out at the Macmillan place, and not much was happening at my place either. Hernández and Hector went into town and made sure that Hernández's truck was fueled up before they drove over to Hector's place so that he could get some fresh clothes and a shower. After they returned, we went out to Mission Deli Mesa Steak House for dinner before coming back to my place for a couple of beers on the porch before getting our heads down again. I'd set the alarm on my iPhone for 4:00 in the morning. Sunrise would be around 5:30 so we needed to be on the road about 4:45 to give us plenty of time to get to the handover on schedule.

None of us got much sleep and nobody was hungry at 4:00 in the morning so we just had some coffee and got an update from Antonio and Miguel. The Riviera Maya boys were awake and kerosene lamps had been lit in the house. Since there was no working plumbing in the house, the men were doing their business in a trench they had dug under a tree on the south side of the house. Earlier they had let the girls go to the bathroom in the woods behind the house, but they had been accompanied by a guard. The good news is that they both seemed to be moving okay and were not injured except for Kassy's split lip when she had gotten backhanded at the shop

We saddled up and hit the road right on the dot of 4:45 and arrived at the turnoff to the dirt road that led off of Highway 160 to the old Macmillan place ahead of schedule. Pulling off onto the dirt road, Hernández shut off the truck while Hector called Antonio and Miguel for a final update and to let them know that we had arrived. Everybody was in the house now, which was expected. What was unexpected is that Miguel had been scouting around and had located one of the Mexicans with another long gun hiding under a tree about 50 yards to their right. Antonio said not to worry as Miguel had it covered, whatever that meant.

Just as the sun broke over Silver Mountain due east of us, Hernández fired up the Raptor again and we slowly drove the mile and a half to the cabin and parked about 20 yards from the front porch steps with the truck facing the house. We all had our pistols tucked into our waistbands at the small of our backs and got out of the truck and took up positions just in front of the truck with Hector in the middle, Hernández on his left and me on his right.

Eventually Hammerhead Pez opened the front door and strolled out onto the porch along with his remaining crew. He appeared to be dressed as a Mexican version of Wild Bill Hickok with a full-length oiled canvas duster, faded jeans tucked into cowboy boots, a snap button western shirt, a black Stetson cowboy hat and an old tooled leather gun belt slung low around his hips with what appeared to be an old Colt Peacemaker in it. His two day growth of beard and the acne scars completed the picture of what he obviously thought was a proper Mexican badass.

I felt sorry for his crew. I think they were embarrassed by him, but the boss is the boss. The rest of the desperados were dressed more conservatively in jeans, flannel shirts over t-shirts and cowboy boots with not another cowboy hat to be found among them. Nobody else was showing a weapon, but the odds were they had them tucked into their waistbands at the back, just like we did.

"Do you have the gold?" asked Hammerhead Hickok.

I walked back and reached into the back seat of the Raptor and took out two of the canvas bags full of coins and dropped them on the ground halfway between the front of the Raptor and the porch before walking back to the truck. Hammerhead came down the 3 steps from the porch to ground level and walked over to the bags. He unzipped them one at a time and took a good look inside each.

Standing back up he asked where the rest of the gold was.

"Those two sacks are for one girl. We get a girl, and you get that gold. We then repeat the process for the other girl," Hector explained.

Hammerhead made a motion with his right hand, which was also his gun hand assuming his old revolver was strapped to his dominate side. The entire crew came off the porch with three coming up on Hammerhead's left side and fanning out and the other three doing the same on his right. The men closest to the boss had the girls held by the nape of their necks. Coco looked scared; Kassy looked bored.

At a word from the boss, the guy to his right shoved Coco forward and she stumbled into Hector, who passed her to me. I told her to get behind the truck and stay there until this was over.

"Let's see the rest," demanded Senor Hammerhead.

I went back to the truck and grabbed the remaining two bags then dumped them by the first batch on the ground before backing up beside Hector again. The Hammerman unzipped both of the bags in the second batch and took a look inside and seemed satisfied.

Things happened quickly at this point, but I need to set the stage. At that moment we were all standing in front of Hernández's truck. Hernández was about 3 feet off to the left of Hector while I was about 3 feet off to his right. About 10 yards in front of us was a line of 7 desperados; 3 fanned out to the right of Hammerhead, Hammerhead himself, the guy holding Kassy just off Hammerhead's left shoulder, then two other knotheads to this guy's left, or our right. Later I reflected that this was vaguely similar to the set up at Hector's place when Hernández and I had shot paper plates for bragging rights.

We had Miguel and Antonio with a rifle 150 yards behind us and to our right, but according to Antonio, Hammerhead also had a guy in the dormer window above the porch as well as another guy across the meadow near Antonio and Miguel. Antonio had the guy in the window covered and supposedly Miguel would handle their neighbor with the rifle in the treeline. We'd find out in a minute.

Pez Martillo made another motion with his left hand that was supposed to indicate that the guy holding Kassy should shove her forward toward us just as Coco had been. In reality he was using it to distract us as he went for his gun with his right hand and was obviously a signal for the rest of his crew to go for theirs as well.

At this exact moment, if you were listening carefully, you would have heard the sound of a gunshot coming from the tree line across the meadow. Antonio had been watching the dormer window above the porch and saw a guy with an AK-47 getting ready to hose us down. When he exposed himself at the window, Antonio put one of those 75 grain boat tail hollow point rounds from that Larue rifle right through his brain basket.

Back in front of the old ranch house, Hernández, Hector and myself had been expecting such a move from Hammerhead and we were already pulling our pistols out of our waistbands before the Mexicans started reaching for theirs. What followed was a massacre.

Hernández, going from left to right, double tapped each of the three guys on his side so fast it sounded like a single rolling muzzle blast. I on the other hand had to worry about hitting Kassy. Kassy, besides being very easy on the eyes, also had a very good head on her shoulders. When Hammerhead went for his gun, she just dropped straight down like a sack of cement which left her handler totally exposed. I shot each guy once in the center of mass going left to right, double tapped the guy on the end then hit the other two guys center of mass again going back right to left before the first one had hit the ground.

While all this shooting was going on, Hammerhead managed to draw his old Peacemaker, but Hector was quicker and shot it out of his hand, breaking his wrist. While I went over to make sure Kassy was okay, Hernández went into the old ranch house to make sure it was cleared and that the guy in the dormer window with the AK was good and dead. While we were doing this, Hector had slapped the black Stetson hat off Pez's head before forcing Señor Pez to get on his knees with his fingers laced behind his head and his ankles crossed behind him. His broken wrist made this a painful exercise.

Hammerhead was no longer the big bandito badass from south of the border that he had been a few moments ago and he was trying to cut a deal with Hector that would save his life. Hector put his finger to his lips in the universal sign to be quiet. Once the ex-Riviera Maya enforcer had quieted down, Hector began to lecture him.

"Señor Hammerhead, you have made two serious errors in coming after me. The first was your incredible arrogance in thinking that you could simply walk into my backyard and make demands of me." While Hector was lecturing Pez, he was slowly circling to get around behind him. "The second error was taking my family. As a man of Hispanic origin, you should realize that family is sacrosanct. The first error could simply be attributed to ignorance, the second is unforgiveable. Via con Dios cabrón."

Hector placed the muzzle of his old Mountain Gun to the crown of Pez Martillo's head and slowly eared back the hammer so that Pez could clearly hear the cylinder of the revolver rotate into position and the click as the hammer cocked. Giving Pez a few additional moments to reflect on his sins, Hector told Pez to say hello to Ernesto for him before pulling the trigger. That big old 230 grain .45 Long Colt hollow point bullet fired from point blank range simply exploded Pez's head like a cantaloupe hit by a sledgehammer, which was oddly ironic. As the body fell forward onto what was left of its face, Hector slowly reloaded the empty chamber in his pistol, snapped the cylinder shut, slipped it back into his waistband at the small of his back and said, "Okay, let's get this mess cleaned up."

Easier said than done if we didn't want to go to jail. While we were contemplating our options, Kassy and Coco sat in the truck and drank a few bottles of water. They were dehydrated from their ordeal. Antonio and Miguel had walked across the meadow from their hide in the tree line. I noticed that besides my little shotgun, Miguel was now also carrying a nice Ruger Model 77 scoped rifle. When I asked him where he'd gotten it, he said that he took it from another Mexican who was also in the tree line but who would not be needing it any longer.

Apparently, once they had spotted the guy in the tree line with them, Miguel had snuck through the woods and ghosted up behind him and just waited. He couldn't simply shoot him since the gunshot would have let the Mexicans at the house know they had company, and he couldn't kill him before the party started because if he had a radio and didn't check in as required, this would also have let the Mexicans in the house know something was amiss. This being the situation, old Miguel, being an old school desperado himself, simply slipped out the razor sharp 7" Marine Corp issued Ka-Bar knife that he kept in his boot and just waited patiently and silently about a yard back from the shooter, whose concentration was focused on the show taking place down at the old ranch house.

When Pez and his crew came out on the porch, Miguel figured that thing's had progressed far enough along that nobody would be checking in on the shooter laid out in the prone position in front of him, so he slithered over to the man, put a knee in his back while grabbing his hair in his left hand and pulled his head back and up. With the throat properly exposed, old Miguel deftly slit it from ear to ear, grabbed the rifle and the backpack lying there and hot-footed it back to Antonio. I only found out later that Miguel had been a Master Sergeant with the Recon Marines back in the First Gulf War and had retired shortly after that. This explained his skills and the fact that nothing seemed to bother the old guy.

The problem we now had was how to get rid of 10 bodies, including the body of the guy Kassy had plugged and was presently residing in a shallow grave behind the house, two big SUVs and all the evidence without going to jail. Oddly enough, it was Kassy who came up with the plan.

We would drag all the bodies back into the house, including their sniper across the meadow. We would also police the area and pick up all the brass. Since we were the only ones who had gotten off any shots, all the brass was ours. While wearing gloves, we would go through both of the Lincoln Navigators and ensure that there was nothing which could tie them to us or their search for us, but we would leave everything else alone. The SUVs, the clothes, the weapons and everything else had come from Mexico and we wanted the finger to point there.

We would leave the doors to the house open and wait a few days for the wild animals to do their thing once they smelled the blood and decomposing bodies before one of us would come back and set fire to the old, dry timber house. The smoke would draw the fire department, which would draw the law enforcement community once the bodies were discovered in the ash. By that time all the evidence and the DNA should be so convoluted that nobody could possibly figure out what had actually occurred at the cabin. By the time this was all accomplished it was after noon. Everyone piled into Hernández's truck with Hector and the girls in the back seat, Antonio and Miguel in the bed and the passenger seat up front left open for me.

I went through the house one final time to ensure we hadn't left anything incriminating and wiped off any surface that one of us may have touched with my handkerchief. While I was doing this, Hernández had hopped out of the truck and cut down some serviceberry bushes and tied them onto a rope attached to the rear bumper, he also used some of the bushes to wipe out any of his previous tire tracks that wouldn't be obliterated as we drove off dragging the pile of serviceberry bushes. Good thinking on his part.

We drove Antonio and Miguel back to Antonio's truck, which they had left on the Jeep trails about a mile north of the Macmillan place before they had walked in. They got in the truck and drove off ahead of us so that Hernández could come in behind them dragging the bushes and wiping out all of our tracks. Once we got back onto Highway 160 heading back to town, we untied the serviceberry bushes on the back of the truck and dumped them in another bunch of serviceberry bushes off the side of the road. We figured it may draw attention to us if we drove back to La Veta dragging a bunch of bushes behind us. We all found this highly amusing so obviously the tension of the day was wearing off.

CHAPTER 32

HERNÁNDEZ DROPPED ME OFF AT my house before he took everybody else back to Hector's place. I grabbed my kit and carried it into the house and dropped it on the kitchen floor before going upstairs for a nice hot shower and a shave. Coming back downstairs, I started putting together a huge ham and cheese sandwich. About this time, I heard Miguel and Antonio pull up to Antonio's house across the cul-de-sac so I whistled at them and told them to come on over.

Since I was already making a sandwich, I just continued on and made two more big sandwiches. I took the plate of sandwiches out to the front porch where Miguel was on the swing and Antonio was in the rocking chair on the other side of the front door. Passing out the sandwiches I went back into the kitchen and got three beers out of the fridge. I passed out the beers as well before sitting down on the swing beside Miguel to eat. This is when I found out about Miguel's Semper Fi background.

While we ate, I brought up the fact that Hector had made a damned fine shot this morning, the one where he shot the gun out of Pez's hand not the one where he blew his head off. Miguel just started laughing.

"You young bucks think that you are so hot with your fancy guns and

~ 226 ~

other toys and tend to forget that it was us old hands that developed those toys and techniques. When Hector decided to pack in the smuggling routine, he got into the IPSC, the International Practical Shooting Confederation, as a hobby. He actually won the revolver division two years running at one point, although not under his real name. Old Hector's got some skills."

When we had finished eating and drinking our beer, I told the guys to just leave all the guns with me and I'd clean and oil them. Antonio took Miguel home and I got busy in the kitchen disassembling the Larue rifle, the Honcho shotgun, my Colt Gold Cup and the newly acquired Ruger 77 rifle. Although the shorty shotgun and the Ruger hadn't been fired, I find cleaning weapons to be very therapeutic, so I just cleaned and oiled them as well.

A few days later I went back to the old Macmillan place and once again came in from the north over the Jeep trails and parked about half a mile away and walked in. By this time the smell of putrification coming out of the old house was almost tangible. The wildlife had been busy and there were some bits and pieces of ex-desperados out on the front porch and outside the back door as well.

I'd carried in two 750ml bottles of Bacardi Superior rum with me on the way in along with a couple of rags and a Zippo lighter. The old ranch house was so old and weathered that this should be sufficient to burn it, and everything in it, to cinders. I fashioned two Molotov cocktails out of the rum bottles and rags. I lit the wick on one of the cocktails and winged it hard through the front door and heard it shatter against a wall. Going around the side of the house to the back door I did the same. By the time I had walked across the meadow to the tree line, wearing an old pair of sneakers which I would throw away later, I sat down to make sure that the place was burning nicely before I walked back to my truck and called Hector and let him know that the deed was done before driving home.

As expected, the smoke drew the attention of folks living in the area who were always on the watch for new wildfires springing up. The Forest Service responded but were too late to do anything about the house but they were curious about the two late model Lincoln Navigators with Mexican license plates parked outside with nobody in attendance. Once the embers had died out, a cursory inspection of the burned out cabin revealed several sets of human remains, which brought in law enforcement and things progressed from there.

As we thought, the scene was such a convoluted mess of foreign vehicles and unidentifiable bodies that eventually the law enforcement agencies went home and none of our crew were ever approached or questioned.

After a suitable amount of time, Hector got in touch with his lawyers and made arrangements to have the centenarios returned to the bank in Mexico anonymously. At this point we may have been able to hold on to it after the little party out at the old Macmillan place, but it just wasn't worth the risk of another encounter with the Riviera Maya crowd. One stipulation that the lawyers were instructed to make to the bank was that the return of the gold must be mentioned prominently in all the major newspapers in Mexico City. If the gold was now back in Mexico there would be no reason for anybody to come up to Colorado to look for it.

A celebration was now called for. Hector set the date, and on that day, everyone involved showed up at Hector's place around noon for a proper parrillada, that's a barbeque to us white folks. Hector, Hernández, Antonio, Miguel, and myself were there along with Coco, Kassy and Coco's beau Tim from the submarine races episode earlier. Alejandra was also there to keep an eye on Antonio and Gabriela, Miguel's wife, had come along to keep an eye on him as well.

Needless to say, those who were not present at the Macmillan place that day wanted a blow by blow description of the action. This naturally led to a discussion as to who was the best pistol shot out of the crew; Hector, Hernández or myself. Another shooting competition was organized while the barbeque pits were warming up, but we had an issue. Hernández's Sig held 15 rounds, Hector shot a wheel gun with 6 rounds and my old Colt held 8. How could we have a fair and equitable contest?

Alejandra piped up and suggested that we should go with the lowest common denominator and only load 6 rounds in each gun. That was okay, but this would not really test the speed portion of a 'speed and accuracy' competition. After much contemplation it was decided that we would only load 6 rounds per gun, but that each contestant had to fire all 3 pistols. The event would be timed from the moment a contestant picked up the first pistol, shot 18 rounds and then placed the last pistol back on the table.

Now we had to figure out what the targets would be. Antonio remembered that he still had a pack of NRA 25 Foot Slow Fire Pistol targets out in his truck, so he ran off to get them while we picked up and moved one of the picnic tables over in front of the split rail fence at the end of Hector's backyard and set it down exactly 7 yards away from the fence as paced off by Coco, our official pacer.

When Antonio got back, we stapled the first set of three targets to the fence about a yard apart from each other and placed the three pistols; my Colt Gold Cup in .45 ACP, Hernández's Sig in 9mm and Hector's old Mountain Gun in .45 Long Colt, on the picnic table, one in front of each target. Each shooter would be required to load each weapon with 6 rounds prior to the event then to shoot at the specified target for each gun moving from left to right. First would be my Gold Cup and the target furthest to the left, then Hector's old revolver and the target in the middle before Hernández's Sig and the target on the right. The spectators would time each shooter, put up new targets and tally the score for each shooter after his round.

Since Hector was a revolver specialist from his IPSC days, this really wasn't fair to him as he'd have to shoot two unfamiliar automatics, but since it was only for bragging rights he really didn't care. We drew cards to see who would shoot first, second and third. I drew a trey, Hector drew a 10 and Hernández drew the king of spades so Hernández would shoot first, Hector second and I'd be third.

Hernández stepped up to the table and loaded each weapon with 6 rounds in either a magazine or the cylinder depending on the pistol. Standing with his hands to his sides and shaking his wrists loose, he said he was ready. Coco yelled, "Go", and Hernández flew into action. Picking up the Gold Cup he leaned into the gun and fired six shots before laying it down and sidestepping to the next gun. Picking up Hector's revolver in a 'cup & saucer' grip he fired off another six shots before putting the revolver down and picking up his Sig and ripping off six shots before laying it down and yelling "Clear!"

We had decided earlier that the times and scores would not be revealed until everyone had shot, so after new targets had been stapled to the fence and he had loaded each weapon with 6 rounds, Hector stepped up and signaled that he was ready. Once again Coco yelled, "Go", and Hector ran the guns. He may have been marginally slower with the automatics, but he was much faster with his revolver, which was to be expected from a former IPSC revolver champion.

Now it was my turn and I was sweating a bit. Both Hector and Hernández were formidable competition and my previous comments about the Alamo and Mexican shooting skills would ensure that I'd never live it down if both Hector and Hernández beat me. I got up to the first shooting position, took a deep breath and said that I was ready. Coco again yelled, "Go". I grabbed that old Gold Cup and fired just as fast and as accurately as I could before laying it down and moving on to the Mountain Gun. Grabbing it in a two-handed grip I fired as fast as I could while concentrating on the front sight picture before laying it down and moving to the Sig. The Sig was a nice piece of kit, a semi-auto and chambered in 9mm as opposed to .45 ACP in my Colt. The recoil was much less and easier to handle than what I was used to. I yelled, "Stop", as soon as I laid down the Sig. Now it was up to the judges.

The judges huddled around the pistol table for a while before calling us all to attention. Apparently all three of us had timed out at exactly 11.2 seconds! The bragging rights would now be based on the total score from the 18 rounds fired by each contestant. After much deliberation, arguing, browbeating and attempted bribery, Hector was awarded 165 points, Hernández was awarded 167 points and I walked away the winner with 168 points. My bragging rights were secure at least until the next competition. The fact is, that at this level of freehand shooting it is mostly a case of who is a fraction better on any given day, not that I would ever admit that to Hector or Hernández.

Now the fiesta could begin in earnest. We ate, drank, danced and bullshitted until well after the sun went down. I got in some good quality time with Kassy but sadly the zipper on her 505 Levis stayed ''high and tight throughout the night', but you can't say that I didn't give it my best shot. As an old bard once said, 'Alas, it is better to have tried and failed than to never have tried at all.' Actually, I just made that up in an effort to justify my unsuccessful attempts to get that zipper tab to hit bottom and stay there.

I didn't drink too many beers that day and was okay to drive when the party finally fizzled out around 10:30 in the evening. This could not be said for most of the Hispanic contingent, which was essentially everyone except me and Coco's boyfriend Tim, so I borrowed Antonio's 4 door pickup and got Alejandra, Antonio, Miguel, Gabriela and myself to our respected domiciles and would get a lift back to collect my truck once Antonio's hangover receded tomorrow. Except for the issue with Kassy's zipper, it was a very nice fiesta and I once again had bragging rights to hold over Hernández.

The next morning, after Antonio got some breakfast down his neck along with a few cups of coffee to ease his pounding head, he drove me back to Hector's so that I could get my truck. Hector answered the door and seemed in fine shape. Hernández was still asleep on the couch, but Kassy was up and about in a t-shirt and shorts and from what I could see her shape was fine as well.

As Kassy walked me to my truck, I asked her if she was always going to be getting in trouble and needing bailed out. So far this summer she'd had her car die on the road, two guys came into her shop and tried to kidnap Coco and then we had to consider the recent incident which came to a fiery conclusion at the old Macmillan place.

"Well of course I'll continue to get into trouble and you'll continue to come to my rescue. This is how the game is played and let's face it, you'd be bored otherwise."

"True," I replied. What else could I say?

EPILOGUE

A few weeks later, after I had taken Kassy out for dinner at the Legends on Main restaurant in town, we were once again just relaxing on my porch swing watching the shadows lengthen to the east as the sun went down in the west. Kassy had her head resting on the arm of the swing closest to the front door and her ankles crossed in my lap. We had been getting a lot closer in our relationship since the one sided shootout at the old Macmillan place, but the clock was still running on the required 'commitment phase'. I hated this whole commitment, platonic relationship, testing period thing, but I was resigned to staying the course and seeing it through to the end.

Just as the sun went down, Kassy stood up and leaned back against the porch railing facing King.

"I think that I will go into the house now and prepare for a performance of the 'Danza de la Virgen Reformada," she informed King.

"That sounds like some Catholic religious thing," I replied.

"You are making that assumption simply due to the fact that I am of Hispanic origins and that I was raised as a Catholic. You automatically presumed that the term 'Virgen' referred to the Blessed Virgin Mary. This evening, for arguments sake, let's say that I was hypothetically raised as a devout Baptist. In which case it would be unlikely to be a Catholic religious thing and the virgin referred to may not in fact be Mother Mary."

"Fair enough, but I was under the impression that you Baptists did not believe in dancing. Doesn't the term 'danza' refer to a dance?"

"Mr. Fisher, the 'Danza de la Virgen Reformada' is not actually about dancing per se, as much as it is about the celebration of life," she said with a sly, mischievous grin.

"Sorry, my mistake. So, what is this 'Danza de la Virgen Reformada' thing then?" I was getting curious now.

"It is the 'Dance of the Reformed Virgin'. To perform it correctly takes skill, patience, timing, emotion and stamina."

"Did I ever tell you that in my younger, wilder days that I was well known within the virgin reformation community?" I asked.

"No, you did not. It must have slipped your mind. Getting back on topic, to perform the dance correctly requires two people and could take hours to perform correctly and with feeling. Would you like to participate in this dance? Do you think that you are up for it?" Kassy questioned.

"Honestly, I think that I have been up for it, since I first met you on the side of the road with your broken down Mustang," answered King.

"Hmmm… These past few months must have been extremely uncomfortable for you. I am sure that if you were to join me in performing the 'Danza de la Virgen Reformada' that any pent-up frustration and anxiety which you may have been experiencing over the past few months would be miraculously relieved."

With that said, Kassy reached down for King's hand and pulled him up off the swing and led him into the house. It appeared that the 'commitment phase' may have finally run its course and was about to come to a mutually satisfying conclusion.

A u t h o r ' s   N o t e :

THE READERS SHOULD EXERCISE THEIR imaginations at this point to complete the tale to their personal satisfaction.